# BAD BOY BRODY

## TIJAN

Copyright © 2018 Tijan
ISBN-10: 163576422X
ISBN-13: 978-1635764222

Edited by: AW Editing
Proofread by: Kara Hildebrand, Paige Smith,
Amy English, and Rochelle Paige
Cover designer: Hang Le, www.byhangle.com
Formatting: Elaine York, Allusion Graphics, LLC
www.allusiongraphics.com
Cover image: Depositphotos 15561905

# BAD BOY BRODY

This is for my father, who loved to train horses,
even though it wasn't his job.

This is for my sister, who brought our own Taffy into the family.

This is for my cousin, who showed so many his love of horses and
that he could stand on two separate horses at the same time.
I think he even had a third in the middle too.

And this is for my own nieces.

Lastly, this is for all the readers out there
who are awed by the beauty of horses.

It truly is majestic.

# CHAPTER ONE

## Brody

Los Angeles
*Seven months earlier*

There was press everywhere. The camera lights were flashing. Glitzy people were all over the room, but I looked around, watching from the back corner.

"Brody."

I frowned at my publicist, who was heading over to me. Before Shelby could say anything more, I asked, "Have you seen Kyle?"

"Kyle?" She pretended to be confused, patting her hair.

I cut her another look. She didn't like my brother, never had, but she could suck it. Honestly. This was my big movie premiere, and I wanted my fucking brother there. He promised to show.

"Shelby, don't fuck with me."

Her confused look melted into a sultry one as she pressed her body against mine, her hand playing on my arm. "But I'd love to fuck *with* you. You know that." She made sure to rub her breast against my arm before standing away from me.

This was Shelby's game. She was one of the best publicists out there, and most of the time she acted as my manager too, but she'd never made it a secret how much she wanted my dick. To her credit, she'd had it. I'd been acting for two years. She got my dick on a regular basis for the first six months of our relationship, but then we started a professional one, so I ended things. I wasn't a goddamn idiot.

I knew where I wanted to be, and being single would help.

That made me sound like a manipulative asshole, but I didn't give a shit.

I had been an extra on movies before moving to small parts. Supporting actor roles had been next, and finally, I landed the movie role that was already promising to launch me into the type of movies I needed.

I was going to be a goddamn A-list actor, but my fucking brother wasn't anywhere he was supposed to be.

"He said he'd come tonight."

We had no parents. They both died too young from cancer, so it was just Kyle and me, and he had always been supportive.

Something was wrong.

I couldn't shake this feeling. It was nagging me, and I couldn't shake it. It was growing more by the minute. Something was off.

A waiter passed with a tray of champagne, and I reached out, snatching one of the glasses. I threw it back, still straining to see around the filled movie lounge. People were looking over at us. I saw the interest, and that was fine with me.

I knew I commanded it. I wasn't an actor who put my life out there for the magazines to know. I kept the interviews to a minimum. I did the press junkets only when I needed to. I showed up on time. I knew my lines before walking into the studio. I rarely flirted. I shook hands with whomever I needed to. I played golf with them too. I did just enough so people knew my name, but not enough for them to know me.

And no one knew about Kyle, but this night was for him too. It was a celebration of the hard work and sacrifice we'd both gone through to get me here. He and his wife put me up so many times that there was a permanent indentation on their couch. Countless nights I'd eaten spaghetti or ramen noodles, until Cheryl wouldn't take no for an answer and demanded I join them and their two kids for dinner.

God. A wave of nostalgia rose in me.

I loved his family.

Ambrea and Alisma were like my own little girls.

One day, I promised myself, one day I'd do an animated movie and they'd be my dates for that premiere. I might have to do it sooner rather than later since they were both drawing past eight and ten years old. They'd be adults in the blink of an eye.

I glanced at my phone again. It was still blank—no calls from him. Kyle was supposed to have been here forty minutes ago.

"Something isn't right." That sick feeling wasn't going away.

"Come on." Shelby's hand curled over my arm. She indicated a couple drawing close to us. "That's the president of Dreamepics Productions. They want to meet you. They already sent an email about working on a project with you later in the year."

I glanced up. Edward Branch and his wife were almost to us. I saw the keen look in his eyes, but that wasn't what I was preparing myself for. It was the wife. She had the same stark hunger in her eyes so many other females in my life had. Catching my gaze, she smiled coyly and licked her lips.

Yeah. She was going to be a problem.

Fuck this. I pressed Kyle's number and murmured in Shelby's ear, "Stall for me."

"Wha—"

"Bro—" Edward Branch started to say, but I ducked out from behind Shelby.

It was rude. And stupid. Okay, it was ridiculously stupid of me, but I had to check on Kyle.

She twisted around, and I mouthed *Stall* to her again before slipping into a back and more private hallway.

It was almost time to go in.

I couldn't shake the edginess. It was a feeling of doom hanging over me.

Kyle's phone rang, and then I heard his voice message. "Yo. This is Kyle. Do your thing. *BEEP!*"

"Kyle, fucking call me. Where the hell—"

*BEEP. BEEP.*

I glanced at the screen, saw he was calling me back, and switched to that line. "Where the hell are you?"

"I'm coming. I'm sorry. Cheryl and I had a fight."

"Again? You guys have been fighting a lot lately."

There was static in his background. He was straining to speak on his end. Pressing a finger in my ear, I moved farther down the hallway. I had to find out what was going on. "Kyle, where are you?"

"Listen, Brody, I'm damn proud of you. I can't wait to get there."

My throat was swelling, tightening with emotion. Goddamn. "Where are you?"

"I'm in your car."

"My car?" *The fuck?* "Are you close? I gotta go in pretty soon."

"No—" A screeching sound cut through his words, metal on metal slamming together.

"Kyle."

No answer.

"Kyle!"

No.

No.

No!

I knelt, hunching over. I was in some corner, hidden by a fake plant. My palms were suddenly ice-cold and sweaty as I gripped the phone. My pulse sped up. My heart was trying to thump its way out of my chest.

"Kyle, answer me!" I was desperate. My throat was dry.

Someone touched my arm, and I shot to standing.

I rounded, finding Shelby standing there.

Her hand went to her chest. Her lips parted on a startled gasp. "Brody?" Her eyes went to my phone. I had it in a death grip, pressed so tight against my ear it could've drawn blood. Her throat moved. She was swallowing. "Wha-what's going on?"

I shook my head. I couldn't talk, not to her. I was too focused on full-on shouting into the phone. "Kyle!" People were coming from the main lobby to see what the commotion was about.

The line . . . there was still nothing on his end.

4

"Please, Kyle. Answer me." I was begging. My voice cracked from the pressure. Shelby's hand covered her mouth. She choked out a sob. I watched as the blood drained from her face.

The line went dead.

"Oh my God. Oh my God. Oh my God—" Shelby was scrambling for her phone.

I couldn't do anything.

I . . . my brother . . .

I heard her punch in some numbers, then a faint, "9-1-1, what is your emergency?"

# CHAPTER TWO

## Matthew

Pryor Mountain Range, South Montana
*Present day. Early May.*

A car crept up the driveway.

Its tires crunched over the gravel, moving closer to the large three-story home. There was a crisp chill in the morning air, which didn't seem to bother the man who got out from the driver's side. Standing over six feet tall, Matthew Kellerman ran a brisk glance over the Kellerman estate. It'd always been a gorgeous home.

He could already see telltale signs that it was empty. The grass hadn't been mowed. Paint was stripping from the sides of the house. The shrubbery in the fields that would normally be trimmed low looked untouched.

He sighed.

Of everyone, the only one who remained at the house was his stepsister, and he found his eyes tracking out to the fields surrounding where he stood on the mountain as if he could see Morgan. He couldn't. The house was nestled into a side cliff, just short of one of the higher peaks on the hill. He was able to see some of the land around them, the spots that weren't hidden by dense forest and the river that swept its way around the mountain, winding to the end and leading into a lake that was hidden in the valley between two other mountains.

He could already feel the effects on his body from the altitude. His mouth was parched, and he felt the beginning of a headache forming just behind his temples.

Yes. He looked back to the stately home. It'd been too long since he'd been back.

Way too long.

Grabbing his bag from the trunk, Matthew went inside, using the keys that hadn't been used in four years.

The second he stepped inside, memories came at him with breakneck speed.

He could hear Morgan's laughs of glee as she raced around the house. She was the youngest of them and was brought into the family when his father and her mother married. Either he or one of his two other siblings always raced after her. Finley and Abigail doted on Morgan as much as he did. The twins might've only been two years younger than him, but they were four years older than Morgan.

The last time he'd seen her, which was four years ago, he had hardly recognized her. She would've been twenty-four then. Her hair had darkened, but there were still streaks of blonde in it from her time in the sun. Her skin had been golden tan. And she held the same smell of the wild mixed with the scent of the horses she spent more time with than she spent with humans.

Even then, he saw how wild she was. He also saw just how much like her mother she looked too. She had the same slender build, the same striking beautiful hazel eyes, and the same cheekbones. Yes. Morgan had been stunningly beautiful back then. He couldn't help to wonder how much more so she had become, but glancing out the window, his thoughts were interrupted.

Another vehicle was pulling up outside. Matthew heard the same sounds of the tires moving over the tiny rocks, and he went straight for the coffee machine. Seconds later, laughter pealed through the air.

"Holy shit. It hasn't changed up here."

"Are we looking at the same house?" A feminine voice laughed. "This place is a mess. Morgan hasn't been keeping it up."

A snort from the other. "Are you kidding me? Taking care of a house isn't in her repertoire. We all know that."

A trunk slammed shut as Matthew was pouring the full-sized pot of water into the machine. He was rummaging through the cupboards when the door opened and his two siblings walked inside.

Finley dropped his bags onto the floor with a *thud*. His eyes lit up when he saw his older brother, and his arms spread wide. "Matt! You're a sight for sore eyes."

Abigail laughed as she came in next, dropping her bags next to Finn's. "And when he says sore, he means it. He's been complaining about his back for the last hour."

Matt and Finley caught up in a hug, smacking each other on the shoulder. Pulling away, he turned toward his sister and pulled her in for a tight hug. "Man. I've missed you guys."

Abby let out a soft sound, wrapping her thin arms even tighter around him. "Not as much as we've missed you." Tears filled her brown eyes, and she wiped them away. "I'm already crying. What a mess." She waved her hand in the air, drying her face and letting her gaze travel to the opened back of the coffee machine. "Oh, I didn't think Morgan would have coffee stocked for us."

"Well, I haven't actually found any, but I was hoping."

"Nope." Finley shook his head as their sister left the house. "Abby knew this would happen. She made me stop in Silver Springs on the way because of it. We all know Morgan is outside as long as the weather allows it."

That was most of the year. Even back when they were kids, she took to the mustangs living around the property like a fish to water. It was an old cliché, but the best way to describe it. It wasn't normal, but it *was* special. She was "adopted" by one mare, and since the first day Morgan had clambered onto Shoal's back, she lived more in the mustang world than the human one. He had hoped growing up, getting her high school diploma, and then an online college degree would urge her to become more ingrained in their world. His world.

It hadn't.

"Have you seen her?"

Finley was going through his phone but paused and looked up. His features tightened before he shook his head. "I was hoping maybe you had."

Four years. That was a long time.

Abby returned, carrying three grocery bags. Finley took them, setting them onto the counter, and Abby opened the one closest to her and pulled out the tin of coffee grounds. "Now we have coffee." She laughed again and ran a tired hand down her hair. "The essentials."

Finley reached into one of the other bags and pulled out a bottle of bourbon. "Speak for yourself, Abs. This is my essential."

"Speaking of." Matt pulled out three glasses. Inspecting them for dirt, he raised his eyebrows. "They're actually clean." He put them in front of his brother. "Fill me up, Finn. It's been a long day of traveling for all of us."

Finn opened the bottle, pouring a double shot in each before offering the bottle to his sister. "You want in on this?"

She grimaced. "No, thank you." She moved to the coffee machine, measured out the grounds, and then hit the brew button. "Coffee will do the trick for me." She pulled open the cupboard closest to her, saw it was more glasses, and moved to the next. She pressed her lips together. "I'm in shock. Morgan must've been here recently. Maybe she's more human than horse, after all."

They all paused, sharing a look before bursting into laughter.

Abby shook her head. "Whatever she is, she did the dishes. They're freshly washed."

"How can you tell?" Matt had moved to the other side of the counter so he was standing next to Finn. Both brothers wore custom-tailored suits, but while Matt kept his dark hair a couple of inches long so he could tuck it behind his ear, Finn's was trimmed short. All three siblings had dark, almond-shaped eyes and dark hair; though, Matt's had a touch of blond in it.

Abby took out a plate and held it up. "It's still warm to the touch." Biting her lip, she put the plate back and opened the fridge. She gasped in surprise. "And stocked the fridge too."

One bin was filled with lettuce, tomatoes, green peppers, and onions. A crisper had oranges, apples, strawberries, and raspberries. She pulled out a ketchup container and twisted off the top. It still had the seal over it. "She went shopping for us."

She opened the freezer. "Holy crap. There's enough chicken in here to last us till the movie's done."

The movie. The reason they were all there.

A grin tugged at the corner of Matt's mouth, and he crossed the kitchen to the two large French doors. Standing there watching the horizon, the mountainside, he held his glass of bourbon in one hand and slipped his other hand into his pocket.

She was out there, and he had a hunch she was watching him back.

Finn moved to his left side, and Abby moved to his right.

All three Kellerman siblings looked out at the same time, each wearing a different expression.

A touch of wonder hit Abby's eyes. A slight grimace flashed over Finn's face, but Matt just kept looking. Unlike his two siblings, who had come to the house for the same project that would bring trailers of movie equipment within the week, he was home for a whole other reason.

Abby rested her head on his shoulder, saying softly, "I wonder what she's doing right now."

Finn grunted, finishing his bourbon. "Who cares? She wants to live out there with the herd of wild horses, that's up to her." He moved around to refill his glass. "Makes no difference to me."

Matt didn't say anything, only transferred his glass to his other hand and reached to grasp Abby's arm in a half-hearted embrace.

Morgan was ten when everything fell apart, but they had gotten four years with her. Four years after their father married her mother and moved them into this house. Four years before everything ended in travesty.

Abby murmured again, "I can feel her in this house." She shivered, looking around. "And it's weird. It's as if I can also feel Morgan." Abby lifted her head, peering at her older brother. "Is Dad coming?"

Matthew shook his head with the slightest of movements. "You know how he is."

Abby grunted.

They had two days to get the estate into shape because, within the week, actors, grips, the director, producers, and everyone from the catering staff to the actors' assistants' assistants would start arriving.

They were coming to film a movie about Morgan's mother, about how Karen Kellerman was murdered.

# CHAPTER THREE

## Morgan

I saw them.

I was across the valley, standing on my own cliff while they stepped out onto my porch. I knew why they'd come. I went to the same meeting to approve the movie script, but that'd been so long ago.

Shiloh stepped close to me, nuzzling my shoulder. Her black nose, smoky grey coat, and mane rubbed against me. Her mother had almost been like mine, but since Shiloh was foaled, she and I were sisters. She could sense my unease as distinctly as I could.

This movie would be done. They would all go away, and they wouldn't return. In the meantime, I reached up behind me, grabbed some of Shiloh's mane and half-jumped, half-lifted myself onto her back.

She turned as soon as I settled, and the rest of the herd lifted their heads. They all turned down the path, heading to the better grazing in the next valley over.

Glancing once more back at my home, I mentally said hello and goodbye at the same time.

I was given human privileges, ones that I never took for granted. My mother's inheritance granted them to me. I was able to stay where I was. I could avoid humans as much as necessary. Some knew about me. Some whispered about me. Some thought I was a ghost. Only my stepfather, stepsiblings, a few others knew the truth.

One day, I would have to join their world.

That wasn't today.

I bent and laid my cheek to Shiloh's back.

# CHAPTER FOUR

## Brody

"Brody." My new manager leaned over from her seat and shook my shoulder lightly. "We're here. Wake up."

My sunglasses hid my eyes, so she didn't see I was already awake. Had been since the plane landed. The touchdown was rough, but it always takes a bit before we got to the private plane hangars for deplaning. No reason to move and upset the hangover headache that was already pressing behind my forehead.

I grunted my acknowledgement before sighing and sitting up.

A ghost of a frown crossed her face, but it was gone as soon as I lifted my head toward Gayle. Her eyebrows pinched together slightly, forming a middle wrinkle in her forehead. I almost grinned at the sight of it. Shelby would've panicked at the idea that she could even move her eyebrows. She would've fainted at the thought of a wrinkle up there. And that was one of the reasons why I enjoyed working with Gayle over Shelby.

There were others too.

Gayle was in her fifties, wore her greying hair long, and had a whole maternal side mixed with a kick-ass attitude. She didn't take shit, but I knew she'd come to care for me over the last few months, and I saw how she was with her children. They were adult and grown, but they called almost daily to check in. That spoke volumes.

I knew she was wondering if she should say something about the headache. But she knew why I drank. Her familiar inner conflict shifted to if she said something about the drinking, then what? Then it shifted yet again to a resolute no. I was her client. I wasn't her kid. If I'd been her kid, she would've kicked my ass in gear long ago, but no. She would round back to the fact that I was her client. She managed me. She didn't raise me.

Or, at least I assumed she was thinking all that. Since replacing Shelby in the managing and publicist aspect, I'd witnessed the storm of expressions play out over her face too many times to count.

In the end, she kept quiet.

Like always.

But the same instinct that told me something was wrong with Kyle also warned me that there'd be a time Gayle wouldn't keep quiet.

"Will there be water in the car?"

"Of course." The attendants were already helping with our bags. Gayle turned to thank one as hers were passed to her, and then headed down the aisle. "If you need a painkiller . . ." She let the sentence hang as she disappeared down the stairs and onto the tarmac.

My bag in hand, I nodded my thanks to the pilot and attendants and then dipped down to follow. I had to take the sunglasses off. The sun had been high when we left California, but I was surprised by how dark it was. "There's a time change, right?"

It was fucking cold too.

Gayle was greeting our driver. She nodded, pointing to the bags that had been placed on the tarmac. As he went to put them in the trunk, she glanced to me. "Yeah. We lost an hour. It's about ten right now."

"It's dark, and cold."

"Yeah. It gets cold here at night, so make sure you always have a jacket with you, at least at night." She frowned again before ducking once more and getting into the back of the car. She slid over as I sat next to her. Reaching for her seat belt, she said, "They're hosting a party for your arrival. If you need a minute, we should stop somewhere."

I switched from frowning to feeling a slight surge of irritation. I masked it. In some ways, Gayle had saved me over the last few months. I'd been an asshole to almost everyone. I didn't need to start in on her too. It had been my choice to drink the bottle of Patrón last night. Not hers.

The driver shut our door, and we were soon heading from the airport. I rubbed at my forehead. I should've shaken the driver's hand, been all gracious, which was what everyone wanted to see from a celebrity when they met one. I did none of those things.

Another asshole moment for me.

I'd have to give him a good tip when he dropped us off.

"Brody."

"Hmm?"

"Do we need to stop or not? It's an hour drive to the Kellerman estate."

An hour-long drive? We were in fucking no-man's land. "What's going on again?"

She closed her eyes for a second, her mouth tightening before she let out a soft sigh. Her tone was markedly calm when she spoke. "We're here to do the Karen Kellerman movie. You're remembering that, right?"

I scowled. "You don't have to treat me like a dick." See. She was starting.

"Then stop acting like one," she shot back.

I waited.

Her eyes widened, and she turned into a statue watching me.

I laughed. It'd been the first time she had let out Mama Gayle. "Wondered when that side would come out."

I stretched my legs out in front, and right away, her shoulders loosened. She sank back into her seat, her hand falling to her lap. "You aren't mad at me?"

"Gayle." I covered her hand with mine and squeezed once before letting go. "I have been a terror to people in the last seven months. Trust me, I try to hold back with you, but I know some of it slips out."

She laughed softly, her head falling back to rest against her headrest. "You can be . . . trying, yes."

I chuckled. "It's okay to want to strangle me. Just refrain from actually doing it."

Her mouth twisted down. "You have reason, Brody."

I felt a punch in the stomach. Yes. I listened to my brother die. I needed a drink. The need just made my headache triple.

She reached over and patted my hand this time. "Plus, the whole reason I'm here is because Shelby was a calculating bitch."

My scowl was firmly back in place.

Shelby had been the only other person who heard the call, and the bitch had her phone recording the whole goddamn time. She sold it to the media, and gave a few interviews hinting that my brother's death hadn't been an accident. There'd been no evidence that he killed himself. The police had looked. There'd been no suicide note, no indication that it was even a possibility. An eyewitness collaborated that he simply lost control of the car, but she dropped the seeds. No matter how much I loathed Shelby, I couldn't shake the question if something else happened.

And the bitch was shocked and pissed when I fired her ass.

I growled, remembering the fucking lawsuit pending against me for unlawful termination.

Gayle was three times the manager Shelby had been, though. When Gayle came on, she'd been the one to push this Kellerman project.

I had wanted to do a superhero movie, which was still on the table. But Gayle had dug her heels in, claiming that my public image had turned to shit since Kyle's death. I got a momentary grace in the public eye. Lots of sympathy and blessings, etc., but that had only lasted a week until I punched another actor at a bar. The media hadn't cared that the dick called a friend of mine a slut. Phone videos and images had been sold, and the story had started a whole host of bad publicity for me.

As if overnight, I had gone from Hollywood's heartthrob to their bad boy.

And that brought us to the whole reason I was being driven to somewhere I didn't want to be to work on a movie I didn't want to be a part of.

Gayle pitched the movie script to me, promising there would be Oscar buzz. That sounded amazing to her. Not me. Oscar buzz meant work. I had to be the good guy until I finally won, and that was *if* I won. The budget wasn't huge, so I wasn't getting as much money, but Gayle got this project as an attachment to the superhero one. If I didn't do this one, they wouldn't bring me on for that one. They were "concerned" about my behavior. I needed to be on time, be gracious, be professional, and act my way to an Oscar trophy.

I still wanted to know how the fuck this movie got tied to that one, but everyone got quiet whenever I asked questions. Gayle only kept saying that I would thank her later, and to be honest, I didn't have much fight in me. Not for this, anyway.

Showing up and acting in this movie was small potatoes compared to the real shitstorm inside me.

Forty minutes into the drive, I reached for one of the bottled waters. "So, tell me about this family and what's going on tonight?"

"Right." Gayle put the movie script she'd been reading aside and dug in her bag. She pulled out a huge packet of papers. "And before we get there, movies like this usually take five weeks, but this one might take longer. But don't worry. I have everything handled with your schedule and, take this." I did, and as I started to look through it, she started talking. "Peter Kellerman. He's the main attraction for this movie because it's based on his last wife's death. The first one died long ago. Something health-related."

Peter Kellerman. His photo and bio was on page one, along with an image of his latest hotel opening. "He has that hotel franchise?"

"Kellerman Hotels. It's a global franchise, but his children are all in his newest venture. Realty. His oldest, Matthew . . ." I turned to the second page and there was Matthew's image, along with a photo of him shaking the president's hand. "He works for Peter. He oversees their operations on the East Coast. The other two are twins."

I flipped the page again, and there were two separate images. A girl was first, and the guy on the bottom half of the page.

"Abigail and Finley. They are both developers, and Kellerman Realty is currently on the rise in California because of them. They're both good, damn good, at their jobs. Early thirties, thirty-two. And"—she motioned for me to turn the page again, so I did—"Finley is engaged to Jennifer Court. Now . . ." She took a breath, leveling me with a look. "Here's the problem I see. I know you know Jennifer, but do I need to know how well you know her?"

My lip twitched into a crooked grin. "Are you asking if I slept with her?"

Her face remained impassive. She didn't break a smile. "You don't have female friends, and because you know her, I already know you slept with her. I'm asking if she is going to be a problem? Is there a reason for her to harbor resentment for you or hope to start up an affair again? They're all going to be there. This movie is a big deal to them. It was their stepmother who was killed, and I've been told Jennifer is showing up too."

Shit. "I know I'm an asshole, but I'm not the cheating kind of asshole."

"You aren't answering my question. Is she going to be a problem?"

I looked down and began reading through the bio Gayle had for Jennifer. "No, she won't be. We parted on good terms, *friendly* terms." I stressed the friendly part because it was true. Finishing reading what she had, my grin turned a little cocky. "And I know something you don't have in here." I held up the binder. "Jennifer is madly in love with her fiancé. The only way she'd look in my direction is if he turned out to be a cheating asshole and she found out about it." I saw the warning flare in her eyes. "And no, I wouldn't touch her even then. You have nothing to worry about. I will be professional."

She grinned faintly. "Bad Boy Brody won't make an appearance?"

I grimaced at what the media had dubbed me. "Bad Boy Brody will only show if I'm locked in my room and drunk and I don't have an early call."

Her lips pressed together again. "We're in the middle of the mountains. I hope you use this project as a cleansing retreat. All that scenery and mountain air and shit."

"I said I'd be professional. I'm not going to turn into a saint."

She didn't show any reaction, but I felt the disapproval from her.

Good thing I didn't give a shit about that type of stuff either. I asked, "I read the script, but they never said why Karen Kellerman was killed."

"What?"

I waved my finger at her, my grin mocking. "See. I pay attention. I have half the script already memorized."

She shifted in her seat. "You're one of the most sought-after actors right now. If you didn't work hard before, none of that would've happened. I'm not surprised that you've read the script."

No. She was surprised I already had half of it memorized, but she was right. Before Kyle's death, I was one of the hardest working actors in the business. All the assholery had happened after. Still, I noted her surprise and made a mental note to maybe let up on some of the drinking for this movie. Some, not all. A guy still had his haunts.

"She was murdered by her first husband, right?"

Gayle nodded, turning to look out the window. After leaving Livingston, we'd turned onto a winding road, going up the side of a mountain.

She said, "The script just says it was a domestic abuse situation. She hid from her ex-husband, and when he found her, he murdered her."

"Hmmm." I shrugged, thumbing back through the binder she gave me. I paused on the bio about Peter Kellerman. This was my role. I needed to understand him the best I could. "He never remarried."

"What?"

I tapped his image. "He never remarried. You said his last wife. That happened, what? Twenty years ago?"

"Eighteen years ago, and you're right. He never did."

He wore a fancy suit, no shock there. Unsmiling. His eyes were flat. His hair perfectly combed to the side. A speck of gray was showing, but most of it was black. Tanned so he spent time outside, but his hands were folded under his arms. It was as if he was squaring off against the camera, or whoever was behind the camera, or hell, maybe he was already challenging who would see this image of him.

But he didn't remarry.

That stayed with me.

"Did we reach out to him? See if I can meet him before shooting starts."

"Yes, *I* reached out to him, and no. We won't meet. He said to ask his children for any insight needed."

The guy sounded like an asshole.

I doubted I'd ever meet Peter Kellerman, and I was fine with that. He was just one role I would be playing.

The car braked suddenly.

"*Oomph!*" Gayle shot forward, but my arm was already there, protecting her from hitting the seat in front of her before I turned my body. I molded around her so I was half-shielding her.

The intercom crackled on. "I'm so sorry. I'm so sorry—"

His words were drowned out by a thundering sound. It grew and grew until they broke from the trees in front of us.

# CHAPTER FIVE

## Morgan

The horses wanted to run tonight.

So did I.

There were people at the house, people I didn't know, people who didn't know me. But they were there, and my stepsiblings were wining and dining them. I heard the laughter, saw all the cars. The lights were on in the house, and people were spilling out onto the patio with blankets pulled around them. It was a large party, too large.

A car pulled up as I was there, and I watched a couple get out. The woman was dressed in one of the most beautiful dresses I had ever seen, and as they ran inside the house, it billowed out round her. The guy had on a suit, one of those that Matthew always dressed in. I knew Finley had to wear them, too, but they signified a different world.

Not my world.

Matthew, Finley, and Abby brought their world there.

It was crashing over mine, and the horses could feel it. We didn't like having these newcomers at home. I knew they would leave, but I couldn't relay that to the herd.

They were scared and pissed, and they had to run.

I heard them starting when I was at the barn and took off. If they were going, I wanted to go with them. And like another time, so long ago, I ran and jumped onto Shiloh's back. After that, she kicked her hooves harder into the ground so we could catch up to the herd because they weren't waiting.

The stallion was leading us away from these interlopers. We were going to the next mountain, but instead of going down into the valley and following the river that wound its way around our mountain, he was impatient. The stallion had us go right, and I braced myself. I knew what we would be crossing.

Then, spying headlights as a car wound its way around the mountain, I could only hope they would be past where we would cross the road. The stallion wasn't stopping. Car or not, we were going.

The herd soared over the road.

The stallion broke through the trees first, rearing his strong head up, but the mares were right after him. They were hot on the others' heels and sometimes a group of six horses would cross at the same time. Shiloh and I were near the end, but the car had stopped. They were waiting. I was holding onto Shiloh so my entire body was flat, and I would normally just bury my head into her mane. But this time, I didn't.

I looked over. I didn't sit up. I didn't lift my head. I just merely turned. Even with her mane half-blinding me, I was still able to see them.

A driver's eyes were bulging, his hands gripping the steering wheel, and his mouth was hanging open. He couldn't believe what he was seeing. My eyes trailed past him to the couple in the backseat. The woman was down, hunched over, and a guy was almost hugging her, but his attention was toward the road in front.

Piercing eyes were staring straight at me, and his dark hair looked as if he'd raked his hands through it a few times. The moment was brief, but he was seared into my memory. Everything about him was dark, brooding, dangerous. He wasn't gaping at me like the driver. His eyes were alert, clear, and intelligent.

Then we were gone, disappearing back into the trees, but I felt him. I felt as if he was inside me somehow, and as Shiloh carried me deeper into the woods and I was blanketed by the other mares, I couldn't help myself. I looked back, and he had moved so he was watching me from the back window.

I felt like I knew him, and I didn't like that feeling.

Shiloh's head jerked back. Her nostrils flared. Her body tightened under me. She felt my fear, and she didn't know how to handle it.

I buried my head back into her mane and stroked a hand down her neck. For the first time, I wasn't sure who I was soothing.

# CHAPTER SIX

*Brody*

The party was in full swing when we pulled up to the house.

I laughed to Gayle. "This is the house?"

She gave me a tight-lipped grin back, but she knew what I was referencing. The home was like a lodge, big enough for thirty guests. There was a pool, a tennis court, and a huge barn with white fences that ran back behind the barn and all the way to where the driveway turned into a clearing. There were buildings farther down by the barn, but I couldn't make them out. A row of trees blocked my view.

"Brody!"

The front door opened and out spilled some images I'd recently looked at in the car. Matthew, his siblings, and others that I didn't recognize.

A small crowd was soon forming behind him.

"Gayle." Matthew led the charge, giving her a hug before extending a hand toward me.

I nodded, shaking it. "Matthew Kellerman."

"Yes." His grin widened. "It's nice to officially meet you." He stepped back, indicating his siblings. "This is Finn and Abby, my brother and sister."

Finn gave a nod and a handshake, but Abby looked like a fan. Her eyes were wide, and she held her breath as I shook her hand. Then, ducking her head, she asked, "Can I get a hug? I know this might not be appropriate, but I'm a big fan."

This relaxed me. Seeing wild horses burst through the trees? No. A fan? Absolutely. Abby just became my favorite Kellerman.

I went into full movie-star mode. Upping the smoldering effect on my eyes, my grin turned so it was half-cocky but also half-genuine as I hugged not only Abby but also the other females that approached. A few of the men wanted a hug, but most were fine with a handshake. I always got the once-over—the look each guy gave me to see what separated me from them. It was damned good genes, my mother's high cheekbones, the square jaw from my dad, and a body that training seven days a week in a gym couldn't get me. I did that, or I had until Kyle, but I still had muscle definition. I'd have to slip away for a run to tighten everything back up, but I knew I was blessed.

After all the introductions were done, most of the group returned back to the house, but Matthew stayed back with Gayle and me. The driver remained by the car, waiting for instructions on where to put our bags.

"How was the drive up?" Matthew's smile seemed normal as he asked the question, but there was an edge of caution in his voice.

"It was eventful, that's for sure," Gayle said dryly, shooting me a look.

I narrowed my eyes, studying Kellerman as I stated, "A herd of horses ran in front of the car."

He looked my way. That smile slipped a bit, tightening. "Horses?" His Adam's apple moved up and down.

I glanced to Gayle and the driver. "I would've counted thirty or forty, maybe?"

"Those aren't the horses we're using for the movie, are they?"

He shook his head, saying to Gayle, "No, no. We have a few from a nearby ranch we're using."

"Are those your horses?" I was going over the script in my head. The few scenes that had horses in them were mild shots. There were no action sequences. The notes said the characters would go on an easy ride, with the focus on the conversation. There'd be the usual close-ups and a zoom-in of Karen holding hands with Peter.

"No. Uh." He shifted his champagne glass to his other hand and scratched behind his neck. "There *is* a herd of mustangs in the area. The sanctuary here runs on some of our land, but I thought they had been moved to a different area. I'm sorry to hear that they ran out in front of your car. That isn't normal. I guarantee."

"Thank goodness for that. They were beautiful to watch, but it was so sudden. We could've had a nasty car accident . . ." Her voice trailed off, hearing her own words, and she turned to me. She reached out. "Oh, Brody."

I'd already been thinking of Kyle and clipped my head in a brief nod. A damn drink would be nice. "Don't worry about it. We can talk about car accidents. It almost happened just now."

But I saw the guilt linger in her eyes.

"Ma'am."

A soft cough from the driver.

"Oh!" Her hand pulled back. She asked Matthew, "Where do we unload our bags?"

Kellerman's shoulders relaxed a little. "Yes!" He gestured toward the barn. "There's a cabin down there where we put Brody," he said and then turned to me. "We know you wanted your own space for privacy. Gayle, we have you in a room in the main home."

"Excellent."

She was in work mode. Her bags were taken out, and she went inside with the driver. I waited by the car, and Matthew turned to me again, his smile a bit hesitant. "So, Brody."

I prepared myself. I'd heard the same tone from lawyers, reporters, and almost everyone else. It was the voice of someone who didn't know me but thought they did.

He asked, "Are you comfortable with horses?"

I hadn't expected that question. "I rode a few times as a kid with my brother, but that was probably twenty years ago."

"Yes, yes." He was nodding as if he knew what I was going to say before I said it. "So they didn't scare you that much?"

I frowned. That was an odd question. "What do you mean?"

"I meant—" He stopped, his eyes narrowing for a bit. "Uh, I mean. Wild mustangs. They must've been a shock to see, right?"

"Yeah." He was fishing.

"You said there were thirty or forty. Were you able to really see the horses? I mean, did you notice which one was the stallion?"

His questions weren't what he wanted to know. He was asking something else.

Then I got it.

He wanted to know if I studied the horses—the image of that girl flashed in my mind again.

It had been her hair that had caught my eye. She'd been hugging her horse, her arms and legs wrapped around, and if I hadn't been looking closely, I wouldn't have seen her. Every inch of her had been plastered to that animal, as if she were an extra layer of skin on the mustang. And those eyes. I still felt the impact of them.

She'd only been wearing pants and a shirt, which was odd since it was fucking cold out.

I couldn't get that out of my head, and I couldn't get *her* out of my head either.

It was as if she stuck her hand inside, took hold of my organs, and crawled in beside them. I still felt her.

*That* was who he was asking about.

"No." I shook my head. "I didn't see the stallion."

He was still watching me closely.

I added, "They were running so fast that it was done within a few seconds."

At that, his shoulders fell back, smoothing out. "Ah. Yes. I do hope to section off the lands where we'll be shooting for the movie, so hopefully you won't see the herd again." He nodded past the barn. "You can't see it now, but they typically run on the other mountain over there. If you see 'em again, it'll be far in the distance."

The image of that girl flashed in my head again.

Her dark eyes. Her dark golden hair. I only got a glimpse, but she was stunning, and I found myself saying, "I hope not."

I wanted to see her again.

And I ignored the sharp look Kellerman threw my direction.

# CHAPTER SEVEN

## Morgan

It was four in the morning.

The last of the strangers finally went to bed, and I heard their snoring as I tiptoed through the building. I hadn't wanted to come back, but I needed clothes. It was getting colder at night, and though Shiloh and Shoal broke the night wind if I stayed with the herd, they couldn't completely ward off the chill. I was used to the extremes with the weather. My body adjusted long ago, but I still got cold. I stayed in the house nights during the bad weather and in the winter. On those nights, I'd usually slip into the second floor of the barn. The house was mine, but I always felt like it was theirs: my stepsiblings, my mom, and him. The apartment felt more like home to me. It'd been renovated so it looked like a normal apartment, but that wasn't where I'd gone.

I wanted to see them.

I was standing above where Abby was sleeping. Her face was turned toward me, her arm was thrown up on the pillow, and her body was twisted the other way. She'd have a kink in her neck when she woke, but she looked happy.

I knelt, looking closer.

There were no bags under her eyes, but the laughing lines still around her mouth made me smile. Yes. She looked happy. She wasn't the frail, thin girl I last saw when I signed for the movie. That was years ago, and I'd been worried about her. I didn't know what was going on with her then. I was glad it had worked out, whatever it was.

Tiptoeing out, I checked on Finn next. I didn't go all the way in. His covers were pulled down so I could see the bare skin of his thigh. He was sleeping naked. Same Finn. He groaned about wearing boxers around the house when we were kids. He hadn't changed.

That made me smile.

Matthew would've been using the main room, and I was coming down the hallway when I heard the neigh in the distance. That was Shiloh calling for me, so I bypassed the stairs. I was going past the kitchen table when I looked down and stopped. The script was there.

*Unbroke.*

That was the name of the movie, a term used about a horse that wasn't trained.

I frowned slightly, feeling a tug in my stomach, and reached for the script.

The movie was about my mother, but why would they use that term? She'd been broken.

"So you *do* come to the house every now and then?"

I whipped around, seeing Matthew in the threshold of the open patio door. He wore the suit he had worn for the party, but his shirt collar was open, the top few buttons were undone. He'd pulled the shirt out from his pants, too, and unlike Abby, the bags under his eyes fell halfway down toward his mouth.

My hand snapped back to my side. Ducking my head a little, I went toward him. If he woke the others, there'd be conversations I didn't want to have. And I heard Shiloh's neigh again. She was worried about me.

Matthew heard her, too, looking back over the fields. "That Shoal?"

He stepped back, and I moved past him, shutting the patio doors behind me. "Shiloh."

"Shiloh?"

"Shoal's daughter. She's a little darker gray than Shoal."

"Ah." His nostrils flared. I felt a wave of anger from him. "That makes sense. It's like you have a new sister."

I watched him warily, moving to the edge of the patio. I murmured, "You look well."

His nostrils flared again. Heat pooled in his eyes. "You don't."

I flinched, looking away.

He cursed under his breath. "Sorry. I'm sorry. Your hair is more blonde than I remembered. You're still so thin. And I want to hug you, but I'm scared if I try, you'll take off like a damned deer."

I looked back up, and there was a yearning in his eyes that had me swallowing over a knot. He moved to take a step forward but stopped, and in a low voice, he asked, "Can I hug you, Morgan? Can I hug my sister?"

"I'm not your sister." I paused a beat. "Or your stepsister."

Not anymore, but once we had been. We'd been a family.

That was a long time ago, and years passed.

*He* took them from me when I remained at the house. Peter Kellerman used my inheritance to pay for my homeschooling, but that was it. And a part of me always wondered if that'd been at Matthew's insistence. When my mom was murdered, my stepfather wanted nothing to do with me. Staff moved into the house, acting like my keepers.

Not that I was bitter. I wasn't. Peter Kellerman always scared me, but he took my siblings away. That'd been the one thing I was angry with him about.

I recognized the look in Matthew's gaze. Ownership.

It reminded me of how my stepfather looked at my mother.

He took another step toward me, and I jumped back, hitting the railing. "Don't." I spoke quickly because he was right—if he pushed, I would run. It was how I was.

His head fell back, and he cursed again under his breath. "You're still like a wild animal." He looked out over the fields, over where I could hear the river trickling and where I could already smell the dew forming on the grass. I could hear the horses on the field across from us, on the other side of the river, but I also knew he couldn't see or feel or hear any of those things.

He just saw darkness because the sun had yet to crest the horizon.

I almost felt sorry for him.

I was a wild animal, yes. I could live out there with them, but I was also human. I would always come back. This was my mother's home. Normally, I felt her when I came back, but I couldn't feel her right then, and I didn't like it.

I looked back inside the house. "There are so many people here."

He nodded, his hand going into his pocket. "We changed the ending."

It was an abrupt change of topic, but I went with it.

I frowned. "You did?"

"Yeah." There was a glass of champagne on the table. He picked it up, tipping his head back to take a swallow. "The studio that invested with us thought a happily ever after ending would do better in theaters. Also . . ." His eyes narrowed, lingering on me. "You aren't in the movie."

I fell silent.

"Dad went to great lengths to hide you so no one knows about you. We thought about writing you in, but there would have been questions. A mysterious Kellerman daughter, even through marriage, who lives alone, and that's *if* she's even in the house?" He laughed to himself. "There'd be a media storm around you." He waved a hand around the place. "No one knows about you, well, except maybe one."

"Finn's fiancée?"

He did a double take. "How do you know about her?"

"Voices travel." I touched my ear. "I have good hearing."

He grunted. "I suppose so. She's coming later, if you want to meet her." His mouth flattened again. "Are you going to see Finn and Abby too? And not where"—he gestured back inside the house—"you see them, but they don't see you. I know Abby would love to hug you."

I heard the sadness again from him. I knew it was from him, that he wanted to hug me and couldn't. Maybe I should? But the thought of feeling his arms circle me, of being crushed to him, made me want to recoil. No. I couldn't. He wanted more than a hug. I could feel it from him.

I chose my words carefully, deciding on, "It'd be nice to talk to her too."

He laughed again. "Could you do me a favor? If you have any pull with that stallion, can you keep the herd from the humans?" Another drip of bitterness. "Your herd almost took out the star of the movie."

They weren't my herd. It wasn't like that.

"Star?" That was who that guy was?

"Yep. A goddamn A-list star. We got him because he needs a good movie for his public image. Couldn't afford him otherwise." He glanced over again. "He's playing Peter. The script is mostly the love story that Peter and Karen had, the good parts, anyway. He's playing the side of Peter we all wanted to have growing up."

The fairy tale.

Matthew downed the rest of his champagne and picked up the bottle to pour himself some more. I finally felt a small ease in the air from him. "The script is getting award buzz already."

He was using words I didn't understand, so I only nodded. I didn't want to tell him that. I didn't need to remind him how different I was from the rest of them, from him.

Shiloh neighed again, this time the sound was closer. She was coming to look for me.

"Shit." Matthew glared in the direction the sound came from. "You gotta go to her. I can't have a feral horse walking around on our property. We could get sued if she hurt anyone."

I threw him a look but started from the patio. "She wouldn't hurt anyone."

"She wouldn't hurt you, but she'd run someone over if she felt threatened, so yeah, she would."

Another whinny. She was growing more anxious.

I avoided the last few steps and jumped over the barrier. I glanced back. Matthew was watching me from above, and I ignored the anger he didn't know he was broadcasting. "I'll come back."

Immediately, the anger waned, but only a bit.

He held up his glass. "Be safe, Morgan."

I began running, moving soundlessly over the rocks. I was to the barn when I heard him add under his breath, "I love you."

I paused for just a second before I grabbed the post and launched myself over the fence.

He never knew how much I could hear.

Shiloh was waiting for me. There were two fence lines. She'd come all the way up to the end of the first field. It was the closest she'd ever been to the main house, and at the sight of me, she began moving around. Restless.

I was halfway to her, far beyond what Matthew could've seen, but I felt eyes on me. Someone was watching me, and like a deer, I froze. My head cocked to the side as I tried to feel where the eyes were coming from.

I turned, feeling my attention pulled toward one of the private cabins, and there he was. The star Matthew talked about. He was standing on his bedroom porch, a bottle in his hand. I could smell the booze despite the distance between us.

He shouldn't have been able to see me. It was dark, a black canvas to a normal human, but I knew he could. I felt it low in my belly. A different wave of awareness swept over me.

It felt strange, alien.

I picked up my pace and sprinted for Shiloh. She waited on the other side of the fence. Once I got there, I clambered up and threw a leg over her. She turned for the river the second I was settled astride her.

I didn't look back, but I couldn't shake the feeling of him watching me.

# CHAPTER EIGHT

## Brody

Goddamn.

I cursed when I woke the next day and glanced to the clock. If I got up, I'd make it for lunch. I was pretty sure I had a folder given to me with the itinerary, and they had times allotted for every meal. I shouldn't have been able to eat. I drank an entire bottle of bourbon last night, but my looks hadn't been the only other genes I inherited from my family—my stomach of steel had come from my uncle who had been a raging alcoholic. I could inhale an entire pizza with breakfast.

"Brody."

Gayle knocked on the outside door.

My voice, which was half-gurgle, half-shout was not made of steel. "Go the fuck away!" Pain ripped through my head. For further effect, I reached down, grabbed a shoe, and hurled it across the room. My bedroom was inside the small cabin, but I buried my head back into my pillow. If I heard them, I was hoping they heard me.

She added, quieter, "I claimed jet lag for your absence this morning, but if you don't get that million-dollar ass out here, I will personally book you a ticket back to Los Angeles."

I was at the front door in a flash, reaching for the knob. Pausing, I glanced down. Yes. I had underwear on, and then I ripped open that door. I held up my hands. "Gayle, I'm so sorry." I would've gotten on my knees if I thought it would help. Real shame laced my veins. "I'm an asshole in recovery."

She came inside, shutting the door. "You're a grieving brother. I don't care about whatever you threw at the door. I care that you missed a breakfast meeting we had scheduled with the producers."

"Producers?" I scratched behind my ear. "I thought I met them last night."

"Not the Kellermans. I meant the production company they're working with on this."

"What?" I was searching my memory. I had faults, but forgetting meetings was not one of them. "I had no idea. Really."

"Oh." Her forehead wrinkled again. "Maybe I forgot to tell you." Then she waved it all away, shooing me. "You're too young for me to ogle anymore. Take a shower and be up in the main house in twenty minutes. Got it? The director will be there, and you better not miss that meeting."

The director. Fuck. I nodded, my hand twitching at my side ready with a salute too. "Got it."

She started to leave, but turned back. "Oh, hey."

"Yeah?"

"Kara Toilley is arriving today. Don't fuck the lead actress. Got it?"

I smirked but bit my tongue. "Not a problem."

Her eyes narrowed. "You're smirking. Why are you smirking?"

"Huh?"

Comprehension dawned, and her eyes rolled to the back of her head. "Are you kidding me, Brody? You already screwed her, didn't you?"

Three times, in fact.

I lifted a shoulder. "We did a commercial together. It was momentous."

"Is she going to be a problem? Who haven't you slept with on this movie?"

I raised an eyebrow, giving her a pointed look.

She started laughing as she shook her head. "Don't start fluttering those long eyelashes at me. You're a boy in my opinion."

She waved a hand up and down toward me. "Your body might be all man, but I view you like one of my kids. That pecker better never harden for me. Got that?" She ended with a bark.

I did salute her this time. "Yes, ma'am." But I was grinning. She said I was all man. It shouldn't matter one bit, but my ego felt a bit stroked. Or maybe it was hearing that she viewed me as one of hers.

I scratched the side of my neck. "I'll be good. I promise, and don't worry about Kara. She's a hit-it-quit-it type, so I'm sure I was a notch on her bedpost."

"Aren't you to everyone?" She held a hand up, moving through the door. "Just keep the pants on, Brody, and you have fifteen minutes!"

The shower was quick. Getting ready was even quicker. I put some gel in my hair, letting it dry messy. The look tended to work on anyone who liked guys. Jeans and a shirt were next. I didn't put on anything super trendy, just simple. When I left the cabin, I knew I was the vision of a celebrity. It was what they hired me to be, so it was the mask I wore for them.

"Brody." Kellerman approached when I stepped inside the house.

"Matthew." I shook his hand and, recognizing the woman next to him, I nodded. "Shanna Michaels. Hello. It's great to see you."

The director was in her forties, had sandy-colored hair, alert blue eyes, and the same attitude I felt from Gayle. She was no-nonsense and whip-smart—at least that was her reputation. She seemed it in person too.

She shook my hand, a slight grin tugging at her mouth as if she thought I was being funny. "We've met before, Brody. Have you forgotten?"

*Did I sleep with her?*

No. I would've remembered. Then I did. "The audition! Yes."

"Before that as well."

Maybe I *had* slept with her.

She said, "You hit on me at a premiere party."

I stilled.

Not good. Not good at all.

"Shit." I held up my hands. "I'm sorry. I—"

She laughed. "Don't worry. It didn't go further than that. I knew I'd want you on one of my movies one day." She caught my hand in a surprisingly strong grip and leaned in close before she murmured in my ear so no one could hear. "But if you weren't such a damned gifted actor, I would've taken you up on that weekend offer."

Great.

Fuck.

I used to be professional . . . at some point. "I'll take that as a compliment then."

She leaned back, her eyes twinkling in amusement. "You should, and we should get down to business. We have the table read scheduled for today. Kara will be arriving shortly."

Matthew was rolling up the sleeve of his shirt. Khaki shorts. Loafer sandals. A slightly pink buttoned-down shirt. He looked like the epitome of every Harvard jackass.

"Did you sleep well, Brody?"

Once I passed out. "Yes, I did. You?"

He hesitated before clipping his head in a nod. "Of course. This mountain air tends to calm me. Always has."

Interest stirred in me. "You lived here when you were a kid?"

"No." He began scanning the room. "When I was a teenager, and even then, it was only for a few years. When Karen . . . when Karen died, we mostly all moved away."

Mostly?

The image of that girl running away flashed in my mind again.

I'd been sitting on the second floor patio last night, toasting Kyle, when a flash of movement had drawn my attention as it streaked across the field in front of me. It was only after I watched her run to the fence that I realized a horse was there. I was starting to wonder if the girl was a ghost. Maybe Kyle was messing with me, making me see shit lately.

"Who's the 'we'?"

He stopped scanning, freezing a moment before looking back at me. His eyes were clearer than before. "What?"

"You said 'we mostly.' Who else was here?"

He held my gaze steady, unblinking. He kept it tight to the vest, more so than others, but I knew this guy was close to shitting his pants.

An unnatural smile broke over his face, giving him a plastic look. "My siblings and I. Peter kept the house, but we all moved back to Livingston and then to L.A. later."

Not Dad. Peter. That was interesting. "How old were you when . . . it happened?" It. What did they say when they referred to their stepmother's murder?

Matthew waited a beat. "I was sixteen when Karen was murdered." His Adam's apple moved up and down as he swallowed. He coughed, clearing his throat. "The twins were fourteen then. And—" He stopped himself.

I found myself leaning toward him. He was about to say something else, maybe add someone else to the equation. That girl? There was a story there. She was someone to him, someone to this place.

I didn't think I was seeing a ghost.

Or hell, maybe I was. I'd already gotten called out for hitting on my director. I was pretty sure I'd been wasted at that party. Play along? Keep my trap shut? Make sure I didn't land myself in another heap of trouble.

Looking over, I saw Gayle watching us as she ignored Abby and a girl from the crew who were talking next to her.

As if knowing what I was thinking, she moved her head from side to side. It was so slow the girls with her didn't notice, but I did. And I knew what she was saying.

Yep. Got it.

Keep my fucking mouth shut.

So, I smiled and said the most generic thing I could think of, "How about that weather you guys have here, huh?"

# CHAPTER NINE

## Morgan

*One week later*

I was stretched out on my back on top of Shiloh.

The sun beat down on us, but there was a slight breeze that broke up the heat. The sky was bright blue with cotton-candy-like clouds.

Shiloh's head was bent so she could graze. Her mane was half my pillow, the bottom of her neck the other. My feet were crossed over each other, resting on top of her back end as the rest of the horses were around us.

This was a favorite pastime of mine.

I slept while Shiloh ate, and if I weren't sleeping, I'd let my mind wander as I watched the clouds.

Yes, I was usually content if I was with Shiloh or Shoal, but sometimes I got bored. Those were the days I'd venture to the neighbors' house seven miles away, or even farther down to see what was going on in the local small town. The trip there and back would usually take a few days. There were other times when I'd lay high above the highway. I could feel the breeze against my hair and skin and watch the birds fly below me. Every once in a while, tourists would come along, see the eagles or a bear or even a moose. They'd stop and take pictures, their excited shouts ricocheting up to me. They never saw me. They never looked high enough, and if they had, I would pull back beyond their eyesight.

The best days were spent at a nearby watering hole. It was shallow enough that it warmed quickly. I loved being there.

And other days, if I was more bored than usual, I'd go to the house. I'd try to pretend to be human, but then weird feelings would move up inside me, feelings that I didn't know how to handle. So, once that happened, I'd go back to Shiloh.

I knew it didn't make sense to others, but it was my life. It was my world. It was the way I made sense of the senseless.

But today, I did none of those things.

Today, I thought of him.

As the days wore on, as they continued to make their movie, he kept showing up in my thoughts. I'd gone back a few times just to watch. One time, I left the barn to sneak into his cabin to watch him sleep.

He'd been restless, tossing and turning. A bottle of alcohol on the floor next to his bed, within reaching distance. Every time I watched him, he had one of those bottles keeping him company, but no one else. Feeling a stirring in my chest, I always thought I would find a woman with him, but I never did.

I tried telling myself I didn't care.

I thought he had caught me the time I snuck in. His eyes had fluttered open, and he had lifted his head, a sleepy groan escaping his parted lips. "Wha—" He had shaken his head, but the alcohol took control over him again, and his eyelids weighed heavy. His deep breathing told me he fell asleep the next instant.

I smiled to myself, remembering that night.

Alcohol and sweat filled the room, but there was another smell. It was manly, somewhat pine-scented, but it was him. I'd been around enough people to know each person had their own smell, and I liked it.

I liked him.

I might be only half from his world, and Matthew said he was the star, but he was different. He wasn't like the others. He was more. He commanded more. He demanded more. There was a sizzle in the air around him. It wasn't just me that he affected. I watched the females. He affected all of them, too, even the older ones. It might not have been in the same way, but he still drew them to him. One grey-haired lady looked after him like a mother; another female who was always barking at people, pointing around as she stood by the cameras, had a fondness for him. Her voice was softer, more patient with him.

I lifted my hands, holding his shirt as I buried my head in it. I breathed him in again. I'd have to take it back and swipe another. His smell was fading, being replaced with Shiloh's and mine. But until then, I draped it over my chest.

It had come to be my favorite blanket.

The stallion whinnied at that moment, and everyone looked at him.

Grazing was over.

# CHAPTER TEN

*Brody*

"Cut!"

We were filming on the back of the river in a valley between the Kellerman's mountain and the other. There was a clearing on our side, giving us enough space to comfortably set everything up, but trees and vegetation filled the other bank. Higher on the adjacent mountain was a clearing like ours. I found myself looking up every now and then, wondering if I'd catch a glimpse of the girl. Then again, that'd been the theme for me over the last two weeks.

Everywhere we went on the Kellerman's lands, I always wondered if she was out there. If she was watching. If she was with her horse. If I'd get another glimpse of her.

A hand fell down, grazing over my groin, and I stiffened.

"Oh. Sorry." Kara laughed, but her hand came back for another rub.

She didn't sound sorry.

We'd been filming the last scene for the twentieth time, and Kara kept forgetting her words. Normally, I wouldn't care. This was part of the job, but it was a scene where I had to keep shoving my tongue down her throat. Every time she slipped up, her hand fell to my ass, and she'd squeeze, pressing against me.

I was half-grinding against a woman. My dick was up, but it wasn't her in my head when we were kissing. It wasn't her body rubbing against mine. It was the damned ghost that had been plaguing my dreams and thoughts since I'd gotten to this place.

I could've sworn she had been in my room one night, but when I woke, there'd been no evidence she'd been there. The doors were all locked and no window was left open.

Still, I couldn't shake the feeling she'd been there.

Shanna's hands cupped around her mouth as she yelled, "That's a wrap. Start taking everything down. We move locations tonight."

"Thank God." Kara pretended to pout, her slim body leaning into mine. Her hand traced down my arm. "If you want, we could take this back to your place?"

The diva was given her own cabin like me. They thought she'd want privacy. Apparently, it'd been too far away for her to walk every day. She demanded to be moved, and she'd been given the master bedroom instead.

I grinned down at her. "Not a chance in hell." My hands went to her arms, and I shoved her away, one clean push to get her body off mine.

I turned to leave.

"Ass."

I paused but then let it go.

I'd spoken too quickly to Gayle. Kara *was* a problem, and I had a feeling she was going to continue to be until I shoved my prick into her. She'd been breathing down my neck, and her hands had been trying to rub my groin since she arrived for the table read.

"Brody." I was walking past the director when she waved me over. She was standing a few feet away from the camera crew.

"Yeah?"

"Are you fucking Kara?"

I gave her a sharp look. "No."

She raised a disbelieving eyebrow. "Come on."

"I'm not."

"She's damned near molesting you, has been this whole time."

I grimaced. The feel of her hand brushing against me came back to me. "I'll deal with it."

"You shouldn't have to. That's what I'm saying. If you aren't sleeping with her, I'm assuming it's because you don't want to. Am I wrong?"

I gave her a crooked grin, tapping the side of my head. "Shit's kinda messed up here right now. Sleeping with my co-star isn't something I can take on."

"About your brother?"

I caught a twinge of pity in her eyes.

I nodded. "You could say that." I was keeping company with all sorts of ghosts lately. Girls. Kyle. I didn't need to add any more regrets to the list.

"Well." She sighed, glancing over to where Kara was glaring our way. Her assistant was next to her, trying to talk to her. "If that's an issue you want help resolving, let me know—"

A scream cut her off.

We both turned, but the sound of stampeding hooves drowned out any other screams. Everyone froze.

High up on the clearing on the other mountain, the horses were sprinting from one side to the other. Even with the river and tree line between us and them, we had a panoramic view of the creatures.

The stallion, which stood a few hands taller than the size of the rest of the herd, was pure white except for two black spots on his backend.

"Oh, whoa." Shanna stepped closer to them, snapping her fingers. "Carl! Get that camera out. Get those horses on it."

He nodded, swinging his lens around. "On it."

Everyone was watching the horses, their mouths hanging open, but I was looking for her. She must be with them. Unless, I glanced to the trees above the horses. No. I looked at the tree line on the other side of the river. No. I didn't see her.

I looked back to the herd. They were almost past us and would be out of eyesight soon. I was studying each one, but they were going so fast.

Then . . . there.

I saw the gray mare she'd been riding the first night, but she wasn't on her.

No.

A foot.

I almost laughed aloud. Her foot was the only thing visible, resting on top of the mare's back. She was riding on the side of her, hidden from sight.

It happened so fast that, by the time I turned, they were already gone. Everyone just seemed stunned. I didn't hear any questions about the girl, or the foot.

"Goddamn." Shanna swore under her breath. "There's a herd of mustangs. Kellerman should've told me that."

"He didn't?"

She looked at me sharply. "You knew?"

"They almost took out our car on the first night. I thought he cleared them with you."

Her jaw firmed, and she ground out, "No. He didn't clear anything with me." She pointed to where the horses had appeared. "There was no fence between us and them. If they had veered this way, someone could've been trampled." She gripped her radio, lifting it to her mouth as she pressed the side button. "I want a twenty on Kellerman."

She let go, the radio crackled.

Someone responded, "He went into town for a meeting."

Shanna pressed down on her button. "Then I want to know the second he's back, not a minute later."

A crackle. "On it."

She gazed up at the clearing again, studying it before she motioned for Carl. "Did you get the footage?"

He nodded, lowering the camera back to the ground. "A good six seconds, I think."

"Fine." She waved her radio in the air. "Pack up! Wait for instructions. We might be changing locations for the night."

"Different from where we were supposed to be?" one of the crew asked.

"Yeah." She swung those keen eyes my way. I could see the steam coming from her ears as she formulated a new plan. "Is there anything else I should be made aware of?"

"Hey." I flashed her a grin, one that usually worked to loosen the panties. "I assumed you knew. I'm only an actor."

She cursed, rolling her eyes. "Wipe that grin off your face. I already told you we aren't going to fuck."

"I know, boss."

She laughed softly, shaking her head. "You're a lot smarter and with-it than you let people see, Brody Asher. Don't think I'm one of those girls who'll fall for your tricks." She pointed her radio at me as she began to walk backward. "You said it. I'm your boss. For a reason."

"I salute my manager sometimes. I can add you to that list if you'd like."

She barked out a laugh before turning and walking back toward the main lodge. "Didn't realize you were funny, Brody."

I was a whole lot more than that.

She could add crazy to the list too.

# CHAPTER ELEVEN

*Brody*

Shanna was upset about the whole mustang situation, so everything was put on hold. She claimed there needed to be litigation about safety zoning and a whole bunch of other legal and technical issues. All I knew was that we got a night free from shooting. Most of the crew went into town to drink at the bars, and while I'd normally be on board, I found myself heading down a walking path instead. I was alone. I could hear the soft sounds of a river just ahead, and I thought I really had lost my mind. I was pretty sure because while my boss was livid about the safety risks of a herd of mustangs in the area, I was hoping to run across them tonight.

Not them.

Her.

So, when the path came to the river, when I could hear it around the corner, I paused for a moment.

Thousands of women wanted me in their bed, and I stood there like a nervous seventh grader for fuck's sake.

I was embarrassed for myself, and rolling my eyes, I stepped around.

I didn't expect her to be there. Why would she? Kellerman told me the horses ran over more than a hundred acres, but dear God, there she was.

Standing on the other side of the bank, she was running a hand through her hair.

I was entranced.

Jesus.

She was like a goddess.

It was like out of a cheesy movie scene. The moonlight sparkled on her golden hair. There were some darker strands that I saw now too. A slight mist was in the air, settled over the river and pooling around her feet. The only thing that was different was her clothing. There was no long flowing dress. She wore what any other woman would've worn, just a sweatshirt and jeans that were snug on her. She'd rolled them up so they ended above her knees, and when she moved back, I saw she wore regular sneakers. They were the kind used for hiking, which made sense.

Christ.

I almost laughed at myself. I'd been so convinced she was a ghost.

"You're a real person."

I hadn't realized I spoke until her head jerked up. Her eyes found me, and she began to turn away.

"Don't!" I started for her, my hand in the air, but I forced myself to stop. I'd spook her for sure then. When she didn't move any farther, I softened my voice and added, "Please don't."

This was surreal.

When I saw she still wasn't leaving, I took a step closer, lowering my hand. "I'm Brody. I'm working here on a movie."

Her eyes widened, but she lifted her head to fully look at me. The flight instinct was waning toward curiosity. I could see how her lips parted, and she moved a strand of hair out of her way to see me better. Her eyes narrowed, and her head tilted up questioningly. "You're famous."

"I . . . uh . . . yeah."

Again. Thousands of women swooned over me. This girl had me stuttering.

After clearing my throat, I said, "Can I ask, just so I know for myself, but . . . are you a fucking ghost?" Shit. What if she was one of those girls who was proper-like? I raked my hand through my hair. "I mean, are you—" Yeah. Anyway I sliced it—even taking out the curse word—I still sounded nuts.

She laughed.

She *was* laughing. Once she started, she couldn't stop. The sound came out of her in waves and then she was shaking her head.

I found myself smiling, but I didn't know why.

"Oh man." She wiped at her eyes, her laughter beginning to fade. "I haven't laughed like that for a while."

"Yeah?" I was an idiot for feeling proud of that. Yep, I even had a boner like I used to walk around with in junior high. What was next? Fucking wet dreams again? I made a mental note to lay off the bourbon at night.

I gentled my smile, ducking my head a little. "I'm glad."

I was flirting with her. I wasn't ashamed. I was going to reel her in because, dammit, I needed her in a way I didn't fully comprehend.

She laughed again. "Thank you. That was nice."

"Can I ask what your name is?"

She swallowed, her eyes widening again.

I didn't think she was going to answer.

Then, so softly I almost didn't hear it, she whispered, "Morgan."

"Morgan." I nodded to myself. "And to be clear, just so I don't think I'm going crazy, you're *not* a ghost. Right?"

"No." A few more chuckles. Her smile came back. "I'm not a ghost. I just spend a lot of time with horses. A lot."

I grunted. "I figured."

She nodded, falling silent.

I was searching for my next question, but I didn't want to overwhelm her. I didn't want to scare her away.

Then she surprised me when she spoke next. "Do you have a girlfriend?"

"What?" My own eyes widened. Her words clicked in again. "A girlfriend? No." Fuck yes. She wanted to know. She was interested.

I had hope.

I added, "I'm all alone."

And yeah, that made me sound pathetic. This chick would think I was a loser. She'd run as fast as she could, and she could run faster than most. She had a freaking horse to do it for her. That would be a new low. A girl running away from me on a horse.

"You drink a lot."

My head moved back. "What?"

She pointed to where my cabin was. "You drink a lot. Every night."

A goddamn smile was stretching on my face. I couldn't stop it. "Are you watching me?"

She shook her head. "I can smell it."

Oh. That was new.

I gulped. "Really?"

Another small laugh, and she nodded. "Yeah." She touched her nose. "I have better smell than normal people."

Not the best way to impress someone.

I could only shake my head. "I don't even know how to respond to that. Yeah." Honesty it was going to be. "I do drink a lot."

"Do you have a problem?"

My eyes narrowed again. There was no judgment from her, just curiosity. This girl wasn't normal, which was a realization that hit me smack in the chest. I knew already, but it was just resonating throughout me more and more.

God. I couldn't let her slip through my fingers, but I had a feeling that was what this girl did—to everyone.

"No, but I shouldn't go as hard as I have been."

"Why?"

I frowned. "Why should I *not* drink as much?"

"Why do you drink so much?"

"Uh." I scratched behind my ear. "My brother died about almost eight months ago. I was on the phone with him when it happened." I was going for broke. "It messed me up real bad."

"But you're an actor? That's what you do for a job?"

"Yeah."

"So, you're working. That's good. You're not so messed up that you can't keep a job."

I frowned at her, then cracked a grin. "Are you Dr. Phil-ing me?"

She frowned this time. "What is that?"

She lived with horses.

"Nothing. Stupid joke." I shook my head and tugged at my collar. Did it suddenly get hot out here? "My manager got me to do this movie, so here I am. Acting. Doing my job." Sounding lame yet again.

She took a step toward me, bringing her feet almost into the river. "I don't know what a Dr. Phil-ing is. Is that something to drink?"

I barked out a laugh and then stopped right away. I didn't want her to think I was laughing at her. "He's a psychologist or psychiatrist, whichever one, and he has his own show. He counsels people on television."

Understanding dawned in her eyes, but she stepped back, her feet pulling farther away from the river. "I know what a counselor is."

I wanted to ask how she knew. The question was burning on my tongue, but it was the same thing. If I pushed too much, would she run? I didn't want that. I *so* didn't want that.

Oh, fuck it. I was going for it.

"So, we've established that I'm somewhat of a drunk, and it's because of my brother's death." I gestured to those woods again. "Can I ask about you? It's the elephant in the room."

She looked around. "We're not in a room. There's no elephant here."

"It's a phrase." Shit. I was going too far. I needed to pull back. "Nothing. Sorry."

I saw a faint grin. She was teasing me.

She asked, "Are you trying to ask me why I spend so much time with the horses?"

"Uh. Yeah."

She shrugged, looking away. "It makes more sense to be with them."

"Really?"

She nodded, turning back to me. "Don't you feel like that? You're here instead of being with the others up there?" She gestured toward the main lodge.

"They all went to the bars tonight. And . . ." Again, I was going for it. "I took a walk tonight hoping to see you."

She continued to look at me. She didn't break her gaze or even blink. Then she grinned, two soft dimples showing. "You're flirting with me."

"Damn straight."

Her mouth parted a little. "When people flirt, are they this honest about it?"

"God, no." I rubbed a hand over my face. Gayle would've been laughing her ass off at me if she were watching. The girl was calling me on everything. "There's usually some innuendos, but nothing so out and out."

"Innuendos."

"Yeah. Where the message is implied but not so explicitly said."

"Ah. Yes." Her smile was fading, but it still lingered a bit longer. The wrinkles around her mouth remained. "I'd forgotten about that. I don't talk to people."

"Like ever?"

"As little as I can." She shook her head. "Talking to people seems pointless to me."

Holy fuck. There were so many questions I wanted to ask just off that one statement. I refrained. People wanted to know my business, and I was always turned off. I couldn't bombard the girl.

"I get it. I do."

She grinned again, and this time, I had the distinct impression she was laughing at me. "You do? You have a band of horses that's taken you in too?"

"Yeah." I didn't remember the last time I'd smiled like this, maybe when I was a kid. "Don't think you're so special. My herd is made up of all stallions. Take that. *All* stallions. How many times does that work out?"

She stared at me and then peeled over in laughter the next second.

This girl. This female. This woman.

I wasn't even sure which I was dealing with, but she humbled me. She wasn't talking to me with an agenda. She didn't want something from me. She didn't see me with dollar signs in her eyes or her next acting gig already lined up. She was pure. She was innocent. And she had no idea how rare she was.

I felt stupidly little in that moment.

She was what every person wanted to find in life.

When she noticed I was looking at her weird, she quieted, a small chuckle slipping out, but she hid it behind a hand. "Sorry. Just—" She looked to the ground. "No one's made that kind of joke to me before."

How many jokes did she hear?

Who *did* make her laugh? *How* did they do that?

But I couldn't ask her that. That was too much, too quick.

Keep it cool and classy and not so desperate. Goddamn I was desperate. I was desperate in a way that I didn't even realize until I saw her up close and in person.

I shoved my hands into my pockets, more to hold myself back than anything else, and dropped my voice low. "Can I ask you a personal question?"

"What?" Her laughter started to subside.

I felt a tug. I didn't want that to happen.

"Can I ask who you are? Who's your family? Why are you out here?"

She stared at me, that same deer-in-the-headlights look coming back to her. I shouldn't have. I'd be cursing myself as soon as she left, but she never bolted. The silence stretched, my question hanging between us, and I was counting my blessings that I hadn't scared her off. Yet.

I didn't expect her to answer. I was thinking of something else to say, anything to keep her there when I heard, "I have family. Kind of."

"Yeah?" Hope slammed into my chest. Hope like I'd never felt before. It sped my heart up. "What do you mean?"

She looked down, kicking at the river with her toe. "My mom died. A long time ago."

Her mom?

Was it . . .

But it was. It had to be. The realization punched me in the stomach. It clicked in place.

"Was your mom's name Karen?"

She nodded, gesturing toward the main lodge again. "It's why you're here, isn't it? How she died." Her eyebrows pulled together. She was frowning so hard that I ached to go over and smooth it out. She added quietly, "Matthew told me they changed the movie so she doesn't die, but she did."

Holy.

I couldn't move for a moment.

Fucking.

*No way.*

Shit!

It was. This girl was a sibling, one who wasn't known to anyone. My heart was beating fast, but I kept my voice smooth and controlled. "What do you mean?"

She rubbed behind her ear before bending, picking up a stone, and tossing it into the river. She watched it sink to the bottom. "He said it was going to be a happily ever after movie." She paused a beat. "He said I wasn't in the movie either." Her eyes were back on me. Judging. Studying. "You can't tell."

It was an accusation and a request at the same time.

I breathed out harshly. "I won't say a goddamn word. I promise." I meant it. I meant every single word, every single syllable.

"My mom died beca—" She stopped talking and glanced behind her. I thought she'd look back, resume whatever she was going to say, but she didn't. She held still, staring into the dark woods. A few seconds stretched to thirty, then a minute, and then two. I waited for what felt like a full three minutes before she looked back to me. An apology was in her eyes as she stepped back toward the trees. She said, "I'm sorry," before she was gone.

She vanished.

It happened in the blink of an eye.

I strained to hear, but there wasn't even so much as a twig snapping under her feet. There was no pounding of hooves either.

55

She was there and then gone.

And despite my earlier questions, I was left standing there, unsure if I'd just had a conversation with a ghost or not.

# CHAPTER TWELVE

## Brody

I was up. I was early. I was not bright.

Gayle put her plate, which held a scone and two apples next to me, her coffee next. I was tempted to grab the coffee, but I knew she'd smack the back of my head and that was only *if* she didn't pour the coffee on my lap.

I sighed, scooting back my chair as she was pulling hers in. "I need caffeine."

"Okay," I heard her mutter, as I walked toward the breakfast buffet table.

I was reaching for the Styrofoam cups when Kara sidled up next to me, a single strawberry on her plate.

"Hey." It sounded a bit breathless, and I watched her as I poured the coffee. I didn't break eye contact, judging from the feel of the heat before I turned off the spout.

Putting the lid on my cup, I pointed at her face. "You've got the sultry smile on this morning. It isn't going to happen."

"The what?" She eyed the coffeepot longingly before following me back to my table.

I went back to my seat next to Gayle. The only seat open was across from my manager, and Kara took it, eyeing Gayle for a few seconds before she sat.

Pointing at her face again, I said, "I know your smiles. I know you name your smiles too."

"I do not." She started to look horrified.

"You do." I picked up a piece of toast. "I've even seen you practice your smiles, and it's not happening."

"What's not happening?" Her strawberry was beginning to look lonely. She was ignoring it.

"You. Me. Put the sultry smile away."

"What? Come on." She let out a nervous giggle, reaching up to pat her hair. "I don't know what's going on right now."

Fuck it. I speared her strawberry.

Gayle spoke up as I did, saying, "He's rejecting you, honey."

"What?"

Another one of the actors, the one sitting across from me, joined the conversation. "Do you guys know what's going on with the movie?"

"Shanna's been in meetings all night and this morning. She blew a gasket about that herd of horses last night," a third member said as she joined us.

"Really?"

The woman nodded to the other actor.

I should know their names. This wasn't me being an arrogant ass or thinking I was better than them, I just mainly had screen time with Kara. I had learned early on that if I got close to the secondary actors, they assume I'd help them become better than I was. Every time I corrected their assumption, it never went well. Gayle said I could choose "softer" words, but the message had to be hard or it wasn't going to resonate. I liked to go for broke in those situations.

Hell. I sighed to myself. Maybe I just liked being an asshole.

I narrowed my eyes.

Did I?

"What are you doing?"

"What?" It was the second actor who asked me that question.

Kara had been watching me, and she grunted, hiding a smile before she looked down at her plate. "Hey!" She slapped the table. "Where's my strawberry?"

It was on the end of my fork. I popped it into my mouth and shrugged. "Maybe it fell."

She groaned, rolling her eyes upward before getting up from the table and stalking back to the breakfast buffet.

The second and third actors were still watching me. Oh right. He asked what I was doing. I countered him with, "What are you doing?"

"Huh?"

I raised my eyebrows. Exactly.

The third actor's eyebrows pulled down, causing a crease in her perfect, marble-smooth skin. I looked more closely at her. She had the beauty to be a lead actress. "What's your role?"

"My real name is Kelly. I play the sister."

Karen had a sister? I made a note to ask Morgan about that. Then the actress said, "Technically, I'm *your* sister. We haven't shot those scenes yet."

Oh. Peter had a sister.

"Do we get along in the script?"

Gayle's head moved back an inch. I could feel her disapproval. "I thought you memorized the script."

"I memorized my scenes in the script, and"—I turned to my on-screen sister—"we don't have any together."

"We do but not till the end. There are some phone conversations, and I comfort you when you think Karen is dead."

"Do you like Karen?"

She started laughing, shaking her head. "God no. My character hates the bitch." She motioned between us. "It doesn't go over well for you and me."

As if on cue, the Kellermans walked into the dining area. Shanna was behind them, steam coming from her ears. As the siblings went to the breakfast buffet, Shanna bypassed everyone and left the room, sweeping outside. I locked eyes on each Kellerman in turn, wondering how much was truth and how much wasn't. The aunt hating Karen made sense. That rang like something true, but I still wanted to know. Was there a real aunt? Did she hate Morgan's mom? Did she hate Morgan?

The whole secrecy about Morgan, knowing she was out there, knowing how much she was out there, made me feel as if a lot of the script was off. I wanted her there, but at the same time, I didn't. I wanted to know her, but I may never see her again.

She was like watching a masterpiece being painted by a painter. You knew the outcome would be breathtaking, but you had to sit back and let the painter do his thing.

And I was officially a pussy with that last thought.

I grabbed my coffee and shoved back my chair.

"Where are you going?" Gayle asked.

Somewhere I didn't feel like such a pussy.

I shrugged. "I want to run over some lines."

"You want company?"

I turned, feeling my jaw clench. "No."

The Kellermans looked up as I walked past.

I was heading to my cabin when I heard someone behind me. The gravel crunched under a shoe, and I looked back.

Matthew held his hands up. "I come in peace." He glanced back over his shoulder, putting his hands into his pockets. "I noticed you take off from breakfast. Is everything okay?"

No, no, buddy. I knew what he was doing. I read through his bullshit. It'd been a guess before, but I goddamn knew. He wanted to know if I knew about Morgan.

"I was hoping to see Morgan." I narrowed my eyes, watching for his reaction.

I promised her I wouldn't tell, but this guy already knew. I wasn't breaking that promise, and I had a strong feeling he was going to dog my movements anyway, just from suspecting I might know.

*I do. Deal with it, fucker.*

He blanched, then gulped, and then narrowed his eyes. "I see."

*Did he now?* A snide voice commented in my head.

"She's the stepsister, right?"

His eyes rounded. "You have *met* her."

"We had a nice long conversation last night." I heard the disbelief in his laugh and added, "Down by the river."

His laugh died. He grew serious again. "I see." That damn phrase again from him.

"She's under the impression she's a secret. My question is: why?"

He started laughing again, saw I meant what I said, and his lips pressed together. "Are you kidding me? It'd be a field day for the media if they found out Karen Kellerman's daughter still lives in the mountains *and* with horses. She'd be a laughing stock, and you know it. Would you want that for her?" His eyes were almost slits. "And how is it your business?"

"The second she told me who she was, it became my business."

"Let me guess." He rolled his shoulders back, shaking his head. "Hollywood *it* guy, who's used to getting all the women he wants, has met someone who isn't falling at his feet, and he's intrigued. She probably ran from you, didn't she?"

I shrugged. That wasn't his business.

He laughed again, almost scornfully. "Yeah. The thing is that I know Morgan." He stepped toward me, lowering his voice. "If you think I'm going to stand back and let you try to sweep her off her feet, you have another think coming. I can already see your intentions from a mile away."

I looked between us. "Pretty sure there's ten feet between us."

"You know what I mean."

"From my point of view, you're the one embarrassed by her. Not me."

This went from one to eight on the intensity scale. We were a few words away from squaring off and proclaiming ourselves enemies, but the problem was that we both knew where the other stood.

I saw the possessive need in him. It was the same look my dad had in his eyes when he drank. The fucker was an abusive drunk before he died, just like his brother, and it hadn't been a good time. He wanted to control everyone. Matthew Kellerman had that look. She might be his stepsister, but he thought he controlled her, or he wanted to control her. And though I cared about her already and wanted her, all I felt right then was this insane need to protect her.

The last time my gut flared up like this was when I was waiting for Kyle at my awards show.

He gritted his teeth. "I am not embarrassed about my sister. I love her, and I do what's in her best interest. She is kept a secret for a reason."

"She was at the river last night. She's been around. I've seen her four different times. If I have, *trust me* when I say that others will, if they haven't already. It's a matter of time."

He lifted his head, his Adam's apple moving up. "Is that a threat?"

"What?"

"Are you threatening to tell everyone about her?"

I shifted back on my heels as anger slammed through me. Christ. I wanted to punch him.

"No, and don't you fucking dare try to turn that around on me. I promised her I wouldn't say anything. I'm talking to someone who already knows about her."

His head lowered, and his voice quieted as he said, "She asked you to keep her a secret?"

I nodded. "Which I think is the stupidest idea ever. Shanna's going to find out eventually." I remembered the fury on her face this morning. "You think she's pissed about the horses? She's going to be livid about Morgan."

"A herd of wild mustangs is a safety factor. They never cross the fences, and them crossing the street in front of your car was a once-in-a-lifetime occurrence. That'll never happen again. That stallion hates humans. He puts up with Morgan. No. She's mad about the safety issues, but I assured her there are none. She won't be mad about my sister."

His stepsister.

I kept the need to correct him to myself. Instead saying, "She'll be pissed that you kept information from her, and she'll be even more mad because Morgan wasn't written into the script."

It hit me then.

That was why he was keeping Morgan a secret. He was right. As I said those words, I knew they were true. Shanna would want to put Morgan into the movie. It would take the script from silver to gold, even though she already thought it was as good as she could get. Right now the movie was an inspirational memoir to the loving memory of Karen Kellerman, the last wife of the man who ran a global franchise of Kellerman Hotels. Put in the surviving daughter who lives with wild mustangs, and forget a movie that might win some awards. She'd have a goddamn blockbuster. It would kill at the theaters if it were all done right.

But Morgan's life would never be the same.

She couldn't be reclusive with the herd anymore. No matter what, people would come to find her. They'd want to see her.

Matthew was watching me as if he could read my thoughts. "Yeah. You're getting it now, aren't you?"

A spark lit my anger again, even though I didn't know which one of us it was directed at: him or me.

"If you don't want Shanna to know, get the whole crew moved into the city. Get 'em out of here. They're going to see her."

"They aren't looking for her. My sister is like a ghost. If she wants to stay hidden, she will be."

"I saw her four times."

"She wanted—" He bit off his own words as if he were being forced to swallow something foul. "You're right. I don't know the other times, but I can say that if you saw her last night at the river, it was because she wanted you to see her."

"She didn't know I was there."

"She has instincts like a deer."

"Deer can be snuck up on."

His eyes went wide again in frustration, and he flung out his hands. "What do you want me to say? Shanna's already looking for reasons to sue. Not disclosing the herd was a breach of contract. I do one more thing like sending the whole crew to the city, and she'll blow a gasket."

"It's better than Morgan being found."

He gripped the back of his neck, his fingers holding tight while he seemed lost in thought. Then he let loose a long, drawn-out breath of air. "Fuck." He raised an eyebrow at me. "I can tell her there is something wrong with the main house, which would make it easier to send everyone into town, but what about you?"

"I'm the only one not in the house." I shrugged, knowing I was coming off smug and not giving one shit about that. "Your siblings need to use the other cabins, but everyone else needs to relocate." I smirked. "For their safety."

"Your manager will probably want to stay in your cabin then."

"She can try."

"It's a two-story cabin. Your main living quarters is on the second floor, but there's a bedroom on the first. It makes no sense that no one wouldn't move in there."

He was right. The cabin was a little fucked up, but I liked it when I saw it. "I need my privacy. Shanna has to go into town too. Both of them."

"Goddamn." Matthew lifted his head, looking out over the fields. "You know what's funny? We have the regular horses coming tomorrow. We even had to get a new door and lock, make sure everything's extra secure so the stallion doesn't steal any of the mares." He flicked a hand toward the barn. "Those stalls are going to be full of domestic horses. Morgan will start showing up because she'll want to check on them and make sure they are cared for. That's just how she is."

"Perfect timing then."

He threw me a harried look, the side of his face of grimacing. "Stay away from my sister."

I felt his warning low in my gut. I ignored it and threw my own challenge back in his face. "So, no more late-night walks to the river?" I gave him a wry smile. "I can't guarantee she'll stay away from me."

He turned to stare at me. All pretenses were gone.

I wasn't backing the fuck down.

# CHAPTER THIRTEEN

## Matthew

Crossing into his office, he could hear the crew in the house, but he was still reeling from his last conversation. Brody Asher. A goddamn Hollywood male diva.

He knew the excitement the females and a few of the males had about this star. He could have anyone, but he had his hooks in Morgan.

Fury started boiling over inside him, and Matthew reached for the armrests on his chair. He wanted to throw the thing across the room. He wanted to trash every piece of furniture in his office, but he *really* wanted to smack either one of the main reasons this movie would get any attention. The director was one reason. Asher was the other. His name would draw all the attention.

Kara was easy on the eyes, but she wasn't Brody Asher.

A growl erupted from him, and he shot back up, stalking to the other side of his office.

"What the hell is going on?"

Abby was in the doorway, her mouth slightly hanging open. She had changed into a sundress and was fixing the ties around her neck. She added, "You okay?"

He only grunted. He wasn't mad at Abby. He didn't want to take it out on her.

"Okay." She sounded resigned, stepping in and closing the office door behind her. All the sounds from the crew were muted to a low murmur. "What's going on?"

"Asher knows about Morgan."

"Ugh—"

He turned to continue pacing but stopped at the window. His hands were on his hips, and he stared out beyond the barn to the field she always ran toward. He couldn't see her, but she was out there. She really was like a ghost.

"Say what?" Abby came to stand next to him.

He let out a deep pocket of air. "He knows about her. He's talked to her even."

That same gargle sounded again, coming out like a wheeze from her.

Reaching up, he patted her on the back, but he never turned away from the view. He knew it was ridiculous. Morgan could hear a cricket moving on a blade of grass yards away. Matthew knew Morgan heard Asher and made the decision to stay.

"She's talking to him."

Him.

Not Matthew.

Not one of her family members.

No, she was talking to this stranger who had a reputation for being an asshole.

A sick feeling spread through him. He already knew what was going to happen.

He wanted to stop it.

He wanted to bar the asshole from his lands, from Morgan, but it was too late. If he did, the asshole would seek her out anyway.

He couldn't control Morgan either. God knew that he'd been trying.

Abby touched his arm, both comforting and seeking comfort. "That's good, isn't it? That she's talking to someone."

Of course, Abby would see it that way.

He wanted Morgan back, so did Abby, and his sister wouldn't care how that happened.

But he wanted to be the one. Not some Hollywood bad boy type. Asher didn't deserve her. Not one bit.

"Yeah." Matthew grasped her hand, covering it with his so he could pull her to him. Dipping his head down to rest against the side of hers, he said gruffly, "Unless he hurts her and she's gone forever then."

He heard her swift intake of breath, but she murmured almost calmly a second later, "We'll just have to make sure that doesn't happen. Or that we'll be there for her." Her hand squeezed his arm. "But she's talking to someone, Matt. That's good."

It was.

It wasn't.

It was the wrong person she was talking to.

"Yeah." A knife was in his belly, protruding out, but he didn't know whose hand was attached to it. Asher's or Morgan's. He said to Abby, "It's a good thing."

# CHAPTER FOURTEEN

## Morgan

I didn't know what I was doing.

Shiloh was behind me, eating leaves from the underside of trees, but we were off on our own. I was standing in the woods, watching. That was what I was doing.

Watching.

Being curious.

Not understanding why.

I didn't think about others. I cared for my siblings, but they had left. When Karen died, they had left. All of them. I had staff, who acted as my guardians, and teachers for my homeschooling, but the people I'd come to consider family were gone. Peter Kellerman went back to his businesses. Matthew, Finn, and Abby returned to their private schools.

I hadn't been given a choice to go with them or not.

I got a new sister when Shiloh was born.

She and Shoal were my family.

Then they came back that day. Car after car. All of them were there, even Peter. My mother used to melt and get a glazed look in her eyes whenever he was around. She had loved him so much, but he had only ever been gruff and distant to me. Still, when he had come back four years ago, he brought memories of my mother with him, and it'd been hard to look at him.

They told me about the movie script, that it would be a commemoration to my mother's life. Even then, I wanted to say no. They said I was giving them permission to shoot the movie on my lands, but my mother was in the room that day. I felt her. I felt how much she wanted this movie done, so I signed.

I had regretted it ever since, until this moment.

I didn't like having strangers around. They upset the horses too. Everyone was on edge, but *he* came, and I talked to him at the river, and I hadn't been able to stop wondering about him.

I wondered what his full name was. Where he came from. What his parents were like. Why did he become an actor? Did he know horses? They shot a scene where he had to ride one, and he seemed a natural at it. He held the reins like it was second nature to him.

There was so much I wanted to know, and then things changed at the house.

All the strangers went away again.

I saw them leave in the cars, but I watched his cabin that night. He remained. So did my siblings. They were the only four there, until the rest came back the next morning. That was the routine. They came at odd hours, sometimes leaving during the day and returning at night. They weren't sleeping at the main house anymore. Matthew must've had them stay at a hotel in the city, but why?

That started a week ago, and every night, I wanted to go and ask why. I wanted to find out so many answers, more answers than I ever cared to wonder before.

I didn't, though.

I always stood at the end of the last fence. It was as if the wild was behind me. The domestic was before me.

If I went in there, I couldn't be myself.

There were expectations. A role. An obligation. Matthew likes those types of relationships.

He was the older brother.

He embraced that role and thought it was his job to care for all of us, to overlook, to watch, and he would try to fix things for us. I could tell he was the same, and Finn and Abby? They had the same spark from when we were kids. Finn always felt he had to prove himself to his father, to Matthew.

Abby was always the peacemaker. If there was a fight, she smoothed it out.

Half the time, I was waiting to see if they would muster the courage to look for me, instead of expecting me to go to them because that was what they felt. I could feel it from them. It came to me in waves.

I was supposed to go to them.

I was supposed to find them.

But there would be more.

I would have to fit into some role that each had for me. It was how they were before, that hadn't left them. I didn't feel that with Brody.

He wanted my body. I knew that. I felt that. I wanted his too. It was more than that, though.

Expectations.

It was the invisible weight crushing them and myself, and they didn't realize it was what kept me away.

Shiloh wanted me to love her, but she didn't expect that of me. Same thing with Shoal.

A twig cracked behind me. I didn't look, but I knew it was Shiloh moving alongside of me. As the cameras rolled beneath us on the hill and the lady yelled, "Action," I reached up, grabbed a fistful of Shiloh's mane, and lifted myself up to her.

She was turning before I sat, and we left again, my back to their world.

# CHAPTER FIFTEEN

The floor creaked.

I was in the dark, a bottle of bourbon half drank on the floor beside me, and I was staring out toward the field. I was on the second-floor patio, the door open behind me. A nice breeze came off the mountain, but it was just me. All me.

And Kyle's ghost.

He was never far away.

But the floor creaked, and I knew it was her.

I felt her in my blood, in the way my skin washed in goose bumps and chills. The recognition slammed full force into me at the same time the need for her rose, threatening to overtake me. When she stepped out through the open door, I didn't dare move.

I feared she'd run like the last time.

It'd been two weeks since I saw her at the river, and as she stood beside me, looking out over the field with me, she was every bit the ghost she'd been that night.

She murmured softly, "Everyone left," before turning to look at me as I took a seat in the chair to her left. "Why?"

"Your brother was worried someone would see you."

Her forehead wrinkled, just a small line. "Someone did. You."

I laughed, a small one. "Someone who wouldn't keep quiet."

"Oh." She bit her lip, moving to the chair beside mine. She folded down, her petite body so strong but so small and graceful. "He cares for me."

I barked out a laugh. "It's more than that, Princess."

I felt her surprise as she looked at me. Her eyes were wide, startled, then a slow smile spread over her face. "That name reminds me of one of the horses."

Great. I gave her the same nickname as a real-life feral horse. Awesome.

"Anytime."

Another peal of laughter came from her. It was genuine, and I smiled along with her. I would give her all the cheesy-ass nicknames she wanted if this was the reaction I got. When she started to fade, I asked, "Why'd you come see me?"

A person with an agenda could've feigned being hurt, saying that maybe I didn't want them to come. I'd have to go on the defensive and tell her I wanted her here. Or even use it as a come-on. Kara, who most certainly had an agenda, would have somehow used the question as an excuse to crawl onto my lap.

Though, I wouldn't mind if Morgan crawled onto my lap.

"Because I'm curious about you." There was no game between us. No hidden manipulation. She was being real, and goddamn, my dick bulged inside my pants. I had to dig my nails into the chair. I needed to calm it down. Otherwise, I'd jump her bones.

I coughed, getting some restraint in there. "What are you curious about?"

"You." She shifted on her seat, pulling her feet underneath her. She was facing me, leaning on the one side of her chair. Rapt curiosity was etched on her face. "What's your full name?"

No thought. I answered immediately, "Brody Josh Asher. Not Joshua, just Josh."

"Are you named after anyone?"

"My mom had a thing for a soap actor named Josh."

"A soap?"

I grinned. That was goddamn cute. "Not something to clean yourself. It's a type of show on television."

"Ah. I had a nanny who watched one, I think." Her eyebrows pulled together again.

I was having a hard time not reaching over and smoothing out the small wrinkles.

She added, "There was a lot of sex."

An awkward laugh from me. "Let's not talk about sex."

Her eyes were on me again. They were full. They were unblinking. There was something there I didn't want to identify. If I did, I would be in her within a minute. I wanted this time with her. It was real. It was the type of shit I didn't want with anyone else.

"Ask me another question."

"Do you want to have sex with me?"

A mangled cry ripped from my throat. "I'm finding the more time I spend with you, the less control I have."

"So you *do* want to have sex with me?"

I saw the knowing look on her face and bit back a groan. "You goddamn know I do." I fixed her with a hard look, letting her know that she may be able to see me, but I could see her too. "You want me as well."

There was no hiding, only the continued spread of that smile. Yep. Tonight was going to be one of the most torturous nights I'd ever experience. I already knew I wouldn't trade it for anything else.

"Yes." She sat up, her feet tucked directly beneath her.

I nodded at her. "I have a feeling you could hang upside down from the post."

"I live mostly in the woods. You develop the ability to climb trees and rocks if you want to survive."

"Horses too."

She nodded solemnly. "Horses too."

"They climb trees?"

She chuckled. "No, but they can climb rocks if they have to. They can also run down cliff edges."

"I've seen *Snowy River*." I suppressed a shudder at the idea of her riding a horse down one of those edges. "It looked damned scary."

"*Snowy River*?"

"It's a movie."

"I've not seen it."

"Do you watch television?"

"I have in the past, when I went to school."

I shot up in my seat. "You went to school?"

She laughed, settling into her seat again. Her feet slowly unwound from beneath her until she looked as if she was almost lounging back. "I had to. I live with horses for a choice, but I'm not a moron. I couldn't give anyone a reason to say I couldn't be with them. Getting a high school degree and," she leaned forward again, a teasing glimmer in her eyes, "a college degree made it so I could do what I wanted."

"You went to high school *and* college?"

She snorted, motioning in the direction where the main lodge was. "No way. I did the homeschooling thing, and I did the online thing for college. Peter made sure there was staff here to take care of me."

I was surprised and impressed all at the same time. "Did you *like* Peter?"

She opened her mouth, but nothing came out. She ended with a shrug before adding, "She loved him. That was all that mattered."

I fell silent, digesting. I was learning so much and not enough. "I'm playing him in the movie, but I've never met him. My manager reached out to see if I could meet him, for research purposes. He said I could ask his children for any insight needed." I remembered when she read the words to me from her phone, reciting them word for word. "He sounds like a peach of a guy."

She laughed a little. "That seems like him."

"When did he stop sending people here for you?"

She mulled it over. Her mouth puckered up again. "When I turned eighteen. He came to tell me everything was legally in my name now. A lawyer came the next day to tell me about my inheritance, and the staff was all gone that same day."

I shot forward. "Wait. These are your lands?"

She nodded.

"Shit." A nice piece of information I was pretty sure Shanna didn't know about.

"Matthew drove out the next week. He took me to the bank and got me set up so I could get money when I needed it. He helped set up other things."

"You don't drive?"

She shook her head. "None of the staff offered to teach me, and I didn't care. Shoal could take me anywhere I needed to go."

"Do you want to learn?"

"Are you going to teach me?"

I nodded. "I would if you wanted me to."

Her mouth opened. She was thinking about it. Then she shrugged again. "Maybe. I don't know."

"Well, think on it." I reached down for the bourbon and took a large swig. God. I needed that burn.

Her eyes were on the bottle as I held it.

"You're still drinking."

I listened for the judgment. There was none.

I relaxed a little, nodding. "It helps."

"With what?"

The air shifted between us. It grew more intimate. It'd been playful, light before. She was getting into a second layer of shit.

I motioned around the patio, still holding the bourbon. "Ever been haunted? Because I have. I am. You aren't the only ghost here."

"I'm not a ghost."

"That's yet to be proven." I grinned at her, but I felt Kyle. He was sitting with us. He was either laughing at how much of a dumbass I was being or he was flipping me off.

I added, "He visits me often."

She leaned forward, reaching for the bourbon. When I relinquished it, she took it and leaned back in her seat. "Does he get stronger when you drink or does he fade?" She took a sip. She swallowed it slowly before handing the bottle back, and I hadn't wanted her as much as I did in that moment. I'd have to readjust in a minute because my hard-on was becoming too uncomfortable. But until then, I took the bottle, as well as a second shot.

I placed it on the floor between us.

I thought back to her question. "He gets stronger, but I can sleep. I can't sleep unless I drink. I don't want to take fucking pills. They mess up my head. If it's going to be messed up more than it is, I want it to be from booze. At least then I can have some fun while I'm at it." I flashed her a grin.

I waited.

Normal girls would try to be cute. Smart girls would try to say something witty. She only reached for the bourbon and took a long swallow. She hissed this time, setting it back down between us.

She coughed, rasping out, "They tried to make me take pills too."

"Whe—" I remembered. "Oh."

"Yeah." Her chin dipped to her chest, and she pulled her legs up so she could hug her knees to herself. "I was young when my mom died. I had to take the pills, but I got off them. I slipped some to Finn. He liked pills back then."

"You saw them after she died?"

She looked down and was silent for a beat. "Matthew brought them out a few times."

But it wasn't enough. They'd basically left her.

My hands went back to digging into the goddamn chair. I wanted to throw the fucking thing at Kellerman, but this time wasn't about the piece of shit. I could hear Kyle telling me to calm down, so I took his advice. I had to. I couldn't scare her away. That was the last thing I wanted.

Forcing myself to chill the fuck out, I asked, "Have you talked to your siblings since we've all been here?"

She was chewing on her bottom lip again.

Between the need to pound Kellerman's face in and the way she was kneading that lip of hers, my dick was raging. I couldn't remember when I had this big of a hard-on. Holy fuck. I tried telling him it wasn't the hottest thing he'd ever seen. I wasn't being convincing.

"I've talked to Matthew but not Finn or Abby."

"Would you like to talk to them?"

Her teeth stopped nibbling. She smoothed her hands down her legs instead. "I always liked Finn. He made me laugh. He scared me a bit because he could be reckless, but he was funny."

I raised an eyebrow. That preppy-looking prick was funny? "Really?"

She nodded. "Abby was too. Both of them would dare each other to do pranks. I remember one time when Matthew had a date. He'd just turned sixteen, and he was so proud of his car. He was taking out Molly Connors. Finn dared Abby to smear peanut butter all over the backseat. Matthew didn't notice when he left, and then it got dark. I guess he found out later when they went back there." She started laughing, her shoulders shaking. "He came home with peanut butter all over him. He blamed Finn the whole time, and I guess it was kind of his fault, but no one told him it'd really been Abby."

Abby. The girl who looked like a strong wind could blow her over. She rarely spoke and stuck close to her two brothers' sides whenever she was around. She had that kind of pranking streak in her?

I grunted, picking up the bourbon again. "No offense, but your siblings have changed. For the worse."

She sobered. A beat later, she said softly, "Karen died. They moved away. Life changes people. They forget."

Life hardened people.

She didn't say it, but I heard it.

I looked at her again, like I was seeing her anew. "That's why you stay out there."

Her eyes widened. She looked stricken.

"You don't want to forget your mother."

One beat.

We stared at each other, both knowing that I crossed the line. I should take back my words, but I couldn't. She was going to bolt. I didn't have time.

We moved at the same time.

I knew she was going to run, and I went for the patio door. I meant to block her, to apologize.

She didn't go back for the door. She launched herself *over* the patio.

"Morgan!"

My heart stopped. Literally.

It was a ten-foot drop.

The world paused in that second, and then I was at the edge. I wasn't ready to see her body there, but my God, if I hadn't known I cared for her, I would've then.

Fear like I'd only experienced one other time crashed through me.

*Not again. Please not again.*

But she wasn't down there. I searched the ground. There was no sight of her.

Shit, shit, shit!

"Morgan."

Where was she?

I scanned the grounds, and then I saw her.

She was jogging down the field, and already knowing what I'd see, I spotted her horse at the end of the fence. She was waiting for Morgan as if the girl had called for a car or something.

A raw laugh ripped from me, and I fell back into my chair.

My heart was racing.

My body heat was a bonfire, and I'd never been so relieved before.

I was happy, but I fucked up, and I wasn't so upset about that, either, because I had my answer. I had suspected before, but I had as much pull on her as she had on me. Whatever we were locked in, we were both in it.

She'd be back.

# CHAPTER SIXTEEN

*Brody*

Thirty minutes later, I'd finished the last of the bourbon and was heading to bed when a tentative knock had my dick hard again. Instead of heading to my bedroom, I kept straight and swung open the door.

"You actually know how to knoc—" My words died in my throat.

I wasn't staring at Morgan. I was staring at her stepsister.

"Oh." My hand let go of the door, and I stepped back.

Abigail Kellerman, whom I met briefly my first night there, was standing on the porch, not a single brother in sight.

I chuckled to myself, pointing to the door. "Is that weird for you?"

"What?"

"Having to knock on your own door? This is technically your place, not mine."

"What?"

"Nothing." She wasn't in my headspace. I waved a hand inside. "Come on in." I held up the empty bottle. "I've had a few, so fair warning."

I didn't mean to, but I knew I was giving her the rakish grin I reserved to turn a woman on. The bourbon was messing with me, making me go into work mode. I didn't want to do that, not with her, at least.

I shook my head, trying to clear the act.

I was about to shut the door but paused. "You're not here to sleep with me, are you?"

Her eyes threatened to bulge out, and her neck reddening as she patted her hair in a nervous habit. "What? No. Oh my gosh. No." She stopped patting her hair, and her head bent forward, her eyebrows pinching hard together. "Though, I suppose that does happen to you."

We were in the clear. I shut the door.

I motioned to the living room. "Did you want a seat or . . ." She walked to the patio, and a whole new understanding filled me.

I almost felt bad for her.

I moved to the doorway and studied her as she focused on the chair Morgan had been using thirty minutes ago.

I said, "You heard us?"

"I wanted to come before, but I was so scared of scaring *her* away. I heard her laugh." Abigail laughed under her breath as she went to the chair. Her hand rested on the back of it. She sounded in awe. "It's been so long since I heard that from her."

Feeling twenty shades of awkward, I coughed. "Do you want something to drink?"

"No." She turned those big eyes on me. "Can I—I mean . . . can you tell me about her?"

"What?"

"Yeah." She sank onto Morgan's chair, folding her hands in her lap. She was almost posing there, just on the edge of the seat. "Matthew's talked to her, but he doesn't freely talk about her. I don't know. I can't get a good sense of how she is from him, but he told me that she talks to you. Could you . . ." She waved for me to sit again in my old chair. "Please."

*"Do it, asshole. She's a sis yearning for her other sis. It's the least you could do."*

I could literally hear Kyle grumbling and sighed, taking a seat. I almost wanted another bottle of bourbon for this, but no. If it'd been Kyle. If it'd been me. I would've wanted to know too.

I raked a hand over my face. "What do you want to know?"

"Is she happy?"

I nodded. I knew that right away. "She seems to be."

A tear formed in her eye, but she ignored it and scooted even closer to the edge of her seat. I eyed her feet, making sure they were planted in place so she wouldn't slip off and onto the ground.

A second question. "Is she healthy?"

Her skin glowed. Her hair was shiny. Her eyes were mischievous. She lit up when she had a grin on her face.

I nodded again. "She looks good. Healthy."

"She's eating enough?"

She was petite but strong. She could move like a panther. "She doesn't seem to be hurting for food. She isn't weak or frail-looking."

She let out a shuddering breath, nodding as she finally reached to brush the tear away. "What did you guys talk about?"

"Ah." An awkward laugh escaped as I shifted. "Well, we . . . I don't know. Just bullshit, I guess. She asked about me, about my life. I told her a little bit."

Her eyebrows pulled together again. The ends of her mouth dipped down. "What else?"

"She told me you smeared peanut butter on Matthew's backseat for one of his dates."

Her eyes widened again. "She told you that?"

"And that Finn took the fall for you."

"Oh my . . ." Her mouth stayed open. Both her hands lifted to cover it and she bent forward, resting her forehead on her knees.

I sat up, cringed, and reached toward her, not really knowing what to do, but then I heard the soft laughter.

My shoulders slumped, and I let my hand drop.

Her laughter grew. Soft at first until her shoulders were shaking, and her laugh was echoing over the field. She sat straight, her face beat red with tears all over.

Wiping at her face, still laughing, she began hiccupping. "I can't believe—" Hiccup. "She remembered—" Another hiccup. She groaned, taking a breath.

She was silent, still holding her breath.

When she exhaled, she leaned back in her seat and let her head rest against the cushion. "Sorry." A lopsided grin flashed for a moment. A few more soft chuckles had her shaking her head again. "I can't believe she remembered and that she told you. That was so long ago."

Her eyes lit up again.

I knew exactly why she began crying again.

I thought of Kyle.

I thought of the laughs we had, the stupid adventures, and I would've been crying alongside her if I didn't have a whole bottle of bourbon in me. It was helping to numb the pain.

"She was so quiet when we moved in." Abigail wasn't stopping the tears anymore. She let them slide freely as she looked out over the field. "We all doted on her. I did her hair. She begged me to show her how to do makeup. Finn brought her along every time we did those stupid pranks. She was his apprentice. That was what he called her. He was going to teach her how to take care of herself, and in his mind, that meant learning all the best ways to trick someone. Then there was Matthew and her. She worshiped him, and he always protected her, and then when Karen died . . ." Her mouth closed tightly, and her throat trembled. Fresh tears slid down her cheeks. "Morgan was supposed to come with us. She was a part of our family. I expected her to be brought to my school, but it never happened. I never thought—" She chewed on the corner of her lip, sounding anguished. "We lost Karen and Morgan that day. We came to visit a few times after, but it was never the same."

I tried to imagine life from her perspective.

Matthew said he was sixteen when Karen died, that would've put the twins around fourteen. She would've been in junior high. I had no clue what happened to their first mother, but she would've been grieving. I heard the love there. She'd been happy when they were here with Morgan and her mother, but I thought about afterward . . .

The new mother was killed.

All decisions should've been pointed toward protecting the youngest. The most vulnerable was always protected. That would've been Morgan.

That didn't happen.

I heard Morgan's explanation, but Abigail was talking as if it were out of her hands, as if she didn't know why Morgan didn't come to her, as if it hadn't occurred to her to make the suggestion in the first place.

Anger rose, and I bit down on it, shoving it back.

Morgan was scared to move on, and these assholes were letting her stay scared.

"What?"

I looked at her. She was watching me, her tears almost all wiped away.

"What?"

She said, "You made a sound. Are you—" Her eyes narrowed. "Are you upset with me?"

Anger flashed back at me, and I saw how she sat up, how she straightened her shoulders, how her little chin lifted in defiance.

There was the adventurous girl Morgan mentioned.

I gestured to her. "You should be this girl more often."

"Excuse me?" Her head reared back a little.

"You walk around like a beat dog with your tail between your legs."

The asshole in me broke the surface. If I was starting, I had to stick with my motto: Go big or go home.

She sucked in her breath. I didn't want to hear her false indignation. I rolled my eyes and said, "Your whole family drives me fucking crazy. You're all moaning about each other, but she's *here*." I shoved to my feet and pointed to the field. "You want her? Go get her! And if you can't find her, turn it around so she has to find you. Get lost. Get into a situation where she has to talk to you. Good grief. And your brother? He looks at her like he wants to control her, and Morgan knows it."

"What?"

*"Kyle, where are you?"*

"A million bucks that's probably why she's staying the fuck away. If I were a girl, I'd do the same. I don't know what your issue is, but if you guys want her, go and goddamn get her. She's here. She's within reach. She's alive. She's breathing. She's still going to be here tomorrow! Don't waste your time."

*"I'm in your car."*
I was breathing hard.
I was sweating now.
*"Brody, I'm damn proud of you."*
The patio was spinning.
I was losing balance.
I heard screeching sounds—then metal crunching.
*"Are you close?"*
I was falling.
I felt myself going down.
*"I can't wait to get there."*
"Kyle," I whispered, my voice heavy and distorted.
I heard screaming in the background, but I couldn't pinpoint where it came from. Who it was.
*That damn dial tone.*
Something crashed and then the world went black.

# CHAPTER SEVENTEEN

*Brody*

A headache greeted me when I woke, but it wasn't the one in my skull.

I opened an eye, saw Gayle, and immediately wished I could go back to sleep. I didn't need to ask. Everything came rushing in.

Talking to Morgan.

Drinking.

Watching Morgan running away.

More drinking.

Then Abigail.

The drinks hitting me.

I groaned. "Am I fired?"

Gayle looked up, folding the newspaper and tucking it back down into her purse. "No, but from what Shan says, you should be."

Shan. "You're on nickname basis?"

My manager grunted, a cocky grin teasing her lips. "Brody, it's my job to be on nickname basis with almost everyone I meet. And to answer your question, you aren't. Abby said she wasn't there on movie business."

Another nickname. I didn't ask this time.

I waited to hear whatever lecture Gayle had in store, but nothing came. Looking at her, seeing her deadpanned expression, it clicked. "No! I didn't sleep with her."

"Are you sure?"

I was in the twilight zone. "Good Lord, did she say we did?"

"No. That's the thing. She's keeping a tight lip on why she was there, but she's only saying it didn't have to do with the movie. Once Shan found out you were fine, she started talking about firing you and backup A-list actors."

I fucked up. Bad.

I squinted, looking around the room. "Where am I?"

There were no call lights beeping in the distance, and I wasn't in a hospital nightgown. An IV pole was next to me and there was a fake plant in the corner, but that was it. The room looked barren.

"They moved you into the main house."

But . . . I couldn't remember Matthew's reason for kicking everyone out.

Gayle's hand pressed down on my arm, reassuring me. "He said the radon test came back fine. They'll move you as soon as you're ready."

Radon? That was the excuse he gave?

I sagged back down into my bed. The headache was beginning to pound behind my temples, but I knew Gayle would drop the hammer real quick. I wanted to get it over with.

"Lay it on me, G. Tell me how I messed up."

That was all she'd been waiting for.

"First"—she held up a hand, her eyes gleaming—"you will goddamn stop drinking! I mean it. I confiscated all of your booze. The crew will be thanking you for their amazing party tonight. Second, you will tell me why Abby Kellerman was in your room. She said you started ranting and raving before you passed out. I know something is going on. You and the Kellermans are the only ones still on the property, and it has nothing to do with some phony radon test. And third, you have to talk to someone about your brother's death. You know it, and I know it. I get it, but enough is enough. He wouldn't want you to tank your fucking career."

My mother just inhabited her body.

I sighed, pushing up until I was in a sitting position. Looking down at my chest, I didn't want to ask where all the bruises came from.

Gayle saw my look. "They had to cut your shirt off to check you over. You fell hard on the floor, then when they were moving you to the main house, you woke up and started swinging. You were going on about Kyle and Captain Morgan."

Captain Morgan?

I was pretty sure I hadn't been adding the "Captain" part. Thank God I was a boozehound.

"Is Abigail mad?"

She frowned. "No, which is the weird thing. She isn't upset at you. She wants to talk to you once you are awake. You ready for that?"

I nodded, sighing. "Better to get it over with now."

Gayle stood, her purse in hand. She paused at the door, glancing back. "You can thank me, by the way, for not letting Shanna fire your ass. You passed out, and they called a doctor to come here. She worried about it being leaked to the papers."

"But I'm good to go?"

She grunted, disapproval lining her frown. "You're good to go. I'll let you yank out your own IV."

I was doing just that after she left, when I sensed someone in the doorway. "You can come in." If it was Shanna, I wanted to get the ass-chewing done.

It was Morgan's sister.

"Hey." I let go of the IV cord, but I couldn't stay in the damn bed. I felt like an invalid. Sitting on the edge, I was glad to see sweatpants, but these weren't the jeans I'd been wearing last night. I was shirtless, and I wished that weren't the case. The bruises were a garish purple and blue. "You can come in, and"—I glanced around but couldn't see a shirt—"I would cover up, but I'm not seeing anything."

She hid a smile, stepping in and shutting the door behind her. "We did call two EMTs that our family knows. They thought it would be funny to change your clothes, hide the shirts. They're both divorced and big fans of yours."

I grunted out a laugh. "So much for Shanna's hope to keep this quiet."

Abigail shook her head, suddenly serious again. "They won't say a word. I promise. We've used them a lot over the years, I mean, when we were here before."

"A lot?"

I eyed her, moving to the chair and lowering myself down carefully.

She nodded, moving to the other vacant chair in the corner. We were watching each other over the bed.

"Finn was always getting hurt. After the first few times, he kind of became friends with them. I think he met them for a beer afterward."

"Good to have resources like that."

"Yeah." She looked down to her lap. She was twisting her hands together. "I went to see you last night to ask a favor. When I got there, I just got so curious. She doesn't talk to people. Ever. Unless you catch her sneaking through the house, which sounds really ridiculous when you think about it, but—"

I cut her off. She had to know first. "I'm sorry for going off last night."

"Huh?" She lifted her head again. "Oh. No. That was fine. I get it. I really do." She lifted a shoulder. "It was pretty obvious you were projecting. I know about your brother." Her eyes grew sad. "Everyone does."

"I hope I didn't scare you last night. I'd never . . . well, you know."

"No! I totally know. I don't want you to think I was scared or anything. It was actually, kind of heartbreaking. You kept saying Kyle's name, and then you started saying things about Morgan. I hid the bourbon, told everyone you'd been drinking Captain Morgan."

"Thanks for that."

Fuck's sake. Morgan's sister was covering for me.

I was such a fuck up.

"You wanted a favor?"

"Yeah." She sat at the edge of her seat, her posture was perfect and her hands were folded in her lap again. "I know you said last night that I should just go out there, try to find Morgan, or have her find me, but I was wondering . . ." Some sweat beads formed on her forehead. "Would you take me with you? Matt said you saw her at the river. I was thinking we could go there. That doesn't seem too far away."

I frowned. She was talking as if she didn't know. "You guys don't go through the lands?"

Her head dipped again for a second and then she looked back up. She shook her head. "No. I know we should, but as we got older, it just started to feel more like Morgan's area. Her horses lived there, and then the whole fear factor kicked in. We could die out there. I don't know how Morgan does it." Her sister kept on, "If you take me out there, she'll come. I know she will."

"Just you and me?"

She nodded, her chin tightening. "Just us. No Matt. No Finn. I want to see my sister again."

Shit.

I was going to do this.

I was going to get involved, and hearing Shanna's voice from the hallway, I knew I was stuck anyway.

I said, "I'll do it if you do me a favor."

"What?"

My eyes cut to the door. We could both hear Shanna saying, "He's awake in there?" Someone replied, but the words were muffled. I didn't have long until she barged in, regardless of whatever they were saying out there.

"Cover for me with Shanna."

"I did." Her attention was skirting from the door to me, the impending arrival of Shanna making her shrink in size. "I told her you weren't to be fired."

"No, I know." I shook my head. Shanna wouldn't be able to find another A-list actor for the salary I was getting, not unless they wanted to put off shooting the movie, which would cost even more money. She knew it. I knew it. I wasn't worried about that. "She's going to think we're sleeping together. You have to set her straight. She's already watching Kara like a hawk. She doesn't want any bedroom shit to land on the movie set. If she thinks we're sleeping together, she won't be happy about that. At all."

The more I talked, the bigger her eyes got.

Then the door burst open.

Shanna came storming in.

Abigail gulped and then jumped up. "We're not sleeping together!"

Yep. That wasn't embarrassing.

Shanna looked from Abigail to me and then back again. A dry chuckle came out. "Well, too bad for you. I've heard he's amazing."

"Not funny, Shanna."

She fixed those eagle-like eyes on me. "I wasn't trying to be funny, but you were. Apparently. Drinking Captain Morgan all night. Then going off on your boss." She gestured to Abigail. "What the hell were you thinking?"

I sighed, leaning back in my seat. "I wasn't."

She was looking me over, lingering on the bruises and then on the IV, which was still in me. "Shit, Brody. What did you do?"

Fucked up. Again.

Exhaustion hit me. I could feel it in every inch of my body. "I'm a mess, Shan."

A ghost of a smile graced her face, but she let the nickname go. If Gayle had nickname status, then so did I.

She jerked her head up and down, briskly. "Okay. Right. Listen, you are going to a brief stay in a rehab."

"What?" I started to stand.

"I talked to Gayle about it. She's got your bags packed already. There's a car waiting outside. We're going to shoot as much as we can without you, so some of the schedule is getting shuffled around, but it'll be fine. As long as you come back in top shape and *sober*, I think we can finish the movie on time."

I'd be gone.

Morgan wouldn't know.

I shared a pleading look with Abigail. If she was going to step in and save my skin, it was a good time to do it.

I waited.

She was quiet.

I shot her another meaningful look. *Right now, Abigail. Cover for me. Right now!*

"Um!" Her wide eyes were locked on mine. "Uh . . . he doesn't need rehab."

Shanna turned to her, an eyebrow raised. "He doesn't?"

"No." Abigail swallowed, her face scrunching and then clearing again. Light bulb. "He already told me he wasn't going to drink anymore. I really think he just needs to sleep, rest. You guys have been shooting at all hours of the day. And you know, what better place to detox than here?" She waved a hand around the room. "It's beautiful here. All the scenery. Crisp mountain air. I mean, we have horses too." She snapped her fingers. "They use equine therapy for rehab. They used to bring patients here when we had domestic horses. We can use the ones they're using for movie. How about that? We can bring in a therapist to work with Brody."

Shanna slowly folded her arms over her chest, leveling Abigail with a hard stare. "Why are you so eager to keep him here?"

Abigail backed up, shrinking even more under Shanna's scrutiny. "I'm not sleeping with him. I'm really not. The—uh—" She shot me a look.

She was struggling.

Good thing I could lie with the best of them. "Because I know things about her family."

Shanna's expression went from mild amusement to sharp alert. "What do you mean you know things about her family?"

I sighed, looking for all the world to be relaxed and unfazed. "Things I can't talk about, and that's why Abigail—"

"Call me, Abby."

"—Abby was in my cabin last night. I've been trying to find out more about Peter Kellerman, so I can better identify with him. I uncovered a secret in the process."

Abby groaned. "Oh God."

"And don't think you can get it out of me. It's a secret I gave them my word I would keep."

"They?"

Shit. Slip up. Still, I stayed in my role, trying to be nonchalant. "Yeah, Matt and Abig—Abby."

I was dangling a carrot in front of Shanna, one of the best directors I'd ever be able to work with, but there was a reason she was one of the best. She was smart, and she was a bloodhound. If there were something out there, something she should know to make the movie better, she would find it out. I just confirmed to her there was something for her to seek.

And she would.

She'd be doing all sorts of her own research.

Maybe I should've done the rehab stint?

No.

If I were shipped away for six weeks, I didn't know if Morgan would seek me out again. That would mean that Abby would never get the meeting with her sister that she so desperately wanted.

I had to stay.

It was the only way.

"I'll meet with a counselor. I'll do the equine therapy, but it has to be here."

"No drinking?"

I nodded. "No drinking."

"You get eight to ten hours of rest a night."

Another nod. "I'll sleep like a baby."

"You take herb supplements if you need help falling asleep. No pills. No prescriptions."

"Yes. All natural. Healthy."

She fixed me with another one of those eagle-stares. Her eyes narrowed to slits, and I could feel she was assessing my bullshit meter. After a full minute, she sighed. "Fine." Her arms uncrossed from her chest, falling to her side. "I'll have Gayle set everything up. We'll be here to shoot in a few days. You can come and watch if you want."

"I will." And I would. Working was not my problem. It was the downtime that was.

"Fine."

"Fine."

Abby clapped her hands together. "Great!"

Shanna and I turned to her, neither of us excited.

With her cheeks turning red, she exclaimed, "I'm excited for the equine therapy. Jennifer's coming soon too."

She almost bounced from the room, and Shanna turned back to me. She cocked her head to the side. "The same Jennifer that's engaged to Kellerman Junior Junior? The same one that I remember you having an affair with?"

Oh . . .

Fuck.

# CHAPTER EIGHTEEN

*Brody*

"I can't believe how you lucked out."

I was sorting through the food Gayle brought for me before she headed to the hotel for the night. Really, it was nothing more than a stall tactic. Even after she and Shanna had gone through the cabin, top to bottom, she was still worried. I wasn't hiding anything.

I wasn't an alcoholic, but I got it. I did. I hadn't been acting like a normal person with normal problems for the last eight months.

I patted her arm. "I will be fine. I promise." I saw her disbelief. Her lips pressed together. "This was a wake-up call." As much as I hated to admit it, it was. "It's time to work through some of my grief about Kyle."

Her eyes clouded over. "You never talk about him, you know?"

"I know."

When I did, I wanted to hurt something. I wanted to punch holes in walls, demolish hotel rooms, shatter glasses. Anything to take it from the inside and put it on the outside.

"I didn't know Kyle, but maybe you should reach out to his wife? See your nieces?"

The man-eating, metal-chewing manager was gone. The mother she must've been for her kids was talking.

I was softening, but I didn't want that. That brought feelings. Morgan.

I'd focus on her.

I saw her horse beyond the fencing. If that horse was there, so was Morgan.

"I'll be fine, Gayle. I mean it."

She quieted, but I still felt her concern.

"I'll give them a call tonight."

"Good." She perked up. "Good. That's so good." She grasped my arm with both her hands and squeezed. "I'm happy to hear that." She was almost shaking me.

"And I'll be fine. I'm going to go on a run, wear myself out, and then sleep. That's it."

"No visitors."

Technically, I was going to Morgan, or hoping to.

"No visitors here tonight." I nodded firmly.

"I mean it, Brody. I know you said you weren't sleeping with Kellerman, but that would be very, very bad if you got mixed up with her. Her brother's protective."

Didn't I know it? I saw the look Matthew Kellerman gave me during the crew dinner the first night. If he could've speared me with a pitchfork, he would've.

"Okay."

Her phone started buzzing, and she looked to read the text. "That's Shanna. They're waiting for me in a car."

"I'll be fine. I promise."

She nodded, going to the door before looking back.

I held my hands in the air. "I'm making you a promise. Once I do that, I always follow through. I will be fine tonight."

Her lips twisted into a half-grimace. "I'm aware you aren't promising other than tonight."

I went to the door and held it for her. She paused there, raking her gaze over me again. Head to toe. She said curtly, "You still look damn good."

I barked out a laugh. "Shanna said if the bruises don't heal by the time I start shooting, they'll work it into a scene."

She grunted. "I'm sure. I wouldn't be surprised if she's in your bed the minute the last scene is wrapped."

That'd be interesting. She'd have a rude awakening.

Her phone buzzed again.

I said lightly, "Go, Gayle. I'm just going for a run tonight, and I'll call my nieces later."

Her shoulders relaxed. Finally.

She began moving down the stairs, waving once over her shoulder once she got to the ground.

Shanna was driving and rolled her window down. She pointed at me, her eyebrows fixed fiercely together. "Rest and healing. Got it?"

I saluted her.

She laughed and then flicked me off as she drove away.

Once the last of the crew left, I knew I was alone for real. The Kellermans had gone into the city for dinner. Abby had texted me to say they'd be back late and would be returning to the main lodge. Shanna said they weren't moving the crew again. Since the EMTs took me to the house, the whole radon lie was done, but she didn't know that. She just said she wasn't flipping the bill to move everyone back. There was enough moving as it was.

Things were becoming a new normal, and it was starting with my changing clothes.

Sneakers.

Running shorts.

A shirt that'd keep me warm.

And headphones plugged into my phone.

I hadn't been lying when I said I was going for a run.

I really did intend to start fixing myself, and that meant getting back to my normal training routine. I needed five miles today, but I started out slowly, turning onto the walking path I'd explored before.

Morgan was out there. Somewhere.

# CHAPTER NINETEEN

*Morgan*

I'd been trailing him for three miles.

He had no idea where he was going. He went to the river, those headphones plugged in. The music was so loud that I could hear it from fifty yards behind him. He was an idiot. He never stopped to mark where he was turning. Just blindly moving from one path to another, until we were winding through a narrow ravine. There was a trickle of water underneath him, and I eyed the cliff walls on both sides of us. A mountain lion could perch up there and jump down. I had no weapon, just Shiloh's hooves if I called to her.

Then again, he would have no idea what was happening until it was too late.

I turned and whistled.

I heard her coming minutes later, and with him still running ahead, I dropped back until I was trailing by another thirty feet or so. I felt her coming up behind me, her hoofs clopping against the rock beneath us. When she drew next to me, I reached up and jumped, curling so I fit snugly on her in one smooth motion.

She was watching Brody ahead of us. The bass was blaring, and he was swinging his arms in rhythm. He was jogging, but he looked as if he was almost dancing at the same time.

I nudged her with my legs. I wanted her to go forward.

She didn't. She swung those dark eyes back to me, and I read her message.

*You want me to follow him? Really?*

I frowned, nudging forward with my legs again. I nodded. *Yes, come on.*

Her nostrils flared out, but she dropped her head and started forward. This canal edged around a cut into the mountain before joining the river again behind us. Most fish didn't travel this way, but every once in a while you might get lucky with a small one slipping through.

As we kept on, Shiloh gave up her search and lifted her head. The trees above us on one side of the ravine caught her eye. Her body tensed, and I knew she wanted to make a run for it, see if she could stand up and catch some of the leaves. There were a few branches hanging low over the side, so when Brody kept going ahead, I let her stop. She reached up, but couldn't catch the leaves with her neck stretched out.

I knew the next step, and I shifted my weight, flattening myself on top of her.

She waited until I was anchored to her, my arms and legs completely around her, and then she slowly stood until she was on her back two hooves only.

She stretched up as far as she could reach and—success. Her giant lips caught one of the branches. Instead of nibbling some of the leaves from it, she snapped the branch off and lowered herself back down.

I started laughing. She looked like a giant dog with a large stick.

Her eyes shifted back to me.

Refusing to feel admonished by her, I nudged her forward again. Brody was almost out of eyesight.

Her entire body shook once before she began forward. She worked her way around the branch, eating the leaves as she walked and I laid on her like I did when she would graze. Except, I didn't lay on my back. I was on my stomach with my feet resting on her back haunches and her head propped my head up, my chin resting in my hands.

As Brody traveled the length of the ravine, he never looked back.

I wanted to yell at him. There were animals around that could kill him, but he only kept going. His breathing started to get winded, so I wondered when he would eventually slow to a walk.

Not that I was complaining.

His shorts slipped low on his hips. He'd pulled off his shirt, knotting it through a loop on his shorts so it bounced behind him.

It was still cold at night, but apparently, he couldn't feel it. If he kept this up, he could get sick. But then I watched his back and the slide of his sweat working its way down around his muscles.

I chewed on my lip, wanting to be the one to touch his back.

It was shaped perfectly. Broad and muscular shoulders, which flexed with every swing of his arms. The skin tightened and slid over them, forming a small ravine of its own that ran down the length of his spine. Every inch of him was strong, hard, smooth. There were bruises over him, but they only accentuated his muscles, giving him a hard and dangerous look.

I never knew the male physique could look like this. He reminded me of the herd's stallion. His own muscles rippled under his coat, and it was the same with Brody.

A throbbing started between my legs, and I shifted uncomfortably on Shiloh.

This was the longest run I'd seen a person do in my life.

He needed to go back to the cabin, shower, and be safe. He shouldn't be out there, and he shouldn't be depending on me to watch over him.

I swung my legs beneath me, sitting upright on Shiloh again.

That was why he was out here and running like he didn't care. Because he didn't. The asshole knew I'd find him.

He was using me and torturing me all at the same time.

Shiloh glanced back to me. She sensed my anger and began shifting around on her feet. She knew I wanted to do something. She was waiting for me to decide, and then I did. I kicked my heels into her stomach, and she took off.

He must've felt her hooves pounding through the ground before he looked back, finally, and his eyes bulged out. We were drawing down on him and at a fast pace, but right before she would've trampled him, I nudged her, and she swung left.

He fell off the trail, and I jumped off her.

I glared at him, standing above him on the trail. He had fallen down a few feet and was already pulling the headphones off.

"You're an asshole." My hands found my hips.

That throb only intensified. My lungs felt like they were going to burst.

"Yeah?" He smirked. "How so?"

His lips twitched as he stared up at me for a beat before he hopped up so he was standing in front of me. He was close, very close. I glanced straight ahead. I was on eye level to his chest, which looked just as good as the back of him. All dips and ridges between his muscles. The sweat was there, too, making his skin almost glisten.

I swallowed tightly, moving back a step. "I don't remember my brothers running without their shirts on."

He tipped his head back, a low and smooth laugh coming from him. "Nah, they wouldn't." He pulled his shirt free from the loop and wiped it over his forehead before his hands found their way to rest on his hips. He was mirroring my stance, but he suddenly seemed a lot more in control than I was. I didn't understand it, but my breathing was shortening.

Tilting his head to the side, still watching me so curiously, he added, "They'd run on some treadmill at some fancy gym, no doubt."

"People don't run out here for a reason."

"You do." He raised his chin as if he were taunting me. No. He was challenging me, but I didn't understand why.

I pulled at the strap of my tank top. There was a nice breeze, but suddenly, I was heated, too heated. The sun had started to wane. We had another thirty minutes before it would be dark. He really needed to get back by then.

"You have to return. You're six miles out."

His lips parted in surprise. "Six?"

I nodded. I looked for Shiloh and spotted her grazing farther down the trail.

I let out a loud sigh. "You're incredibly stupid."

"Why?"

"I have to walk beside you. I have to make sure you get back okay, and I don't have a horse for you to ride."

He looked over to Shiloh, a question in his eyes.

"She's not broken. I'm the only rider she allows." My voice was rising. "These are wild horses. This is the wild out here. There are bears. There are mountain lions." I hit him. I didn't care. And once I smacked his chest, I wanted to do it again. "You're so reckless."

"Hey." His arm snaked around my waist, and he pulled me to him.

I lifted my hand to hit him again.

He caught it, holding it to pull me even tighter against him.

I almost moaned aloud . . . almost. He was rubbing against me, right where I was throbbing, and I wanted him to keep going. I couldn't help it. The desire had been building since I was following him, and now that we were face to face, I saw the same hunger in his eyes too. I made the first contact, hitting him, and it was all he needed.

A spark lit, and he grabbed it, pulling me closer to him.

Hell. He felt so good.

He wrapped his arm around me, catching my hand in one of his. He traced a finger down the side of my face, softly, tenderly. "Hey." He brought it to my chin and tilted my face until I was looking him in the eyes again.

Once I did, I saw he had softened. I saw the remorse, but it only worsened my ache for him.

I didn't think I could walk beside him for six miles.

"I'm sorry."

"What?"

He gentled his tone again. "I haven't been training. I forgot how much I liked to run. I lost track of time."

"You lost track of your sanity."

I saw how he was fighting to hold back a grin before he managed to school his features into a straight line. "You're lecturing me for what? Being out past sunset?"

"It's dangerous out here."

I curled my hand into a fist, but his hand wormed its way in there, and I struggled, pushing against him. I almost groaned, feeling pleasure lace my veins, but I couldn't stop him. His hand got in there, unwound my fist and his fingers slid alongside of mine. They went slow, acting like a caress.

"Stop it." But there was no heat to my words. I knew he'd take it as a submission.

"Stop what?" His finger rubbed against mine. His free hand cupped the side of my face, and I started to close my eyes. I felt myself leaning into him, letting him hold the weight of me up. Then his thumb ran over my lips, and my eyelids flew open.

I was looking into him. He was watching me as if he were waiting for something. I saw the lust there. I knew he wanted me. I could feel between my legs, and just thinking of it, I felt my legs tighten, but he was in there. His gaze darkened. He murmured, "Morgan."

"What?"

My chest started heaving. I was practically panting.

Shivers, tingles, and wanton need coursed through my whole body. I was becoming drugged by him.

He continued to watch me, and then suddenly, his need shone prominently, and he shifted. He let go of my hand, but his arms wrapped around me and he lifted me.

I gasped, my legs went around his waist, and he held me there.

My arms wound around his neck. I was looking at his lips, wanting to feel them.

"We have a situation here," he rasped out.

I laughed, just a tiny bit. We did indeed.

"I could lay you down here on this path. We could satisfy what we're both wanting right now, or . . ." His hand slipped to just under the waistband of my pants.

I jerked from the sensation, but he caught me, holding me anchored to him.

"Or . . ." His hand slid farther down, resting on the outside of my underwear.

I gasped. "There's a water place not far from here."

His eyes sparked. "A pool?"

"It's a hot spring, but not too hot. We should be fine."

As if knowing what I was agreeing to with that admission, my mind started to flee. I wanted him as much as he wanted me. We just watched the other, the air thick with tension between us. I didn't know where Shiloh had gone, but I didn't care.

I wanted him.

I shoved back enough that he let me down, and I led him the rest of the way. It wasn't too far. When he saw the water, his eyes rounded. "Whoa."

It was a small waterfall. The foliage around it kept it private, and there were rocks jutting out so we could sit and dangle our feet into the water.

"This is beautiful." He pulled me against him.

"This is where I bathe if I don't want to go to the house."

"I can see why. It's amazing." He looked up. The pines towered high above us, the tops opening to a small circle where we would be able to see the stars in a few minutes. "Morgan, wow. Thank you for showing me this."

The need for him was still there, but it ebbed a little, enough for clear thinking to return and self-consciousness to take hold, but he was right. This pool was like a home, or one of my areas I considered mine. It was the first time I had shown anyone.

I stepped back from him, but his hand caught mine. He kept that one area of contact, lacing our fingers together as I stepped into the pool.

"You don't take your clothes off?"

I shook my head. "I keep stuff out here. I'll be fine."

He let my hand go, but only to toss his phone and headphones to the side. His shoes and socks were next, then his shorts and underwear. He stood, almost proudly in his nakedness, and gazed at me, watching for my reaction.

I didn't shy away. I knew I would be feeling him all over. I was almost trembling, knowing he would be inside me that night. Stepping out of the pool, I traced a hand down his chest, lingering on his waistline, drawing closer to him, and then, as my eyes went to his, I wrapped my hand around him.

He gasped silently, but he didn't do anything else. He held still, waiting to see what more I would do.

I began to rub my hand over him, softly, going up and down.

He closed his eyes, and as I kept caressing him, his head tipped back. His mouth fell open, and he groaned.

I rubbed my thumb over the end of him, hearing him hiss for a small second. His body reacted to me, making me feel powerful. He was hard already, but he only got harder and harder as I kept stroking him.

My own pleasure was pulsating through me, and before I thought about it, I knelt and took him into my mouth. His head reared forward, his eyes almost black from desire as he watched me. His hands caught the sides of my face, and then paused before he pulled my mouth away and guided me back to standing. As if I weighed nothing, he lifted me into his arms and carried me into the water.

His mouth found mine.

It wasn't like anything I'd felt. A graze of his lips over mine. It was a tingle, spreading through me, and before I realized it, I acquired a thirst for him. I wanted more of this touch and somehow, I knew after this first kiss, I would always hunger for him.

He whispered, "Not this time. Later, trust me. Later." His eyes held so many promises as he pulled back to look me in the eyes.

I nodded, my legs tightening around his waist.

I felt him moving, seeking me out, and if I didn't have my pants on, he would've sunk into me already.

"God, Morgan." He panted softly, sinking into the water and moving so my back was resting against one of the softer banks. "You have no idea how much I've thought about this." A hand slipped under my shirt so he could pull it off. I didn't wear a bra, and after tossing the fabric aside, he grasped one of my breasts, his hand cupping it fully. His thumb went over my nipple, almost teasing me like I had with him.

His mouth found mine again, pressing to me.

I shuddered in his arms.

His lips opened over mine, and his tongue swept in. I was kissing him back, relishing every taste of him. I was moving in his arms, grinding against him.

I wanted to be just as naked as he was.

His hand ran the length of me, a soft rub, and tingles trailed behind. He went to my waistline and paused, curling his fingers around my pants. "Is this your first?"

I shook my head. "A drunken mistake at a barn party once. It was stupid."

His eyes softened, and his hold on my pants gentled too. He began to peel them down, trailing kisses over the length of me as he went, pausing between my breasts. He kissed both of them, his tongue licking, teasing me briefly before he continued. As my pants and underwear were pulled from my legs, his mouth explored my stomach before moving lower and pausing right over my opening.

He looked up at me. The same dark promise there as before. "This won't be a stupid mistake. I promise."

I nodded. I already knew. There was something about Brody that made me not regret anything. Regret seeking him out. Regret looking out for him. Regret feeling myself being pulled more and more into their world. Regret following him tonight, even his stupid mistake of going too far and for too long—I wouldn't regret not stopping his run earlier than when I did.

I leaned down, my hands raking through his hair as I pulled him up to me. He stretched out, half on top of me, but I felt him nudging me. He went to slide inside, but he held back, waiting.

I nodded, letting my lips brush over his. "Yes." I opened my mouth, and he was inside me. He pushed all the way in, and I gasped, feeling him fully. He held still, letting me get used to him, then his lips brushed over mine again.

"Yes," he repeated my word, grinning against my lips.

I felt my own matching grin, but I kissed him, opening my mouth against his.

"God." He breathed out right before he began moving.

I closed my eyes.

My head fell back.

He thrust in deep before pulling almost all the way out, only to slide back in.

He started a rhythm, but I was moving with him. I wrapped my legs around his hips, my ankles locking behind his back.

I wanted him to go faster and harder.

"Morgan," he whispered my name, his hips thrusting into me. He dropped a kiss to my throat, his tongue tasting me there.

I wanted him to keep going.

I was riding with him, our bodies straining against each other. There was something so frenzied about our movements, primal.

Then he paused, a raw tenderness came over him, and he began to explore my body again with his lips. He kissed me everywhere, and I gasped, feeling my insides straining for him to keep going. I needed that release, but he chuckled, knowing the torment he was enacting on me.

"Brody!" I gasped, pushing against him.

His eyes were dancing. He lifted his head to look down to me. "Hmm?"

"You're driving me mad." I reached down, grasping his hips, and I began moving him. If he didn't start again—I growled from frustration.

"What?"

He was laughing.

I smacked him on the chest, but then pushed so he was the one lying on the bank. I rose up, getting my feet under me for better position and lowered myself back onto him. He went in deep, and I stilled. His hand came up my back, holding me, and I half-leaned backward, letting him touch me.

I savored the feel of him in me and began to move.

I was in control and could push down as far as I wanted, which was all the way. When I did, his mouth dropped open and a low groan left him. He was embedded in me, all the way to his hilt, and I lifted up, only to go back down.

I went slowly at first, enjoying the rub of him, but then sped up, rolling my hips forward and backward.

I arched my back as I kept going.

God.

I loved this—the feel of him deep inside me, the pleasure rolling through me in waves as I kept going.

His hand covered one of my breasts, and he lifted so his mouth could catch first one of my nipples and then the other. He was tasting me as I kept riding him.

I started going harder, faster.

I was nearing my climax.

He grunted, his hands flexing into my hips as if he was going right with me. He was slamming me down to him almost ruthlessly.

"Fuck!" He growled, and I was flipped onto my back.

He didn't wait for me to adjust again, he slammed into me, and this time, he didn't stop or let up. He was almost rough as he pounded into me, but I wanted it. I was thriving on it. My entire body was awake and wanted him to keep going.

Then, as he held me still and kept driving hard into me, I almost screamed.

I hurtled over the edge, my whole body climaxed at once, and I went mad. I was trembling, shaking, quivering.

He paused, waiting until the wave lessened, and once he saw I was sated, he grinned lazily down at me. "You ready for me?"

I groaned and wrapped a hand around his neck. "I'm ready."

And I held on as he pounded into me for his own pleasure. As he neared, he paused and then ground into me for a moment before he thrust again, his movements turning jerky as he swelled and climaxed. His body going taut right before he slumped over me.

Holy.

I ran a hand down his back, savoring the feel of him over me and in me.

This . . . this had been nothing like my drunken mistake.

I curved against his body, my lips against his neck as I smiled. He laughed, leaning into my kiss as he curled a hand around my waist and dragged me into the water.

We both went under, but the water was warm from the hot spring. He dislodged from me. I went to the surface first, and then his hands caught my waist. We played after that.

He dunked me.

I dunked him.

I was the better swimmer, so I could evade him if I wanted, but he had a better reach on me. He caught my ankle, pulled me back to him, and it wasn't long before he was inside me again.

# CHAPTER TWENTY

## Morgan

It was close to dawn when I woke.

Brody was half on top of me, his head curled into my neck and his arm heavy around my waist. We'd fallen asleep like this, lying on the bank beside the water after I dug down, putting some heated coals beneath us and covering those with enough dirt to protect us. Grabbing some blankets from a hidden stash, we settled in.

It was cozy where we were, but I knew it'd be cold once I peeled back the blankets.

I looked at him, needing a fast way to get him back to safety.

I didn't want to leave him, but I had to. I edged out, pulling on my clothes from the night before. They were damp with dew, but they would dry within an hour. Once I got my sandals on, I edged out from the hot spring. I started running down the path, and I whistled for Shiloh.

I kept going. She must've gone back to the herd, but I kept whistling for her. I'd been jogging for thirty minutes before I heard her behind me, and because it was like second nature for me, I weaved to the side. She came up beside me, and I reached up, pulling myself to her back. Once I was settled, she could sense my intensity. I clicked my heels in, and she took it as permission. She kicked up her speed until she was full bore going ahead. We skipped the wood trails, choosing to run alongside a cliff's edge instead. There was enough clearing beside the rock where she could go comfortably, knowing there wouldn't be a hidden log or hole in the path.

As she ran, I leaned back.

I spread my arms wide, and as her mane was flying behind her, so was mine.

I'd never felt more alive than I did in that moment.

This was the world I loved. Moments like these, where it was just she and I and our perfect understanding of each other, were what I lived for. She wanted to run, and I wanted to feel like I was flying.

We stayed on the ridge for as far as we could, dipping into the woods again once we neared the main lodge.

I knew domestic horses had been brought in, and I didn't think they would mind if I snuck one out, especially for the star.

We drew up to the end of the field, and I jumped off Shiloh. I scrambled over the fence and then ran the length up to the barn. I would need a halter this time. Once inside the barn, I eyed the saddles, not knowing if he would need one but knowing I didn't have time to grab one I kept going. Part of me churned at the idea. In the truest sense, they weren't supposed to be strapped down with saddles.

Grabbing a halter and lead rope, one long enough for him to hold on to, I studied all the horses. A few didn't want me there. Their nostrils flared. They could smell the wild on me, but one didn't huff or back away. Her eyes were the gentlest I'd seen in a long time. I slipped the halter on, then the lead, and took her out of her stall. Once we were free of the barn and I had shut the door behind us, I tried to swing on to her back. Unfamiliar with the move, the mare shifted away from me, and I had to try again. Only Shiloh and Shoal knew my routine, but once I was on her, I made the clicking sound and urged her ahead. There was no opening at the fence so I had to get her going at full speed. Once we were close, I pulled her head back and she followed my signals. She jumped, her body clearing the fence easily. Shiloh fell in step beside us, following us all the way back to where Brody was still sleeping.

Except he wasn't.

He was walking on the path, his shirt hanging over his shoulder, and his shorts and shoes on. He was looking down at his phone, frowning and only looking up when he heard us coming.

"Holy shit."

I circled him with the horse before I slid down to the ground and handed him the rope. "You know how to ride, right?" I saw him earlier on a horse, but I didn't know his comfort levels about a longer ride.

A gurgled laugh rippled from his throat. He was gawking at the horse, which had started to shift around, feeling his nervousness.

I frowned. "Brody. I saw you before, you were riding."

He shot me a look. "I've ridden you."

I flushed. "You know what I mean. You'll need to ride back. It's a long way."

He grinned, his eyes darkening at me. "I know. Sorry. I rode a long time ago when I was a kid. I agreed to talk to some therapist who's coming today. He or she's going to use horses for therapy."

"Really?"

He nodded, eyeing the horse again. "What's his name?"

"Her." I frowned. "I wouldn't ever get you a stallion or stud to ride. Gelding, yes, but not them."

"Yeah." He laughed shortly, raising a hand to the horse's neck. "Hey, buddy. Hey, hey." He said to me, "I have no clue what you just said. I'll be honest, they all look the same to me."

Seeing a horsefly, I swatted it away.

Shiloh snorted, shifting sideways to avoid it as well.

"What?" Brody jerked around, alarmed.

I flashed him a quick grin. "She's just calling you a dumbass."

He looked at me. "Horses can't understand what we're saying. You can't convince me of that."

"She can feel emotions."

"Oh." He quieted, looking back to the horse I brought him. She was a beautiful chestnut body and mane. "Okay, I guess." He nodded to her. "You and me, huh? I suppose we'll get to know each other eventually." He looked at me, motioning to her back. "How do I get up there?"

I eyed him up and down before doing the same to her. She was giving me a look that said, "Please don't let him hurt me."

I patted her on the neck, crooning, "No, no. I won't." I pressed my forehead to hers, reassuring her I had good intentions. She sensed my calmness, and her body visibly shook as she settled.

I took the lead rope from Brody and motioned to a rock jutting out over the path farther down. "You can get up there, and I'll bring her along in front of you. You can get on her that way."

He looked at her back. "She isn't saddled."

"Are you joking?"

He flushed. "You grew up like this. Being around horses is more normal to you than being around people. I get that, but it isn't for me. I'm used to people, and cars, and motorcycles." He gestured to the chestnut mare, who had a wary look in her eye again. "I can do sex. I'm very good at sex, but as far as riding another living creature like a horse? It's been It's a different ball game for me."

"I've seen you ride for the movie. You handled everything like you knew what you were doing."

He smirked. "That's called acting. It's what I'm damned good at, and that wasn't long term. Those horses were trained. They knew to take me from spot A to spot B, and not to buck me off on the way."

I sighed. I was going to have to ride her with him, and I gestured to the rock. "Go. It'll be fine."

He didn't move. "I have no problem walking back."

I gestured again, my hand flicking more impatiently. "I said go. Get on there."

As he sighed and then climbed onto the rock, I gently pulled myself up onto her back. Motioning her forward, I lined her up in front of him.

"You're riding her too?"

"I have to, or it'll take two hours to get you back. We're seven miles away."

He gulped. "For real? Seven miles?"

I nodded, indicating behind me. "Just gently climb on." As he did, he lined his body up behind mine, and his arms wrapped around my waist. "Don't sneak any feels. I could react, and she might drop us both on the ground."

I didn't add how I doubted she'd do that. He didn't need to know that.

He nodded, but his hand dipped under my shirt. His head dropped, and I felt his lips graze my neck as he said, "I'll do my best." But as we started off, his hand didn't stay still. He had it under my pants and resting at the edge of my underwear before we'd even traveled a mile.

By the second mile, his finger was inside me, and I was leaning all the way back against him.

Somehow, the mare got us back, but I had to admit that I hadn't done much of the steering.

He brought me to a climax, a slow and smooth and sensual one so my body was softly shaking once the chestnut stopped by the fence.

His lips skimmed the side of my neck. "Well, that was the best horse ride ever."

I groaned. "I told you not to touch me like that."

His grin turned cocky when I motioned for him to get off the horse. He slid down, dropping the last couple of feet to the ground. "Yeah, you totally gave me that impression when you opened your legs wider for me."

I barked out a laugh but caught up the reins in my hand. I clicked, turning the chestnut back again. "Stand back. I have to jump her." I signaled for her to go farther. We'd need a running start.

"What?"

I nodded to the end of the fencing. "The only opening is up ahead by the barn, but not down here. I gotta jump her to get her in there."

He was starting to climb over the fence when I turned her back and kicked her into full gallop. She cleared the fence easily, and instead of waiting for Brody, I rode her all the way to the barn as Brody followed on foot.

I put her in the stall, watered her, and was brushing her down by the time he entered behind us. Waiting until I was done, he just stood and watching.

I'd done this act so many times, it was second nature. I'd taken care of horses when other people were in the barn with me, but it felt different this time. Maybe it was because we were intimate last night, or even the ride here, or maybe it was Brody himself. For whatever reason, as I brushed the mare down, as he stood and watched, and as we both didn't say a word, it felt like one of the most intimate moments I'd endured.

My nerves were stretched tight, and I didn't want to question if that was a good thing or not. I just knew that I wasn't surprised when Brody grabbed my hand once I was done. He began to lead me toward the door. I started to go with him. My body was saying yes all over again, but I cleared the fog and dug my heels in.

We were going fast, too fast.

Right?

I asked, "What are you doing?"

"Taking you to the cabin. I have a bed there. A *soft* bed."

I was torn. I wanted to, but . . .

It was becoming too much, too intense too quickly.

I pulled my hand free. "I shouldn't."

"Why not?"

I shook my head. Tucking my hand behind my back, I began edging backward. "I just can't. It's a lot . . . I'm sorry."

"But—" His expression twisted in confusion. "I want you beside me." He stepped toward me again. "I want to hold you."

I wanted that too. And we'd have that. But not here, not in his cabin, not so close to where I felt the world was trying to pull me back into its folds.

I reached for the door behind me. "I can't." I opened it and slipped outside. Before I shut it, I said quickly, "I'll come back."

Then I shut the door and ran back to where Shiloh was waiting for me. She had followed behind us as I hoped.

When I climbed over the fence and onto her, I looked back.

Brody was standing inside that door, watching me. I paused, but I didn't wave. He didn't, either, and feeling myself hardening inside, I dug my heels in. Shiloh didn't need another signal. She tore off, and we veered back to the cliff's edge again, both of us feeling as if we were flying moments later.

Except this time, it didn't feel as free.

# CHAPTER TWENTY-ONE

## Brody

I got laid and rejected, all within twenty-four hours.

And was propositioned by my therapist.

"I thought that was against your code of ethics or something."

She smiled coyly, cocking her head to the side and fluttering those eyelashes at me. I fought against rolling my eyes. It wasn't the best come-on I'd witnessed. It wasn't the worst, but it was among them.

She was stroking the horse's lead rope as if she were wishing it was my cock, or maybe she thought it looked seductive. It didn't.

"I'm not really a therapist. I studied counseling, got into graduate school, and then took a job at a horse ranch. I never finished my degree, but my boss hired me because of work experience. Said my internship was enough. They just can't bill you like a normal client. So voilà. I'm not tied down to the same ethics normal therapists are."

Of course. That seemed like something that'd happen to me: getting a counselor that's not a counselor at all. I think karma was trying to tell me something.

She leaned forward, making sure her cleavage was on full display. I eyed the horse behind her. He'd been eyeing her, too, stomping his foot in agitation. I narrowed my eyes and corrected myself. A mare. Morgan said most of these were mares.

"Any geldings in here?"

She paused, her eyebrows dipping together, but then she nudged the horse back into her stall. She closed the door and followed along as I walked past all of them. There were a good ten horses in the barn, maybe more.

She looked around and shrugged. "I don't know, actually. Matthew Kellerman got these from the Coral Ranch just down the road. They breed mostly quarter horses. I don't think they'd loan out a gelding, though. They'd keep those back." She gestured to the wilderness beyond the field and fence. "Just to be safe, and everything has to be locked up tight. Want to make sure no mares run off with the herd."

"Really?"

"Yeah, especially with that stallion. He's the most male stallion I've ever seen. Not a mild temperament."

I stopped and focused more on her. "What do you know about the herd? Are you from around here?"

She nodded. "I grew up here, came back instead of going to that grad school, and I just know what everyone around these parts knows. They're protected by the government, though the government is thinking about rounding them up and there's legislation that might get them slaughtered."

No—no way. That'd devastate Morgan.

Seeing my look, she rushed out, "But don't worry. I doubt that'll happen to these guys. The Kellermans have been letting them roam these lands all their life, but they're dangerous. I mean, they're true wild horses. Don't get one cornered. They'll fight back. They could kill a person."

She began walking toward the front of the barn and, almost as an afterthought, mentioned, "I mean, except for the youngest Kellerman." I froze, but she was too busy laughing to notice. "If she even exists."

She was reaching for the door.

I clapped a hand over the knob, stopping her.

Her head jerked up, and I smiled, using my best seductive swoon there was. "What do you mean, *if* she exists?"

God. This therapist that wasn't a therapist. I didn't know her name. She was another female that blended in with all the other females in my life, but not Morgan. Morgan was special. Morgan was important, and now this pretend-therapist was *seriously* getting on my nerves.

She laughed, a nervous thread in her voice. Backing away a step, she tucked a strand of hair behind her ear and shrugged again. "It's nothing, just a stupid joke."

"Morgan Kellerman?"

"Yeah. It was the dad that killed her mom."

My fake smile dropped. I clipped out, "What?"

*The dad...*

It clicked then. Everything. It was even in the goddamn script. Karen was hiding from her first husband—Morgan's father.

I looked out the back of the barn, half-hoping that Morgan would be there but knowing she wouldn't be. She was a damned ghost, and another piece of information fit into place about how much she must've needed to be a ghost.

Her father.

The therapist reached around me and opened the door so she could pass. "On top of the murder, the little girl was in the woods. She stayed out there so long that there was an uproar. It was a big deal. There was a murder and then a huge search party all at the same time. The Kellermans organized a manhunt. Dogs were brought in, professional guides, trackers. You name it. It took a couple days to find her. She was curled up behind a log, sleeping soundly. She was perfectly fine, even thought it was a game."

"Was there news coverage about that?"

She shrugged. "Just the rumor mill. We don't have local news like that. There might've been a news article, but everyone knows that Mr. Kellerman had it all covered up, the murder too. He didn't want any of it leaking. Doesn't like bad news spreading, could hurt his big fancy empire or whatever he runs. At least, that's what people around town say."

My stomach was rolling over. "Tell me more about that day, when Karen was murdered."

She studied me a second, her eyes flicking up and down. "It's an inside joke about the girl being a myth. Everyone in town knows she exists. I mean, it's just something stupid we use to help with the tourists, you know? People like traveling up around here, seeing if they can get a glimpse of the 'wild girl.' We're all, actually, kind of protective of her." Worry etched in her eyes, and she flicked them up and down me. "Don't go blabbing this shit to anyone else. Okay?"

I was sick to my stomach.

*Morgan.*

I looked again. Dense forest covered the mountain. There was a river that led into a lake. Crevices. Ravines. Cliffs. There was solid rock in some places and long billowy grass in others.

Then there was a beautiful waterfall and a hot spring.

She showed me all that treacherous beauty.

She didn't hide out there. She lived out there. She thrived out there. She wasn't some mystery to be used to toy with the seasonal tourists, or even a story to be talked about.

She was real. She was so goddamn real.

"You okay?"

"What?"

The therapist had been watching me. She turned toward the forest too. "You see something out there?"

"Nah." Too much. "Nothing at all." I'd seen everything.

"Well . . . anyway." She started for her car. "You obviously don't have a problem with horses. I don't know why they had me come out, but if you need to talk to someone, you should probably see a real therapist."

"Yeah." I muttered, wanting nothing more than to ignore her as she turned back to me. "I'll do that."

"And, uh, could I get an autograph? Maybe a selfie with you?"

I shoved my hands into my pockets. "Not a fucking chance."

# CHAPTER TWENTY-TWO

## Morgan

It wasn't even a full day.

I couldn't last that long.

I felt his touch all day.

I could feel how his lips slid down my throat, over my body. How I felt in his arms, the weight of him above me, the pressure of him filling me. How he gripped my legs and slid inside, over and over again.

I spent the day with Shiloh, but my mind was with him. He never left me. He was whispering to me, beckoning to me, pulling me back to him until I could no longer stay with the herd.

I swung my legs off Shiloh and walked back to him.

She started to follow me, but when she realized where I was going, she trotted up to me and dropped her nose onto my shoulder. I reached up, my hand rubbing over the front of her face where the gray faded to a soft white. I always loved the look on her, and I glanced up, looking into her eyes. She was watching me, a sadness there.

She knew I was being pulled away.

I flattened my hand and ran it all the way up into her mane. Dropping my forehead to rest over the bridge between her eyes, I sighed.

So did she, lowering her head even more so we were almost on equal footing. Almost.

She'd always tower over me, and I pulled back.

I ran my hand through her mane again before moving over her strong cheek and down over her soft nose. "I love you, girl." I bent my forehead back to hers. "Sister to sister."

But I needed to go to him.

There was a stirring in me, and it was alien, but he would calm it. I knew he would, because he'd been the one to awaken it.

I turned back, and it wasn't long before I felt her absence. She'd returned to the herd.

It was late when I climbed to his second-floor patio. He'd left the door open, but the curtain hung there to keep any bugs out. I walked through to his room.

He was there, sleeping. His chest was rising and falling in a steady rhythm.

A part of me was tempted to curl up on the floor. I would've been content just to listen to him sleep the whole night through, but then, as if sensing my presence, he woke. His breathing quieted, and he sat up in bed.

"Morgan?"

His voice was alert, as if he hadn't been sleeping at all, but I knew he had been.

"You wake so alert."

I couldn't see his eyes or mouth in the darkness, but I wanted to. I stepped forward, needing to know if he was smiling at what I said.

He murmured, "I was hoping you would come. I must've just dozed for a little bit."

Another step.

This felt right.

One more step. I was by his bed and able to see his eyes. I saw what he said was true. There was a look in them. He had been waiting for me. Silently, still looking into me as I was looking into him, he lifted his bed sheet, and I curled up next to him.

When his lips touched mine, it felt so much like the right thing to do that my heart broke a little.

Something was changing.

I didn't want it to, but I couldn't stop it.

Because the thing changing was me.

# CHAPTER TWENTY-THREE

## Matthew

He was at his desk when someone knocked.

"Come in."

Finn opened the door. "Got a minute?"

"Always for you." He stood, gesturing Finn to come in. "Close the door."

His younger brother, who was usually carefree, seemed off. He'd been working as a developer for their father's company, a new branch for them, but even the high pressure of that job hadn't seemed to bother him that much. His brother had fallen in love. For the first time in a long time, Matthew had seen his brother truly happy.

That look was gone.

Matthew frowned. Tugging at his cuffs, he ran a thumb over each to make sure his cufflinks were in place. It was a habit he'd acquired years ago.

"What's going on?"

Finn motioned to his chair. "You can sit for this."

Matthew's smile tightened a little, but he tried to joke. "Am I in trouble?"

Finn sat across from him, his legs stretched out toward him and his hands in his lap. Matthew took note of his body posture.

*This should be interesting.*

"I want to know what's going on with Morgan."

Matthew raised an eyebrow. "Where is this coming from?"

Abby had been the one who wanted to know about Morgan and

always seemed close to tears every time her name was mentioned. He added, "I wasn't aware Abby had been keeping you abreast of everything."

"She said that Morgan's been talking to Asher and that you've had cameras installed to watch the actor's place. It's been a week since he's gone on his sobriety stint, and Jennifer is coming to stay until the movie is wrapped. I want in on the loop. She and he have a history and I don't need any surprises."

"Ah."

Yes.

Finn was abreast with everything, except one item.

Matthew said, "I had cameras installed to watch both entrances to his cabin. Morgan hasn't shown up on any of them."

"What?" Finn jerked forward. "Abby said she heard Morgan talking to Asher."

Matthew held up a finger, continuing to speak, "And once I heard *that*, I added another camera toward the patio on the second level. Morgan's shown up there every night, and she leaves every morning."

*She left* almost *every morning*, Matthew corrected in his head. There were two days when she remained half the day.

"What?" Finn barked out right before a wide smile spread over his face. He leaned back, relaxing once again. "Hot damn, little sister's becoming almost human. Nice to know not even she's immune to the Hollywood bad boy, huh?" He kept chuckling to himself, shaking his head. "I'm happy for her."

"Yes."

Matthew wasn't.

Finn admitted, "I was a little worried about Jen. Logically, I know I shouldn't be, but you know. It's ridiculous how girls fall over for him."

Matthew's lips thinned. "I'm sure Asher doesn't even remember it. He's dipped his dick in a fair share of women, hasn't he?"

"True." But Finn wasn't alarmed.

After they talked and Finn got a call and excused himself, and long after he left the office, Matthew was on edge.

He pulled up the footage again. She was on Asher's lap, her lips fused to his.

The image froze there.

He stopped it, and he didn't need to see any more, but it was wrong.

Everything about it was wrong. If Abby were happy for Morgan, if Finn was too, then it would be up to him to stop it. Because that's what he had to do.

He had to put an end to Brody Asher.

# CHAPTER TWENTY-FOUR

*Brody*

Morgan slept beside me, her head resting on her arm and the bed sheet pooled over her waist. She was naked with me, and I ran a hand down her arm, knowing it tickled her a little, and snuck around to grab one of her breasts. I cupped it, loving how it fit perfectly in my hand. She was petite, so her breasts weren't too big, but I loved them. Leaning down, I took one in my mouth, my tongue swirling over the nipple.

I felt her start to awaken, her entire body jerking.

She rolled, her hand coming to my back. Her next sound was a soft groan. "Good morning."

The sun was starting to peek, but only just, so it was probably before six. It was my first day back to work, and I had a scene in the afternoon. I knew Gayle would be coming to check on me, but until then, I rolled on top of Morgan, my mouth switching to her other breast.

Her hand went to my hip, and her fingers sank into my skin as I positioned myself at her entrance. I went in, pushing all the way.

Goddamn.

She felt so good, every fucking time.

I closed my eyes, loving this feeling of my dick in her. It never got old. Every time I wondered if I'd start to get the "used to" feel, but it never happened with her. I'd never experienced this before—wanting back in as soon as I was out of her.

I felt her body warm to mine, molding against me, and her walls tightening around me.

I dropped a kiss to her shoulder and then began to move.

Her legs went around my waist, and she rocked in tempo with me.

I first worried since I hadn't used a condom and didn't pull out, but she laughed when I expressed the concern. She ran a hand down my chest then, saying, "I can't have children."

I caught her hand, asking, "What?"

She nodded. "I don't know why. I don't have a cycle like normal women. I think it's because of how I live, but it isn't something we need to worry about."

Since then, I'd been raw the whole time, and we'd been having sex on the daily this week. As I slid back out, then right back in, I searched for her mouth. I wanted to touch those lips. I wanted to claim her both ways, and like all the other times, she was eager for me. She opened her mouth, her tongue searching for me right back.

This whole week had been amazing.

It wasn't just the sex.

It was everything.

She was with me every night. She was beside me every morning, staying on the days I could convince her Shiloh wanted mother-daughter bonding time with Shoal. Morgan laughed every time, knowing I was just bullshitting her, but she'd stay in the bed, her naked body wrapped around mine.

There'd been no other therapist sessions. Gayle checked in a few times, even coming to visit once. I saw the surprise when she looked at me. I hadn't been lying when I told her I was resting the whole time, and she'd been right. I had needed the week, but it wasn't because I was suddenly doing meditation and finding myself. It was because of Morgan, all of it was because of her.

I felt my release coming, but I wanted to hold off.

Pausing, I reached down and found her nub. I began rubbing my finger there, applying just enough pressure to drive her wild. It was like a magic button. I touched it, and Morgan started going nuts. I waited, caressing her, and when I felt her starting, I began thrusting harder.

"Brody!" she gasped, her body twitching under my hands. She arched her back, her neck exposed, and I clamped down, tasting her there.

Holding her hip as an anchor, I pounded her harder, going all the way to the hilt and then I felt my release.

Holy fucking shit.

I gasped, keeping myself above her. She ran a lazy hand up my arm, cupping the side of my face. She liked to watch me as I came. I didn't know why. Her thumb touched the corner of my mouth, and I grabbed it, nipping it with my teeth, rubbing my tongue around it.

She laughed before pulling it out. Her hand went back down my back, her nails lightly skimming. I loved that. I felt like a damned cat, but it felt so good.

Then, as my release left me, I laid down on her, letting her take almost my full weight. I worried about this too in the beginning. I didn't want to crush her, but she enjoyed it, or that was what she said. I never gave her my full weight, usually shifting to the side so it was mainly my chest and head on her. I wrapped my arms around her, and she began brushing my hair from my forehead.

Those little ministrations? They always relaxed me further. I'd either fall asleep or get drowsy again, like I was this morning.

"You working today?"

I nodded, lifting just enough to look at her. I saw the cloud of wariness and shifted to the side so I was lying beside her. With my head propped up by my hand, my elbow on the bed, I reached out with my free hand to tap her chin lightly. "What's wrong?"

"Our time will be . . ." She hesitated. "It'll be different."

"Yeah." I caught her hand, lacing our fingers and resting them on her stomach. I began rubbing my finger over her, enjoying how even that small touch had her closing her eyes in contentment. "I'll just leave at random times, but trust me, I'll have to go on more runs if you don't come find me first."

She groaned. "Don't ever do that again. I was so mad at you."

I chuckled. "I enjoyed that night. Best sleep I've had for a year." I meant it. I slept better when she was beside me, and it didn't matter if we were outside or in this apartment. Though, I liked the clean sheets if I was given a choice.

I reached up and ran my thumb down a wrinkle in her forehead. "What's really going on? I can tell you're stressed about something."

Her eyes shot to mine. She was chewing on the corner of her lip. "You're going to think I'm stupid."

"Never." I stared back at her. I wanted her to see how serious I was. "Tell me what's wrong. I'll fix it."

"That's the thing. I don't know if you *can* fix it. I've felt off, like something is wrong."

"Wrong? You and me?"

"No, not us." Her eyes shifted. She was staring at the ceiling, but I knew she was lost in her thoughts. "I've just been getting this feeling lately. Something bad is about to happen."

I pulled my hand away and sat up, tugging her with me so she was lying in my arms. "What do you mean something bad is about to happen?"

A fierce need to protect her took over.

This week hadn't been just amazing; it'd also been terrifying at times. I worried every morning she left that I wouldn't see her again. And once she came back, I knew she'd go again. It was inevitable. I was relieved when I had her by me, but the horses and the wild really did call to her. She'd be in my arms, and we'd hear Shiloh neighing for her. A part of me didn't even blame the mustang. She wanted her family with her. She wanted to make sure Morgan was okay.

I would've done the same, but I saw that it wore on her.

She wanted to stay with me, but she also wanted to go to Shiloh.

Every time she chose me, a little lost look entered her eyes.

There were times when she wouldn't know I was watching her, and I saw that look almost overtake her. She was yearning, missing the feeling of being out there. The afternoon trips to Shiloh weren't doing it for her, but then she would look at me and the look would clear. A hunger would appear in her eyes that matched my own.

We'd start kissing, other times so much more.

I ran a hand over her arm and then down between the V between her breasts before I cupped her. This felt right. Every time I could hold her, touch her, I was fine.

I ran a hand down the underside of her arm, caressing her.

I never brought up her mother or what the pseudo-therapist told me, though it was in the back of my mind. I kept waiting for her to talk about it. She never did. And I was unwilling to push her, but I felt like I had to now. "What about your mom?"

Her body grew heavier again as she turned her eyes to mine. "My mom?"

I nodded. "It's the whole reason I'm here, Morgan. You never talk about her."

"There's nothing to say. She died."

I cleared my throat. I was about to ask a prodding question, but she started on her own.

Her voice was quiet again, small like she was embodying the little girl she'd been then. "They don't think I knew what happened when they found me, but I did. I knew that he killed her."

I went still. "He?"

"The monster." Her voice went flat, hollow. "I never knew my father. My mom left him before I was born so I didn't know who he was then, but it wouldn't have mattered. I still would've run. He was there to cause harm." Her body tensed in my arms.

I'd never felt so useless. How do you protect against a goddamn nightmare?

"My mom told me to hide, so I ran to Shoal." Her bottom lip jerked, but that was it. "He searched the whole day for me. He left once, but he only moved his car so that they wouldn't know he'd been there. He parked it farther down the road, pulling off and hiding it behind some trees."

"He was searching for you?"

She said, almost dully, "He looked until *they* started looking for me. I heard the search dogs barking, and it wasn't long after that when his smell left."

"Jesus, Morgan." I rested my cheek on top of her head. "I'm so sorry."

My arms tightened around her. I would've held her for the rest of the day, for the rest of her life. I didn't want to let her go, but she had a different idea. Hunger darkened her gaze, and she turned in my arms. She moved to straddle me, and I knew what she wanted when her lips found mine.

She wanted to forget.

I was sliding into her again moments later, but this time was different. Maybe I was trying to make sure we both forgot our haunts.

Or maybe it was the first time I felt like I was making love to someone.

# CHAPTER TWENTY-FIVE

## Morgan

Brody's manager arrived to drive him to where they were shooting.

I was in his room when she knocked outside, and he dropped a quick kiss to me before going to let her in. As she entered, I exited, jumping down from the patio. Shiloh had been calling for me all morning, so I knew she'd be waiting.

As soon as I climbed over the fence, she was there.

I jumped on, and she tore off.

Our rides had been cut drastically over the last week, but not then. Not today. I wanted to ride with her. I wanted to feel as if we were flying.

I felt her body rippling under me, mirroring my need.

Too much time apart wasn't good for us, *either* of us.

I lie against her back and rested my cheek on her neck, my arms wrapping around her, and I closed my eyes. Wherever she took me, I would be fine.

# CHAPTER TWENTY-SIX

*Brody*

Gayle had been giving me a weird look since she had shown up at the cabin. After the tenth sneak peek, I sighed and looked over. "What?"

She was pulling into the lot, and I watched as she parked behind a trailer. "Nothing."

I climbed out, grabbing my bag of extra clothes from the backseat. Shutting my door, I shot her a look back over the top of the car. "That look doesn't say nothing. It says something. What's going on with you?"

She paused, resting her arm on the car. "It's just . . . you look good, like really good."

I only shrugged. "I worked out a lot. I went on runs every day, and I did a whole bunch of meditation shit."

"You weren't drinking?"

"I already told when you checked on me, and every time you called—no. No booze. I swear. I didn't even leave the property. You bought me enough food to last the week."

"No, I know." She held a hand up, as if she were going to back off. "You look good. I'm proud of you."

I noted, dryly, "I never had a drinking problem. I just drank too much."

"Brody!"

Shanna shouted my name. She waved, trying not to drop the clipboard she was holding, and Gayle and I headed her way.

Gayle said, "You drank too much for eight months."

I wanted to remind her why I started, but bit the words down. It didn't matter. In her eyes, it was time to get moving forward, and I needed to follow through. I signed a contract. I agreed to do this movie, and I was so damned grateful for it.

"Brody!" Shanna said again, opening her arms and engulfing me in a hug. She clasped me to her, patting my back twice. "It's good to see you. Shit. You look good, real good." She held me at arm's length, holding on to my biceps. "You're right, Gayle. He looks a hundred percent better. Whatever you did, it worked. You look like the actor we hired for this movie and not a washed-up drunk. Damn time."

"Thank you."

There were so many smart-ass comments I could've made then, but I refrained.

"No more drinking?"

"No more drinking."

Shanna glanced to Gayle, who nodded. "That's what he said, and it seems to be the case."

I leveled them both with a look. "You guys are so trusting, I'm amazed."

Shanna laughed, patting me one last time before gesturing back toward the cameras. "We had to rearrange the schedule. Did you get the updated script?"

I nodded. "Gayle dropped it off when she checked on me."

"Fabulous." Shanna waved over my shoulder. "Your trailer is behind you, and you have thirty minutes before your scene starts. Now scoot. We've wasted enough time. We only have so much sunlight."

I didn't need the thirty.

Fifteen minutes later, Kara and I were running lines until Shanna signaled for us to start filming. I checked my watch. It was exactly another fifteen minutes later. Shanna was punctual, which was a benefit because everything had to run smoothly or our shooting time would've lasted until the next day. Instead, she called the final cut for the night ten hours later. It was around eight in the evening.

I was doing the math. I could run home and head out for a "run" if I needed to find Morgan, but when I headed back for Gayle's car, Kara stopped me.

"What are you doing tonight?"

She picked up her pace to match mine.

I was ready for the pick-up line or the sultry smiles, but neither came. She'd also been professional the whole day of shooting.

"I was planning on heading back and going for a run."

Her eyebrow rose. She smoothed a hand down her hair, flicking out a piece of grass. "The crew and I were heading to Juan's. It's a Mexican restaurant in town. They have good chips and salsa. Want to come?"

I started to decline, but there was an extra look in her eyes. It wasn't one that I'd seen before, and it gave me pause. I wanted to see Morgan, but having good relationships with co-workers was another leaf I should turn over.

I flashed her a grin. "No bar?"

She ducked her head, the back of her neck reddening as she shrugged. "We're trying to be supportive of you."

I had to go.

"Yeah, I'm down." I turned to Gayle, who joined our conversation. "How about it, boss?"

She barked out a laugh. "Ha!"

"You can have a margarita. I won't be tempted." I winked at her. "Promise."

Her laughter faded. She grew more serious, the old hawk-like look entering her eyes. "Okay. But if you start craving some booze, you tell me right away. I'll leave with you."

The only thing I'd be craving was Morgan. "I'll be fine."

Her elbow playfully nudged my side. "All right. Let's head to town."

Kara asked, "Could I get a ride with you guys?"

"Yeah, yeah." Gayle waved toward the car. She hollered back, "We can take one or two more!"

And in the end, the actress who played Peter's sister, one of the production assistants, and Kara rode with us. They'd sectioned off a private area in the back of the restaurant, and when I stepped inside, I felt like a thankful asshole.

Thank God I had come, and an asshole because this whole thing was for me.

A large sign that read *Welcome Back, Brody* hung from the ceiling against the far wall. Most of the crew was already there, and when they spotted us, they started clapping and whistling.

"You guys." A large smile spread over my face. I couldn't take this in. "This was planned for me?"

One of the actors came forward. "If you didn't come, we were just going to pull the sign down. It was a last-minute idea." He nodded to Kara.

I turned to her. "Yours?"

An almost shy smile peeked out. "I just wanted to be supportive."

"Yeah!" A camera guy held up his glass. "All water."

I laughed and then waved my hands. "You guys, this is amazing, but please, for the love of my sanity, drink. I *was* drinking too much to deal with my brother's death, but I'll be fine. Really."

Gayle stepped around me, clapping a hand on my shoulder. "He really is doing better. He's been glowing every time I checked on him the past week."

"Were you actually resting for the week, or you were jacking off the whole time?" the water guy asked with a wink.

"No comment. How about that?"

They all laughed as we sat. I was at the end with Gayle, Kara, and the girl playing Peter's sister. At one point during the conversation, Gayle leaned in and said, "Her real name is Kelly."

"Ah. Thank you."

Then I remembered I did know. I'd forgotten, but Gayle patted my arm. "Don't feel bad. You're at the top. They just have to know your name."

I lowered my voice. "That makes me sound like an elitist asshole."

Gayle shrugged. "It is what it is. I guarantee that in your first role, the lead roles didn't know your name."

It didn't matter. I wasn't above these guys. I just had more lines and got a bigger check. We were all together in this project, and I hadn't been pulling my weight. Feeling a good dose of humility, I signaled one of the waitresses down. "At the end of the night, make sure I get the bill?"

Her eyes darted around. "We were told to bill the director."

I looked too. "And she isn't here, so it's on me."

She nodded. "Okay." She gestured to my empty glass. "Would you like anything stronger than water?"

"Yes."

Gayle stilled, overhearing.

I added, "I'll take a soda."

Gayle glared. "Jerk."

As the waitress left, I grinned. "That's what you get for eavesdropping."

"That's my job. I eavesdrop on you in general. Haven't you figured that out?"

"Shit." I'd never thought of it that way. "You're right, you do."

"And I'm good at my job."

I saluted her with my empty glass. "Cheers to you for being my own personal busybody."

She laughed and then rolled her eyes. "You aren't that bad of a client."

I grinned lazily at her. I was a hot mess when she took me on, and she knew it. "Really. Thank you."

She nodded back, a tear forming in the corner of her eye. She flicked it away and laughed a little too loudly. "I'm taking you up on that margarita." She raised her hand for a waitress, saying to me, "You might be driving yourself back tonight."

I could do that. Happily. Which is what happened.

I stayed until karaoke began and three of the crewmembers were croaking out "Sweet Caroline" in their best rendition of Blue Whale. Kara promised to take Gayle with them to the hotel, and with that, I took the keys and headed out. I didn't quite remember the way back to the Kellerman estate, so I programmed it into the GPS and kept a cautious eye out for the mustang herd.

The drive there was longer than I expected, but it was uneventful.

I was driving past the main house when the front door flew open and someone started waving frantically, trying to get my attention. Pulling to the garage, I got out. I was pocketing the keys when I got a good look at who was coming down the walkway in my direction.

"Jenny? Is that you?"

She had the same long brown hair, smatter of freckles over her smooth complexion, and dark brown eyes. She ran up to me, looking exactly the same as the last time I saw her, only this time she was dressed.

"You look good." I patted her on the back before stepping back and adding, "Strong."

"Marathon training. I'm hoping to get Finn to run with me."

"How long's it been?"

"Eight months." Her sparkling brown eyes turned somber, and it clicked then.

I was with her that weekend. We had our three-day affair right before the movie premiere. Right before . . . Kyle.

I raked a hand through my hair. The air was suddenly not so light anymore. "I never called you back." At all. "I'm sorry, Jen."

She lifted a shoulder, but her smile slipped a little. "I understood. I tried reaching out."

She had. I wanted to tell her it meant something to me. I listened to her message. Her voice had been friendly. There'd been no anger, or resentment, but I never called her back because I hadn't cared one bit.

I didn't want to lie so I only gave her a half-grin. "I blacked out a lot of that time."

Which wasn't completely true. I forgot parties. I forgot whomever I was using to make myself forget, because the truth was that I couldn't forget anything about Kyle, about the funeral, about the phone call, about the noise of the crash, about the dial tone.

I was raw all over again and needed a drink . . . or Morgan.

I needed Morgan.

"I hear congratulations are in order for you." I made sure to put a cheerful ring in my voice.

She grasped my arm, squeezing me from excitement. "I met Finn that week, actually. Everything worked out."

No.

Everything hadn't.

Kyle hadn't.

"Uh, yeah."

Fuck. Where was Morgan? I had to go.

The front door opened, and Jen glanced over her shoulder, sighing a little. "He makes me really happy, and"—she stepped close—"he's really nervous about you because you're the big-time actor. I know you've technically met, but he knows about you and me. Be nice? Please?"

I heard footsteps on the sidewalk drawing close.

I nodded but pushed her back a little. Once she was at a distance the fiancé wouldn't want to deck me about, I grinned. "You know me. I'm always nice."

Finn drew to us, and I ignored Jen's rolling eyes. My smile widened. "Finn." I held out my hand. "I know we met the night I arrived, but I never congratulated you on the engagement."

He seemed cautious but shook my hand in a firm grip before nodding, "Yeah. Thank you." His eyes darted between her and me. "I wasn't sure if this would be awkward or not." He stepped up, his arm going around her shoulders.

"Not awkward. Not at all." I gestured around us. "Are you two going to tie the knot here? It'd be a beautiful setting." Most people liked that shit.

"Oh—" Jen started, her head tilting back an inch.

Finn spoke over her, "I'd *love* that." His eyes darted around behind me. "Something about this place. It brings the whole family together."

Family.

Yeah.

I understood whom he was referring to, but the burning was still in my throat from my own situation. It spread to my chest, and it was only going to get worse. Kyle's ghost was back full-force.

"Yeah," I said. "I get that."

And then we heard a soft voice say, "You're Brody's friend?"

We turned, and everything stopped in that moment because this was fucking climactic stuff.

Standing behind me, as if materializing out of the darkness was Morgan.

# CHAPTER TWENTY-SEVEN

## Morgan

I walked forward, saying to Brody, "I was waiting for you."

After seeing the car's headlights shut off, I had expected him to walk down to the cabin. When he hadn't, I went outside, and that was when I heard their voices.

I looked at this girl, who was so beautiful my chest felt tight for some reason.

"Morgan!" Brody glanced from me to Finn and then back again.

Finn's arm fell from the girl's shoulders. The blood drained from his face, and he took a faltering step toward me. "Morgan."

I stepped back.

I wasn't there to see Finn.

It wasn't that I didn't want to see him. It was just, he used to be family. And that word, family, brought pressure I never know how to handle so I stopped trying. It muddied everything up inside of me.

I looked at Brody. "She's your friend?"

Brody's eyes were dark, concerned.

I looked away.

But I still heard his soft voice. "She's going to marry your brother."

"Brother?" the girl echoed, her eyes darting back to Finn, who was only watching me.

She wasn't there for Brody. I was beyond relieved to hear that, I felt tears coming to my eyes. I touched one in wonder. When was the last time I had cried? I couldn't remember.

"*Morgan.*"

I turned to Finn then. He said my name with such intensity that I couldn't *not* look at him. And I saw it all on his face.

There was happiness.

There was contentment.

There was nervousness.

He missed me.

But there was peace amongst all of that. It had me looking at her again. She was the cause. I looked at her fully, dipping my head. "You're good for Finn."

"God, Morgan." Finn's voice dipped low. A stark and desperate look came to his eyes. "Can I . . ." He lifted his arms. "Can I hug you?"

It was the same question Matthew asked, but it felt different from Finn. Or maybe I was the one different. I held back, surprised myself when I realized the old fear wasn't there. It hadn't knocked on the door like before when the other brother asked. It slammed me then.

This time, I felt it open. A small crack.

I glanced to Brody, who nodded his encouragement, and whispered, "Okay." I braced myself, but he moved forward and his arms came around me so gently and slowly that my lungs expanded from relief. I didn't feel closed in or suffocated.

He held me, an inch of space between us, and I hugged him back. Tentatively. I placed my palms against the back of his shoulders, which had him sucking in a sharp breath.

"Morgan." A drop of wetness fell on my shoulder. I leaned back to find that he was crying.

I frowned. "I'm sorry."

He stepped back, sliding his hands into his pockets. His eyes were raking all of me, studying every inch of my face, and a hoarse laugh filtered past his lips. "No. God, no." He moved back in to hug me, going slow again. I nodded this time, and he closed the distance, holding me in his arms. His hand cupped the back of my head, and he rested his forehead to mine. "This is . . . I've missed you."

He held me another moment before stepping back. He didn't go far, just a couple steps back. His fiancée went to his side. She slipped her hand into his, and he used his other to wipe over his face. "Man, Morgan. Wow. I can't . . ." He trailed off again, just looking me over. "You look amazing."

His fiancée, Brody's friend, gave him a quizzical look.

He squeezed his fiancée's hand. "I'll tell you later." He asked me, his thumb pointing back to the house, "Matt's at a meeting tonight, but Abby's going to faint when I tell her you're out here. Can I get her? She and Jen are friends. We were having a few drinks to celebrate her coming tonight."

I looked past him.

I *could* go into that house. There was nothing actually stopping me.

Abby would be there. Finn.

Then a surge of need rose inside me. I *wanted* to see my sister. I *wanted* to laugh with her and my brother again. I *wanted* to feel what home used to be like.

I *wanted* to remember.

Before caution or anything else stopped me, I brushed past everyone, climbed the porch steps two at a time, and strode inside.

This wasn't like before when they were asleep. There'd been an eeriness in the air then. I paused, taking it in. I smelled the mix of their wine in the air and the aroma of whatever they were eating. I knew they had put fruit on the table before I stepped in. There were older smells, but I liked the fresh ones better.

The home felt alive again.

Then the back patio door opened. Abby was coming back inside, holding her wine glass. She was saying, "Where'd you guys go? I thought we were moving to the patio . . ." Her voice faded, and her wine glass slipped from her hands. "Morgan!"

She started forward, but I yelled, "No! Don't move." The wine was spreading everywhere and pooling around shards of glass she was about to step on.

"Wha—" She stopped short and glanced down. "Oh."

Finn strode forward. He had hiking shoes on, and ignoring the glass, he swept his sister up and moved her closer to me. He signaled to Jen. "Could you grab some paper towels? I'll get a dustpan and mop."

They went to work cleaning the spill at the same time Abby threw herself at me. She wrapped her arms around me without one ounce of hesitancy Finn showed outside. "Oh my gosh. Morgan." She began sobbing. "Morgan. I've been hoping." She tightened her hold, and as I did with Finn, I patted her on the back. Her body shook as she let me go, her face was drained of color. She continued to stare at me, shaking her head to herself. "I can't believe it. I just can't."

She reached out and touched a strand of my hair. "You're so tan. Your hair is so blonde." She laughed to herself, her hand resting on the side of her own face. She continued to look me over. "You look so beautiful, Morgan." Her voice dropped to a whisper as she added, "Like Karen."

Finn came up next to Abby, his arm going around her shoulders. She fell into his side, and neither reacted at how natural that movement was for them.

My throat started to burn.

My mother would come up behind me, run a hand over my head, tousling my hair, and I'd lean into her, just how Abby rested against Finn.

"Matt's going to pop a vein when he finds out you were in the house and talking to us."

Abby's eyes lit up. "Do you want a glass of wine? Wait." She frowned. "Do you drink?"

I glanced to Brody, who had come up beside me. He met my gaze, both of us remembering the time I drank with him.

I was torn.

His eyes softened, as if he were trying to tell me this was okay to do. He shifted on his feet, the back of his hand grazing against mine.

It was the slightest touch, but Finn saw it. He drawled, "So that's actually happening?"

I tensed.

Brody didn't.

No, that wasn't right. I felt the air around him. He was just as tense as I was, but he didn't look it. He threw a lazy grin back at my brother. "What's happening?"

Abby's mouth formed a small O.

Finn gestured between Brody and me with his free hand. "The two of you. Matt said it was, but it's different seeing it."

"What?" Finn's fiancée asked, joining the conversation after putting away the mop and throwing the paper towels into the garbage. Frowning, she looked at us, noticing how close we were. "Oh," she murmured.

"Matthew did?" Brody clipped out. His jaw clenched. "Really?"

Finn frowned. "Said you guys got cozy during your week off."

Brody's hand left mine as he shifted, almost shielding me. "And how would he have known that?"

"Uh . . ." Finn's shoulders abruptly fell back down. "Shit."

I moved around Brody. The old uneasiness I felt earlier came back, and this was it. It was back and building, burrowing deep into me.

"Finn."

He looked at me.

"How did Matthew know about us?"

He jerked up an awkward shoulder. "I don't know. He—uh—" He flung a hand, gesturing to Brody. "Didn't you tell him?"

"Not about this past week."

Anger was literally rippling from Brody, crashing into and melding with the bad feeling inside me. I was sinking, further and further down.

Abby said quickly, "What does it matter? Matthew knows everything. You're here. You can have a glass of wine with us, right, Morgan?" A nervous laugh rang from her before she closed her mouth, chewing down on her bottom lip. "Come on. Let's sit and talk." Her voice rose up again with a desperate ring. "Or I'll walk back with you to the fence. I want to know how you are. I want to know . . . I want to know everything."

I looked at my sister. I remembered playing with her, having her do my hair, wanting to learn about makeup from her. I remembered how she would let me play dress-up with her clothes or take me to the mall to shop for hours.

I was shaking on the inside, but I nodded to her. "A walk would be fine."

"Yeah?" She perked up and turned to Finn.

He was staring at her, and the two seemed to share a conversation with no words. Finally, he gave her a half-grin. "Go. Talk to our baby sis. Then come back and report everything." He said to me, "I want to know too."

I turned so that my back was to the rest and looked up at Brody. The anger was still there. I saw it flaming, but like Finn and Abby, he nodded to me. I was going to Shiloh. He knew what I was going to do, and he wasn't fearful of never seeing me again like my siblings were.

I reached out, my hand grazing over his stomach. He caught it, giving it a small squeeze before letting go as I started for the door.

"Morgan!" Finn called out.

I looked back.

"Will you—"

I already knew the answer. "Yes." I would see him again. I wouldn't disappear.

# CHAPTER TWENTY-EIGHT

*Brody*

I gave the girls a few minutes to walk from the house. I didn't want them to come running back, but as soon as I was sure they were out of hearing distance, or within reason for Morgan's hearing, I walked toward her brother.

Jen saw the look on my face, and I heard her say, "Oh boy."

Finn was turned to me, watching as I closed the distance between us.

He looked around, but my hand was at his throat before he could take a step toward an exit.

"He—" His eyes threatened to bulge out.

My hand squeezed, but I ignored how he tried to grab ahold of my arms. I walked him back against the wall and lifted him in the air. I didn't give two shits if this got me fired. He could explain why I put my hands on him. I had a strong feeling my reason outweighed his.

When he began making choking sounds, I relaxed my hold, just slightly.

He could breathe, but just barely. He could talk if he tried.

Leaning forward so he damn knew to take me seriously and said, "You're going to tell me how your brother knew about Morgan, and if you don't"—I squeezed my hand again, leaning even closer—"I will hurt you, and trust me when I say that I know how. I got my ass beat by my old man every day I was in his house. I picked up some nasty tricks."

"Brody." Jen started to reach for my arm.

"Don't fucking touch me, Jen. This isn't your fight right now."

"He's my fiancé." She began to reach for me again.

I twisted to her, letting her see how deadly serious I was. When her eyes met mine, reading my intent, she gulped.

Finn started fighting again, his arms and legs trying to hit me.

I relaxed my hold again and shifted my stance so his fists only grazed my arm. His legs couldn't reach me.

"Are you going to cooperate?"

I waited.

His eyes were wild, the need for violence surging to the surface. He wouldn't, but I relaxed my hold and stepped back.

He'd have to try, but if he did, I would teach him. Again.

He rushed me, but I ducked and stepped to the side. As he ran past me, he swung an arm wide to try to hit me. I moved back in, wrapped an arm around his arm, and shoved him against the wall. He went face forward, and instead of holding his throat captive, I had his arm. He was paralyzed. The only thing he could move was his mouth, and he grated out, "I'm going to sue your ass. You're off this movie. My father will—"

I applied pressure on his arm, and he bit out a primal scream as the bone popped out of joint.

"Oh my God, Brody." Jen was behind me again, beginning to cry. "Please stop. Please."

"You won't sue me." My voice was calm. "You won't fire me. If I go, so does Morgan."

Panic flashed in his eyes.

"And you know it. So"—I leaned in again and lowered my voice, almost so I was soothing him—"are you going to talk this time? I can do this all night long if I have to, but trust me when I say I'll learn *how* your brother found out about us. I'll do it with or without you. You and I can be enemies, or I can just be your brother's enemy."

I held his arm until I saw some of his panic fading. He was starting to relax.

I stepped back. Another chance.

He pushed off the wall and swung wide. I hadn't been expecting that, and his fist caught me on the cheek, but I scrambled. I wasn't seeing stars, but it was a good solid hit. Acting on years of instinct, I went to the floor in a roll, getting right back to my feet when I was out of his reach. He was storming toward me, a vein sticking out from his neck.

Jen started to jump between us again. Both of us barked out, "Don't!"

She went back to the sidelines.

I braced myself, saw his hand clench into a fist.

I had my arms up, blocking his punch, but he wasn't stupid. I saw him feign, and his other hand came up in an upper cut. I moved my arms down instead, hitting his leg and using the momentum to bounce back and smack him in the face.

It disoriented him. It was a hard slap, but it gave me enough time to twist around and get him into a headlock. I just had to squeeze. My legs were tight. He could only beat at my forearm, but my muscles were tight. His hands weren't doing much damage, and I looked around, making sure he couldn't grab a knife or utensil to impale me with.

We were a little too close to a fork. I pulled him with me, closer to the front door, and applied pressure again. I wouldn't kill him, but he'd go unconscious.

"Now, we can go this way. You can fall asleep, and I'll search this house without your permission. I'll start with your brother's office, where I'm certain there's other items in there you won't want me to find."

"There isn't—"

"There's always something you don't want to be found. I don't want that. I want to know how your brother knew about Morgan. That's all."

I already knew. We didn't walk around the estate, only the land. Morgan was the one to slip in and out of my cabin. Abby could've said she overheard us, but that was a big fucking leap to go from one conversation to us being together.

There were only two ways. Either he had the cabin bugged or he had cameras on it.

My contract said privacy, so both were cause for a lawsuit.

I wanted Finn to admit it. I wanted one other person to say it, and I knew Jen would back it up. I glanced at her, gauging whether she would lie for her fiancé if he asked.

I wasn't sure. Before tonight, I would've said no, but the terror on her face was genuine. She got a glimpse into the old Brody that I didn't like to visit.

Our odd friendship was over. I saw that.

I squeezed tighter around his neck. "I mean it, Finn. This isn't a pissing match between your brother and me. I'm protecting Morgan. If he has something on me from this week, he might have something on her. We were *together*, together."

"Fine," ripped from him.

He was still struggling.

"Stop fighting."

He went slack, and I let him go. He fell to the floor, and I bounced back on my heels, ready for him to come at me again.

He didn't. He only looked up at me from the floor, his chest heaving as he rubbed the red mark on his neck. "He said he installed videos to watch the outside of your cabin. That's all."

I was right. I knew I would be.

"I want to see the footage."

He started to shake his head. I said again, "I'll find it without you, if that's what you want." I took a step toward him, dropping my voice, "But I *will* find that footage."

He stared at me, glaring. Then he stopped abruptly, the fight finally leaving him.

"Fine. I know the password to his computer."

I motioned to him. "After you."

He scowled at me, rubbing his neck as he led the way. Kellerman had his desk setup on one end of the room, and behind it, large windows showcased the mountains. Two leather chairs were in front of his desk, and there was a couch on the other side of the room. Bookshelves stretched the entire length of the back wall.

Finn went to the computer and turned over the plaque on the desk, revealing the password that was taped underneath. Finn shrugged. "Matt has all the same habits. He just doesn't know that we know 'em." He typed in the password.

I went to stand behind him, watching as he clicked on an icon. Security footage came up, with cameras showing all over the estate. Finn clicked through a few until he got to the ones of my cabin.

The front door.

I said, "Next."

The back door.

Another, "Next."

He hesitated before clicking on a camera feed that was pointing right at the second-floor patio.

I knew what that meant.

I forced myself to wait. I couldn't go nuts, not yet.

"Are those the only three angles?"

Finn looked back at me. "Yeah."

I gestured to the history folder. "Pull that up."

"Look." He straightened away from the computer, motioning toward it. "It's just the doors and your patio. He didn't break any privacy codes or anything. We're allowed to put cameras on our land."

I sat in the seat and clicked on the history folder. As it pulled up all the old footage he saved, I asked, "This house is in Morgan's name, right?"

I was clicking through them. There was nothing incriminating.

When I didn't hear him respond, I looked back up.

His eyes were wide and alarmed.

I pushed from the computer again. "Finn. Am I right?"

"Yes. It's Morgan's land. She inherited it from Karen."

I had already known that, but like the cameras, I just needed one to confirm it.

Jen moved forward. "What does that mean?"

I shot her a look before going back to the saved video footage. "It means none of these cameras had Morgan's permission to be put up." I shared Finn in the same look. "And my contract says *all* privacy. These cameras violate that stipulation. Would your brother bug my cabin?"

"No! My God. Matt isn't some eavesdropping cree—"

As he spoke, I clicked on the last footage saved.

Every cell in my body froze.

Finn's gaze jumped to it. "Oh, fuck."

The image was clear even before I played it.

Morgan was straddling me. We were on that back patio, and I knew exactly what we would be doing when I hit play.

As the screen came to life, Morgan was straddling me, her mouth over mine. I let it play for just a second, but it was a second too long.

Rage was rising in me.

My arms began shaking as I grabbed a USB and copied everything to it.

"What are you doing?"

I clipped out, "Evidence."

I couldn't lose it. Not yet, but that time was coming so close. It whispered to me, seductive and alluring.

I grew up in violence. It had always been hard, abrasive, bitter. And I'd had my fair share of scrapes when I was mourning for Kyle. I always hated it, hated myself afterward, but this was different.

This need for violence was almost sensual, and once everything was copied—I let myself go.

I stopped thinking.

I stopped feeling.

My mind went on autopilot as I destroyed the video, destroyed all of the footage. He violated me. He violated his sister, but I still couldn't vandalize an entire computer.

And then I thought of where that footage ended.

He had watched us kiss.

My stomach churned, not knowing what else he had watched. If he let it play, if he watched her?

I'd seen that look in his eye. He wanted to control her, have her back under his thumb. My dad had the same need. Kyle and I had to wear the clothes he picked. We could eat when he said so. We even showered when he declared it was our time. He controlled everything. It'd been abusive, and I thought that's what I saw in Matthew's eyes, but had there been something else? Something sicker?

I heard a click in my head as somewhere deep down, my mind turned off.

I turned and ripped the hard drive out of the computer and strode into the bathroom. Finn and Jen followed me, and I gritted out, "I need a lighter."

I wanted everything destroyed. I didn't know if I was going above and beyond. I didn't care. I wanted every last scrap charred and burned.

Finn looked at Jen. She hesitated. I said, "I know you smoke, Jen."

She sighed and reached into her pocket. She tossed it to me, and I flicked it on, running it beneath where the magnetism was, melting it. After letting it burn for a few minutes, I tossed it into the toilet. It didn't go out, not right away, but once it did, some of the rage lessened. I felt more in control, slightly.

I looked at the two. It seemed neither were breathing.

"You can tell him my lawyers will be waiting for his call."

I left the house, walking right past where Morgan and Abby were sitting, not far from the barn.

"Brody?" Morgan stood. She could tell something was wrong.

I just waved, not looking over. "Keep talking. I'll be in the cabin."

"What's wrong?"

Christ. I finally looked at her. Could I tell her? He was watching her.

Could I destroy whatever she felt toward him?

I looked at Abby. She'd be told anyway. It would get out.

I shook my head. "I don't want to tell you this, Morgan."

I expected to see her pull away, to become wary. She did neither. Her mouth flattened into a strong line, and she stepped toward me with purpose. Even her voice was firm. "Tell me."

Abby jumped to her feet, biting her lip again. "Is it Finn? Did you hurt him?"

"No." Well, yes.

I couldn't say the words. I didn't want to say the words. Matthew was a piece of shit, but this would send Morgan over the edge. She'd go back to the horses, and even I didn't know if I'd see her again.

"We found video footage on Matt's hard drive," Finn said from behind me.

He was holding tight to Jen's hand.

Abby gasped.

He added, "Brody destroyed it."

There could be other copies besides the one in my pocket. My stomach rolled over on itself. If there were . . . I couldn't go there. My hands were already forming into fists.

Morgan didn't react. Her eyes were just questioning, looking back to me. I didn't look away as I stepped toward her. "Morgan—"

Finn spoke over me, "He had a video of them together." He let his sister comprehend it.

I couldn't look away from Morgan.

She didn't once look away from me, as I scraped the words from my throat, saying, "He watched us."

# CHAPTER TWENTY-NINE

*Brody*

Morgan's face gave nothing away, but she snapped her head toward her siblings. "You won't tell him."

"What?"

She clipped her head from side to side. "I mean it. You lie for Brody. Matt isn't to know it was him."

"His hard drive is destroyed. He had business on there. He's going to flip."

"I don't care. Tell him I did it."

"What?" Abby and Finn shared a look. Abby asked again, "What?"

"I did it. I found out what was on there, and I was the one who destroyed the computer." Morgan swallowed tightly, lifting her head higher.

God.

My heart pounded a little harder.

She took my breath away.

"He won't say a goddamn word then." Morgan turned, her eyes slightly wild, as if she didn't believe what she was saying. She walked toward me, but she didn't stop. She took my hand and led me to my cabin.

I pulled her to a stop before turning to Finn. "You get those cameras taken down."

He nodded, running a tired hand over his face. "First thing tomorrow."

"Tonight." Morgan had turned back. "I mean it." Her face was in a set mask. She was dead serious, and she let everyone see it before she tugged on my hand again. As we went for the cabin, I heard Jen murmur, "Your sister is a badass. And bossy."

No one commented.

I went straight to the liquor cabinet but then remembered Gayle cleaned everything out. "Fuck!"

Bracing my hands on the counter, I leaned down. I was holding on to that thing like I wished it were Matthew's throat. I wanted to strangle him. I wanted to beat the shit out of him, and once he healed, I wanted to do it all over again. And again. And again.

Morgan took a step near me, but she didn't say anything.

A savage growl built in my throat. "I want to fucking beat the shit out of your brother."

I expected her to cower or flinch, but she only met my gaze full on and let out a soft sigh. "That hard drive had his business on it. I'm sure there was valuable stuff on there. He'll be furious."

I straightened, getting a dose of humility. "I won't let you take the blame for that. I did it."

"No." She raised her voice, her eyes urgent. "You can't say anything. He can never know it was you. He'll hurt you if he does. He won't care about the reason you did it."

"Morgan." The house was hers. He put those cameras up without her permission. She had to know. I destroyed his private property, but in the grand scheme of things, Matthew did so much worse.

"I don't want to hear it."

It clicked with me then. She wasn't reacting because she *wasn't* reacting. She was on lock-down. I could feel the distance between us, which only got wider with each flick of her eyes toward the window.

She wanted to bolt. She wanted to go numb to this world again.

"You're going to go."

I wasn't asking because it was inevitable. I wouldn't be able to keep her there. She *needed* to go.

155

She jerked her head in a stiff nod. "I have to. I can't—" She gulped again. "I can't breathe here right now." She looked at me, searching for understanding, maybe even a sliver of permission.

I nodded, giving her both. Giving her whatever she needed. "Go."

She started, not waiting another second.

"Just—"

She was already at the patio door, but she looked back.

I felt for her. There was a look of agony on her face as she waited.

"Just come back. Okay?"

She nodded again, but then she was across the room in a heartbeat. She caught my face between her palms, and her lips were on mine in the next second. She pressed up on her tiptoes, her mouth commanding and loving, harsh and soft all at the same time.

I caught her face in my hands, too, and kissed her back.

She was saying goodbye, but she was also telling me she was coming back. I tasted her, slipping my tongue inside, and she moaned, her hands moving to grasp at my shirt. I tipped her head back, my lips becoming softer against hers, coaxing.

She didn't want to go. I could feel the struggle in her, and the longer I kissed her, the more I knew I could get her to stay.

I poured everything I had into that kiss.

She moaned. It was slight, but I heard it, and then her entire body melted against mine.

I swept her up, bending and grabbing behind her legs. I never pulled away. I never stopped kissing her as I carried her into the bedroom. The light stayed off. Nothing was touched so the window shade was slightly pulled back, letting the moonlight cast a reflection over the bed. As I set her on the bed, I settled beside her, kissing her still.

I think I would've kissed her for the rest of our lives if I had to at that moment. My desperation to keep her with me, to love her, taste her, explore her, worship her was all-consuming. I needed to keep reminding her that she was human.

She wanted to pull away, go hide again, maybe feel the adrenaline rush of being on Shiloh or running with the herd.

I would give her that rush.

I began to explore her body, my hand stroking her stomach and then slipping past her jeans. I didn't wait. As my tongue was brushing against hers, my fingers went under her underwear and slipped inside her. I thrust them deep, and she surged in my arms. She came alive, gasping, and her head fell back to the pillow. I rose over her, finding her mouth again. I wouldn't leave it for long, no way. It was my lifeline to her.

I worked her to a climax, loving how she gasped for me, how her hips began to move with my fingers. Shifting my weight so I was partially resting over her, I used my other hand to touch her stomach. I pushed her shirt up, bending to kiss her there. Then back to her mouth, another long kiss.

My hand caressed her, grazing over her ribs, encircling her breasts. I dropped to kiss her other breast. Then, as my thumb rubbed the moisture from my mouth away, I went back to kissing her. All the while, I kept sliding my fingers in and out.

I could feel her body lifting off the bed with each stroke. She began to shudder, and I paused.

I kissed her throat, tasting where she exposed her neck for me, how she was moving to lead me where she wanted me to taste her. I moved around her throat before dropping my lips back to her breast. My tongue laved over her, and she moaned again, grabbing the back of my head.

Her hips were moving still, lifting and rotating with my fingers.

She was going to come soon. I felt her tighten around me, the spasms rolling over her, but I kept moving my fingers.

She gasped, arching up completely.

My mouth was on her breast, but then she choked out a gasp and scrambled toward me. She grabbed my shirt, pulling it up and then off.

My dick was so hard that if I let go of the top button, he would bust the zipper open. I knew I shouldn't have, but as she climaxed in my arms, I pulled my fingers out and then rested over her. We were groin to groin, and I could feel her entrance. I wanted *in* her.

God. Fuck.

I didn't know if I could hold out.

I wanted to savor this, draw it out, and make her addicted to me.

Holding her thigh flat against the mattress, I ground into her.

Her legs twitched. She tried to tighten them against me, but I didn't let her.

She looked at me, biting back a grin. I gave her a wolfish grin in return, my eyes eating up every inch of her exposed skin.

Perfection.

And every inch of her was mine.

I let out a growl again and bent, my teeth lightly nipping her breast.

She cried out, but when I thought she would catch my face and lift my mouth to hers again, she pushed my hand aside and reached for my pants. She had the zipper down in a flash, then I was out, and she wrapped a hand around me.

We rolled and she rose above me.

Still holding me, her eyes holding mine at the same time, she impaled me, sheathing herself down on me, and then we both went still at the contact.

I let out a shallow breath, my eyes darting to hers.

She was grinning, and she bit her lip again.

I groaned, catching her lips with mine.

Laughing softly, the sound caressing my mouth, she began to move for me. Her hips rolled back and forth, and then I took over. I couldn't hold back.

I pulled her back underneath me.

In.

Out.

I began moving faster as she deepened the kiss, her tongue finding mine.

I couldn't get close enough to her. I wrapped my arm around her back, crushing her to me. I thrust in, going deep. I pushed all the way until I felt her wall before pulling back out, only to go in again. I paused there, grinding into her, and she began to whimper. Her mouth fell open, a throaty moan leaving her.

This wasn't enough. I needed to be deeper inside her.

"Do you trust me?" I panted as I ground into her again.

Her lust-filled eyes held mine. "Yes."

I shifted, pulling her legs from around my waist and lifting them so they rested on my shoulders. Then I slid back in, and this time I could go deeper than I ever had been. Her mouth fell open, a silent cry ripping free as her back arched and her eyes darkened further with hunger and pleasure.

"Harder. I want you to fuck me."

Holy shit.

My dick twitched in need. "You sure?"

"Yes." She grabbed my hand and pulled me down so I was staring right into her face. I braced myself with my other hand, but I had her hand pinned to the bed on the other side. Her knees bent, resting over my arms. "Goddammit, Brody."

I groaned. I was addicted to her. I knew this wasn't just fucking. I wasn't just reminding her that she was human. I was trying to brand her. I was trying to make her feel she was mine so deep inside that she'd never leave again.

My hand flexed around hers, digging into the sheets, and then I did as she asked.

I fucked her, rough and hard—unrelenting.

My body stretched out, and I kept thrusting into her.

I felt her come again, her back arching off the bed as she gasped, letting herself shatter, but I didn't stop. I needed my release. My body was demanding it, burning for it. I still held off. I kept sliding in and out, going deeper and deeper until I couldn't stop my release from ripping through me. It was like a rope stretched as tight as it could go, and then it snapped, recoiling with passion.

My body was convulsing.

Pulsating.

Trembling.

So was hers.

As I slipped out of her, I searched for her mouth. It was becoming a drug to me. I nuzzled her jaw, and she turned, her lips finding mine. It was a soft and sweet kiss, drawn=out, and I was panting afterward.

So was she, her chest lifting up and down as she caught her breath.

I held on to her, wrapping her tight in my arms, and I buried my head into the crook of her neck and shoulder. She smelled of the wild. Fresh air and the earth with a slight hint of vanilla, and she was mine.

I dropped another soft kiss to her shoulder.

We didn't talk the rest of the night, and I rose above her once more.

But she never left.

She never left.

# CHAPTER THIRTY

*Morgan*

I was in the barn a week later.

I wanted to check on the horses because they weren't getting brushed down or washed at the end of their long days. The staff wasn't taking appropriate care of them, so I got into the habit of sneaking in at night and doing it myself.

Four days ago, Brody woke alone and came looking for me, and since then, he had helped me when they weren't shooting late into the night. So as I was finishing putting Butter into her stall, I didn't react when I heard the barn door rolling open.

The thought that it was Brody settled me, but then I froze.

An alarm went off.

He was working tonight and said he wouldn't be back till four in the morning. Plus, he never used the big door. He jumped the fence and came in through the back.

"The horse handler thanked me for brushing down the horses, or having someone do it. I didn't know what she was talking about, and then it hit me yesterday."

My frozen state didn't thaw.

Matthew had been gone on a business trip, and while I knew Finn told him what happened, he hadn't been back since.

Seeing him a few feet away—he was back now.

His arm rested on the barn door like he would block me if I tried to run out that way.

Seeing I didn't bolt, he nodded to himself, his hand dropping from the doorway and sliding into his pocket. He was dressed like he'd come straight from a meeting, but his collar was pulled out and the top few buttons of his shirt were undone. His hair wasn't slicked back like it normally was. It was messy.

He looked tired. There were bags under his eyes.

"You're almost becoming normal again, a regular tenant of the Kellerman estate."

Was that true?

Since the night Brody destroyed his hard drive, I hadn't been able to pull myself from his arms. I slept in his bed every night, left to go see the herd when he was working, and timed it so I was always back around the same time he was.

It gave me a thrill every time I walked in to find him already waiting for me, knowing I'd be in his arms within moments. He always showered before coming to bed, and I showered with him those times. I no longer smelled like one of the herd, and the stallion hadn't liked it. He had taken to rearing back when I approached, but Shiloh never left my side. Shoal didn't either. After a while, he accepted my new scent, but I knew he was unsettled by it.

"What do you want, Matthew?"

His head lifted, resignation weighing on his shoulders. He swallowed once and then murmured, "I'm told you destroyed my computer."

I lifted my head. "Not your computer. Your hard drive."

"And what gave you the impression you could touch my computer, much less destroy it?" His eyes were narrowed to slits. His anger just underneath his surface.

It struck me then how much we had both changed.

A month ago, Matthew would've just been happy to be talking to me. That was gone.

"You violated my privacy, and the evidence was on that computer. You're goddamn right I destroyed it." I narrowed my eyes to slits. "I'd do it again too."

His head bobbed back a centimeter. I had surprised him.

"You saw?"

Sensing my unease, Butter popped her head back over the stall door and began nuzzling my cheek. She was not only trying to soothe me but also seeing if I had an extra treat for her. I reached into my pocket and pulled out a small apple. I palmed it as she leaned forward, nibbling gently.

"I know what was on that hard drive. I saw where you paused it." I was lying, but I didn't care. I wished I had been the one to destroy it. I would've had the entire herd run over it.

He jerked back, his eyes rounding.

"You are here because I allow you to be here. You *continue* to be here because I allow it."

I turned back to Butter, sliding my hand up her neck, my fingers running through her mane. "I won't be spied on. By you or anyone else." I faced him again in time to see him flinch.

"We were so happy to have you and Karen in our lives," he said in an almost hoarse voice. As if that could excuse what he'd done.

I turned back to Butter, but he kept talking. "We lost our own mom, and our dad." He exhaled sharply. "You know how he is."

I heard the snap of the straw under his feet as he took a step closer. Only one.

I jerked, but I was remembering.

Peter Kellerman scared me. He always had.

"She softened him, somehow. And for a moment, I thought we could have a family. We all did. Us. Karen. And you. You were our littlest sister, and we all adored you."

He was right. She made Peter Kellerman happy, but she made all of us happy.

Then she was gone, and I was back there that day.

*I heard the pounding on the door.*

*I was running for the door until that sound, and then she screamed my name.*

And like then, ice ran through my veins.

It was taking me away, pulling me back to memories I didn't want to remember.

His voice drifted to me again, softer. "I can't imagine what you must feel—"

He kept talking, but a buzzing sound drowned him out. It was growing louder and louder.

*"Morgan," she whispered, kneeling before me.*

*I saw the terror in her eyes, and that pounding kept going.*

I gasped, silently, but Matthew didn't notice. I slammed back to the present day, but feeling faint, I grabbed on to Butter's stall. I was going to fall. Pressure pushed down on my chest. I felt my lungs shrinking in size, and I gasped silently, struggling to draw air in.

I couldn't.

I was choking.

I was going to die.

I could hear his voice, a blast of bass sounding from the distance, but it was as if there were thick walls separating us and his words couldn't penetrate them.

Then, while I clutched on to Butter's stall, the pressure started to dissipate. I felt my lungs growing back to their normal size, and suddenly, I could breathe like normal again. My mouth opened wide, and I gasped in large mouthfuls of oxygen.

I grew light-headed and dizzy from the abrupt change.

My arm was shaking hard enough that Butter looked to see what was rattling her door. She began sniffing at my hand. My other had fallen, dropping the last little bit of apple onto the ground. She was searching for more.

I couldn't move. My arm was too unsteady. I would fall completely.

"—that had always been my hope growing up, and you've grown into a beautiful woman. You're smart. You're strong. I know how much strength you have—"

My head felt as if it weighed five tons as I lifted it enough to look at my stepbrother.

He'd been watching me, talking, giving me his pitch, and he hadn't noticed a thing.

Relief knocked my knees together, almost sweeping me down from the movement. I called for Shiloh. I had to. I let out a high-pitched whistle.

Then another.

"—can do so many things. You don't have to waste your heart on this man. He'll break your heart. I know this. I know guys like him. You might not believe me now, but I want the best for you."

What?

I opened my eyes wider, trying to see Matthew more clearly, but my vision was swimming. He was going in and out of focus. He just kept talking. He just kept saying things, not seeing that I was struggling.

Was that a good thing?

When we were kids, he was always the one to protect me. He would have seen that I was struggling, that I couldn't breathe, and he would have helped me.

He wasn't that Matthew anymore. He changed over the years. I sensed the shift the night he had me sign the papers to approve this movie. He was desperate, hungry, and motivated. And angry . . . so, so angry.

It was there when they began the movie too.

Except his desperation switched. He had gotten what he wanted. He wanted the movie. He was going to use it for something, I didn't know what. Fame? Power? Money? I had no idea. I didn't care, but the movie was underway, and I stayed away. But Brody brought me in, made me feel safe and protected. Yet, there I was in the barn, experiencing an attack worse than any I'd had since I was ten years old, and Brody wasn't around and Matthew didn't care.

A whinny.

A lifeline.

I whipped around, almost drunkenly, and my shoulder slammed into the other side of Butter's stall door. She was nibbling at my shoulder, only her lips. I managed to lift one of my hands to pat her on the nose, to reassure her I was fine and that I wasn't hurt. She nudged me again before shifting and stomping and moving her body in the stall.

"What was that?"

Finally.

Matthew stopped talking. He strode toward me. I tensed, flattening myself against Butter's door completely.

Matthew went right to the back door, bypassing me, and throwing it open. He paused on the threshold, squinting out into the darkness.

A second whinny, closer this time.

It was Shiloh. She never came this close, but I knew without having to see her that she had breached the fence. She was coming up the field.

She was coming to me.

God.

Matthew was in front of her. If he was angry, she might react. I couldn't let that happen. She couldn't hurt him. I shuddered, not wanting to think what he would do in retaliation.

"Matthew," I croaked.

He turned to me and finally saw I was struggling for breath. "Oh my God." He rushed to me, but I waved him away as Shiloh came running through the open back door. Her eyes were wild and panicked as she tossed her head back and forth, searching. When she found me, she bucked up onto her hind legs, preparing to kick at Matthew. She thought he was hurting me.

"NO!" I shoved him as far away from me as I could.

He fell to the ground, frozen with his eyes fixed on Shiloh.

"ROLL!" I screamed, hoping to get him moving.

He did, rolling right into an open stall. Her hooves just missed him as they landed hard on the wooded floor.

"No, Shiloh." The screams had taken everything out of me. I waved my arms to get her attention. Her one eye turned to me, seeing me. She didn't know what was going on, she just wanted to help, so I reached up, grabbed her hair and a section of her coat and tried to heft myself onto her. I couldn't get up in one jump, so I tried again, scrambling until I was lying safely on her back.

I didn't have it in me to sit upright, so I nudged her back.

She resisted. She wanted to go after Matthew.

"No, Shiloh. Home."

Her head swung back to me.

"Home."

Her nostrils flared before she wheeled around and took off at a gallop.

I grabbed her mane and tried to keep from falling.

# CHAPTER THIRTY-ONE

*Brody*

Kara was pressed between my legs. I had her backed up against a tree, my mouth hovering over her exposed neck, which was where it had been for the last hour. We kept fucking up the shot. Either the wind was in the wrong direction, Kara was hiccupping, my "smoldering" was all wrong, or Shanna wasn't happy with a line delivery.

To make matters worse, I had to keep my groin pressed against hers because I didn't have a hard-on and I was supposed to for this scene.

"BRODY! BRODY!"

"Cut!" Shanna cried out, throwing her hands in the air as she whipped around. "What the fuck?"

I backed up, and Kara leaned against the tree. She muttered, "Thank God. My back is killing me."

I grunted. She and I both.

"BRODY!"

I turned and thought I saw Matthew careening over the field toward us. It was dark, but I recognized his voice. He was waving his arms like a madman, and I scowled. I hadn't seen him since I ripped out his hard drive.

Finn and Jen were on set that day, and right away, Finn started for me.

I pointed at him as we fell in step together and headed in Matthew's direction. "If he fucks with me today, I swear to God, I'll rip him apart."

I hadn't eaten all day since Shanna wanted my muscles to be as defined as possible. I was cold from the damn water being thrown on us, and I'd spent hours pressed against a woman I couldn't stand. I wasn't in the mood to deal with Matthew's shit on top of everything else.

"Excuse me!" Shanna went to get in his way, her hands planted on her hips.

She had a coat on, unlike—I glanced over my shoulder and saw an assistant wrap a heavy blanket around Kara's shoulders—me. I didn't even know where my shirt was.

"Brody!"

Matthew was almost to us.

Finn held his hand out. "Let me talk to him."

"Fuck that." He was saying my name. I clenched my jaw. If he wanted a fight, so be it.

"Brody!"

I strode ahead, ignoring Finn.

Matthew looked as white as a sheet, but he couldn't catch his breath. He got to me, but couldn't talk. He held a hand up, bending over and resting his hands on his knees.

I started to get it then.

He wasn't here to fight, and then the panic started.

It was Morgan. There was no other reason he'd seek me out. And if he was coming to me for help—I stopped thinking then.

Something was wrong, really, really wrong.

"What happened?" I barked out.

Shanna yelled, coming over, "You interrupted a shot that's been taking forever to get. There better be a good reason for this."

"Morgan," he gasped.

"Who?" Shanna asked.

Ice went down my spine

"What happened to her?" I barked at him.

He didn't answer right away. He still couldn't.

"Matthew!"

I started for him, but Finn jumped in front of me, his hands in the air, his palms toward me. "He can't breathe, Brody. Let him have a second."

"Something's—" Wheeze. "Wrong—" Another wheeze. "With Mor—" He bent over, still gasping for air.

I'd had enough. Storming past Finn, I grabbed Matthew's shoulders and pulled him upright. "What happened to her?"

I looked in his eyes, and his own panic had that ice lining my stomach.

I stepped forward so we were almost chest to chest. "TALK! What happened to Morgan?"

Everyone had fallen silent around us, but no one and nothing else mattered but the answer to that question.

Matthew, closed his eyes, took a deep breath, and let it out slowly as he stepped backward. Finally. He managed, "Something's wrong with her. She couldn't breathe."

The world went away.

I was only on him.

"Where is she?"

"Shiloh."

Oh good God, no. I let him go, not caring that he collapsed to the ground. If she was on Shiloh, that meant she was in the mountains. She was out there, and no one could get to her. I had to—there were two horses here for the scene.

"Brody." Finn tossed me a sweatshirt.

I caught it, taking off in the opposite direction.

They were being taken care of by a handler, who started when she saw me racing toward her. The horses stepped to the side.

"Wha—" Her eyes trailed behind me.

I heard Finn, who was right on my heels, say, "What are you going to do?"

Ignoring him, I focused on the trainer. "Which one is the fastest?"

"What?" Her mouth was gaping open. Her eyes were skirting from Finn to me.

"Brody!"

I ignored him. "Which one?"

She flung one of the leads to me. "Her. She's the faster one."

It was a brown mare, and she was watching me, but she wasn't scared. I ran a hand down her neck, soothing to her at the same time, "Hey, hey. Listen, Horse. I don't know you that well. You don't know me, but I need your help."

"Brody!"

Gayle was joining the fun. I didn't look for her, but I knew if I had, I would have seen the look of complete disapproval on her face.

"Brody." Finn tried again. "What are you going to do? You'll get lost up there."

Morgan was in trouble. Nothing else mattered.

"Brody." He grabbed the horse's bridal as I climbed up on the saddle.

"Let go." One warning. I'd run him down if I had to. "I mean it, Finn."

His eyes flared from urgency to me. "You cannot ride."

"I've been riding the last week."

"Not enough. Not for those mountains. Not for where she went."

He had a point, but I didn't care. "It's Morgan. I'm *going*."

"Give us time. We can organize a search party. We've done this before. I told Jen to call Abby. She is probably already making phone calls to get people out here."

I shook my head. "That could take hours." She might not have hours. She might not even have one hour. "I have to go, Finn!"

He still wouldn't let go of the bridal. "I'm thinking about you too. It isn't just Morgan. She's done this before. She's probably fine, but you won't be. You'll get lost. You'll get stuck out there for hours." He nodded to the horse. "This mare isn't equipped to be out there."

It was the fastest way to Morgan. That was all I knew.

I pulled on the reins, jerking the horse's head away from Finn and ripping the bridal free from his grip. Kicking my feet into her side, her rear end came around, knocking Finn to the side.

I twisted around and said, "I don't care." Then I leaned forward and kicked my feet into her side again.

I wanted her to run.

As she did, tearing up dirt, Finn yelled behind us. "You're not going to help her like this!"

Maybe.

Maybe not.

All I knew was that I had to get to her.

# CHAPTER THIRTY-TWO

## Morgan

Shiloh took me to a cliff before dropping her head to graze. There was a small smattering of grass there, but I know she took me there for a reason. It was the highest point we could comfortably get to. I was far away from everything—from the herd, from the humans, from my old life that was trying to pull me back.

I slid off her back and slumped to the ground.

This was what I needed.

Crisp mountain air. My lungs felt as if they were burning, but there was nothing like the feeling of being above it all. I felt close to the sky, and I lay on my back, gasping, dragging in air. I looked up, and it was as if I could reach up and touch a cloud.

I hadn't had an attack like this since after my mother died. The counselor pushed too hard, asking me to recall details I didn't want in my head.

Maybe it was because of the attack, or maybe it was because Shiloh brought me to this particular cliff, but I felt her again.

It was as if she were smiling down at me, and maybe because of that, I curled in on myself and slept.

When I woke, it was to the sound of someone calling my name.

"Morgan!"

"Morgan!"

I sat up, squinting a moment. Brody wasn't near me. I wasn't in his bed. It took a second before it all rushed back to me.

I felt the winds pick up, shifting from the valley below and blowing harshly against my cheeks. Shiloh lifted her head, her nostrils picking up Brody's scent.

That wasn't my mom calling. I scrambled to my feet. "Brody?"

"Mo-Morgan! Where are you? MORGAN!"

I went to the edge and saw him by the river below us, all the way in the middle of the valley. "Brody!" I yelled, feeling Shiloh coming up behind me. I was close to the edge, too close. I felt her unease and reached back, touching her face. If she jerked it away, the movement could've had enough momentum to push me over. She was completely still.

"Brody!"

His head was whipping back and forth. "Morgan!" He lifted himself in his saddle, almost standing as he called out, "Where are you?"

"Look up!"

He did, and then he dropped abruptly back to his saddle's seat. He gulped. "Wha—what the fuck are you doing up there?"

Good question. I tried for a small smile, but figured he couldn't see it. I called back down, "I'm coming to you. Don't leave that spot."

I heard his wry laugh as I took a step back from the edge. "Yeah. That isn't a problem."

Shiloh eased back with me, and once we were far enough away, I swung up to her back again. She turned for the trail that'd take us down to where he was, but it was close to the edge of the mountain. I hated these trails, but I trusted Shiloh. She wouldn't go somewhere she couldn't get us out of. Brody, on the other hand, wasn't prepared for the sight when he lifted his head to see us picking our way down the side of the mountain to him.

"Holy shit," he said. His eyes were wide. "I'm not religious, but I'm going to start praying. I'm praying to God. Your horse is nuts."

I was thinking the same. The trail was as wide as her body. There was no leeway there.

Once we set down on level ground with the river, Brody was off his horse and running to me. Shiloh reared back, jumpy from his fast arrival, but I hurried off her and went to meet him. He grabbed me as I splashed my way to his side of the bank and had me up in the air in a second. He folded himself around me completely, burying his head into my shoulder. "I was worried about you."

I ran a hand over the back of his head, burying my own into the crook of his head and shoulder. "I'm fine. I'm safe."

He pulled back, concern dilating his eyes. "Matthew crashed one of the movie scenes, he was that worried about you. Said you took off and you couldn't breathe. Are you okay?" He was feeling all over me. My forehead. My mouth. My chest. He was looking at my back, making sure I was still in one piece. "I don't get it." His eyebrows dipped together. "You look fine." His gaze lingered on the bags under my eyes. "Tired, though."

I caught his hand, squeezing it. It felt good to be touching him, even if it had only been a few hours since I'd seen him. "I'm fine. I had a panic attack when I was talking to Matthew."

"Panic attack?" His eyes darkened with anger. His head straightened back. "I didn't give myself time to think about why you were talking to Kellerman. What the fuck did he want?"

"To talk about the hard drive."

"Oh."

I grinned, ruefully. "Yeah. Oh."

Shiloh was slowly making her way through the river to us. It was a small enough creek that the currents weren't dangerous. She was moving at a lazy pace, drinking as she did.

I glanced at her as she came onto the bank, smelled my shoulder as if to reassure herself I was fine, and then moved around us. I watched as she and the other mare began grazing together.

"You rode a horse here."

Brody groaned. "Yeah." He raked a hand through his hair, letting the ends stick up into a deliciously rebel look. "Don't know what the fuck I was thinking about. I grabbed the first thing that'd get me to you." His eyes narrowed, studying his horse. "I think I bonded with that thing."

He said it as if it left a bad taste in his mouth.

I hit his shoulder. "That thing is a mare. Her name is Taffy."

"Taffy? What the fuck kind of name is that?"

"A good name." I nodded to the mare. "It's her name."

"Hey." A playful grin tugged at his lips. His arms went back around me. "I should warn you. Cat's out of the bag. Between Matthew, Finn, and me—everyone's aware there's someone named Morgan that we all care about."

He grimaced.

I ran a soothing hand over his cheek before letting my thumb linger on his lips. "Why are you worried about that?"

A somber look settled over him. "Because things are going to change for you. People know about you now."

I didn't say much after that except, "We should go back."

Brody rode Taffy, and I rode Shiloh next to him.

I was impressed by how he did with her, only cursing a few times when she balked at his orders, but it was his mistake. He wasn't reading her correctly. When we got closer and the buildings started to take shape through the trees, I thought back to his words.

Were things really going to change for me?

If they were, wouldn't I have felt a sense of gravity weighing me down? I thought for a minute, searching for the knot I would expect to be twisting in my stomach, but there was nothing. I had a hard time imagining the world actually finding me. They might at the estate. That was different. No one could take that away from me and no one could keep me from coming back to the mountains.

We stopped at the end of the second fence. There was still an entire field between us and *them*.

Two ambulances and dozens of cars—both police cruisers and regular vehicles—lined the driveway. Some tents had been put up on the front lawn, and there seemed to be people everywhere.

A chill went down my spine.

It was déjà vu. They were organizing a search party for us.

I fought back a wave of unwanted memories. I hadn't wanted them here then, and it was the same today.

She left that day. No. My hands balled into fists. I pressed them down into my leg—she was taken from me that day.

And I had felt her earlier. Shivers went up my spine.

A shout rang out. Someone spotted us.

As one, all of their heads lifted, and they looked at us.

Brody glanced to me in concern.

This had happened before in my life. They would be upset with me, having to go through this work to pull their resources, and l was healthy and fine. Again. There'd been tears before. And lectures, so many lectures. Angry words. Biting words. It was the last thing I could take back then.

Seeing Matthew and Finn racing towards us, I braced myself for the same treatment.

A black car was pulling to a stop just behind the tents at the same time they opened the gate by the barn and sprinted down the field to us, stopping a few yards away. Matthew got to us first. His panic was clear in his eyes, which were still wild. "You're okay?"

I didn't respond.

I couldn't tear my gaze away from that car.

Shiloh jerked backward. I reined her in, warning Finn and Matthew in a low voice, "Stay over there." I still moved her back, just in case. Brody shifted, trying to put himself between Matthew and me. "She's fine."

Finn gave us a shaky smile. "Well." He glanced over his shoulder to the whole scene spread out. Among the cops, ambulances, tents were the crew and actors for the movie. They were dressed as volunteers, wearing a bright red vest, so if they got lost in the woods they could be seen easier.

I was almost wistful of them at that moment.

They didn't want to get lost. That implied they wanted to be found.

Getting lost and hiding have two different connotations, but the act is the same. If they disappeared into the woods, like I wanted to do right now.

I knew who was in that black car. That was a gravity weighing me down, and no one else seemed to be aware of him coming.

Finn added, laughing a bit, "My guess is that you're unofficially part of the movie now. Welcome back, baby sister."

Yeah.

Right.

I swallowed back the knot in my throat. I could handle whatever came with that, but not that car.

I gripped Shiloh's mane tighter and leaned forward.

A driver got out, went to the back door, opened it, and . . .

My stepfather stepped out.

Peter Kellerman had arrived.

# CHAPTER THIRTY-THREE

*Brody*

The blood drained from Morgan's face and in the same instant, her body curled in. She seemed poised to flee.

Matthew, Finn, and I all turned to look at what had her spooked. It took a second for me to spot him.

The man was wearing a business suit. His hair was thick and silver, not quite white but not really gray. That was the only indication of his age. He kept himself trim.

Yeah. I recognized him.

Peter Kellerman was bigger than his two sons.

I skimmed a look over at Morgan. "Did you know he was coming?"

She started at my question, as if she had forgotten we were there. "No."

Matthew was looking between the two, frowning. "Yeah. That's my fault. I had to call him, Morgan. I'm sorry."

Morgan's head lowered, as if she wanted to curl into a ball.

Finn rolled his eyes, focused on his brother.

Matthew ignored Finn, saying, "You couldn't breathe when you left. You were in the mountains. I didn't know if Asher would bring back a body or if we'd have to go in and find two of you."

"I told him to relax a little." Finn was speaking to Morgan. "I thought maybe you'd be fine." A look passed between the two.

I was watching the guy, who was being introduced to Shanna. I looked for Abby and Jen but didn't see either before I turned to the two brothers. "Is he going to be a problem for Morgan?"

Peter Kellerman was my father without the boozing, whoring, and beatings being handed out. By all accounts, he was ruthless, sharp, and didn't give one shit about Morgan. He would hurt her. That was what I knew, and I would stand in his way every time if I had to.

I knew all of that within two seconds of seeing him.

When neither answered, I narrowed my eyes at Matthew. "Maybe I should be asking if *you're* going to be a problem for Morgan?"

We still hadn't had our talk, and I really wanted to have that talk. What I did to Finn would be tame compared to what I still wanted to do to the elder brother.

Finn grunted. He knew exactly where I was going with this. He stood to the side, stepping away from his brother.

Matthew noticed, his frown deepening, and then he swung his gaze to me. "What?"

I gestured to where Kellerman Senior was. "Who are you loyal to? Him or her?"

"What?"

I leaned forward on my horse, making sure he could hear me clearly, though I wasn't sure how much more frank I could put the question. "If a pissing match happens, if he's here to hurt her and not help her, whose side are you on? Let's get it fucking clear right now before we walk into something we can't control. You on your pop's side or her side?"

Matthew swung his horrified gaze to Morgan. "Morgan . . ."

Two figures broke from behind the fence, hurrying down the hill toward us before a third joined them and, a second later, a fourth behind them.

Shiloh started moving back at the sight, her nostrils flaring.

"Shhh." Morgan bent forward, crooning to her. She ran a hand down her side, but they retreated a few more feet.

Finn swore under his breath and then sighed. "It's Abby and Jen."

I recognized the two behind them. My hands tightened around the reins. "And Shanna and my manager."

Morgan looked at me. I registered the look from the corner of my eye, and I wanted to turn to her. I wanted to reassure her everything would be okay, but I couldn't lie. I told her things would change for her, and that had been the truth.

Shanna would want to know everything about Morgan.

Gayle would want to know everything about our relationship, and I'd have a hard time suppressing the desire to tell them both to fuck off. As much as I wanted to tell them to mind their own business, my business *was* Gayle's business. Shanna, however, was my boss. If she wanted to grill anyone about Morgan, she could go to Matthew or Kellerman Senior, since he decided to show up.

"Morgan." Abby was blinking back tears. "You're okay." She stopped, her hand reaching out like she wanted to go to her sister. Finn drew her to his side, his arm around her waist, and he pulled Jen against his other side.

"Brody." Shanna drew up to the group, wrapping the ends of her sweater together in front of her. She looked from me to Morgan, paused for a minute, and then turned back to me. Gayle came to her side, but Shanna cleared her throat. "You're okay?"

"I am."

Her eyes kept going to Morgan. Her eyebrows pulled together, but she murmured to me, "I see. We were all worried."

Gayle's eyes were wide and accusing.

I ignored her. "I needed to make sure Morgan was okay."

"Yes." All eyes turned to Morgan. Shanna wasn't even trying to disguise her interest. "I see. And you were okay?"

Morgan nodded. "Yes. I am fine."

Finn laughed. "I'd bet a hundred it was you who found Brody, not the other way around."

Morgan just looked at me.

I grunted. "I was lucky to stay on the damn horse, and yes, she found me."

"Well." Morgan folded her hands together over Shiloh's mane. "You technically did find me. You just didn't know it."

I cringed at the memory of looking up and seeing her on the edge of that cliff. It didn't matter that I knew different—she looked supernatural in that moment. It had been eerie. She was defying gravity by being up there, and even more so as her horse picked their way down the side of the cliff.

I didn't reply.

"So, I'm assuming we can send the search party back? We won't be needing it?"

Matthew jerked around to Gayle. "Yes." He motioned back to them. "I'll deal with all of that." His gaze went from mine to Morgan's and held there a second. "I'll—uh . . . I'll talk to my father as well."

Morgan didn't reply or move, and once he was halfway back up the hill, Finn asked her, "Are you really okay?"

She nodded. "I'm fine. Yes." She motioned to the party. "I'm sorry about all of that."

He shrugged. "There's a difference between you running and hiding and you being hurt." The side of his mouth curved up in a wicked grin. "Besides, it was really for the Hollywood golden boy."

I barked out a laugh, gentling it as Shiloh's head reared up. "Right. Say what you want, Kellerman Junior to the Junior, but that's twice now I've ventured out there and come back alive. Can you say the same?" I was teasing, and when Finn threw his head back and started laughing, everyone else realized it too.

Shanna and Gayle exchanged mystified looks while Jen and Abby just seemed relieved.

Abby held up a hand toward Morgan. "Can I . . . this is Shiloh, right?"

A whole fence between us and them, and they still remained back by fifteen feet. At Abby's slight approach, the mustang's head reared up. Her ears perked forward.

"Is that—" Shanna's lips dropped open as if she were only just noticing the horse Morgan was astride. "Is that one of the wild herd?"

Morgan was still running a hand down Shiloh's neck. It wasn't working. The mustang started to back up the louder we talked and the closer Abby got.

She said to Abby, "Brody's presence has been forced on her, but she isn't tame. She'll run if you keep approaching. I won't be able to stop her."

Abby stopped approaching. "She's beautiful, Morgan."

Morgan looked to Shiloh, who swung her head back to her. They looked at each other a moment, and Morgan grinned. "Yes, she is." She bent forward and patted her neck, laying her cheek against her before sitting back up again. "Beautiful but wild."

I was staring right at Morgan as she said those words.

When she lifted her gaze to mine, she saw my own message to her, and her eyelashes fluttered closed a little before her gaze cleared. She lifted her head higher, staring back at me steadily.

She was beautiful.

She was wild.

She was the untamed one.

Unbroke. I didn't realize how perfectly the movie's title fit until that moment.

An emotion shifted deep in me, deeper than I'd ever felt. It was something I'd only felt toward family before.

I shoved it aside. This wasn't the time to proclaim feelings and shit like that.

I said to Shanna, "Is Peter Kellerman being here going to be a problem?"

She hesitated before replying, "For the movie? No. We have contracts in place in case he tries to change anything. For others . . ." Her eyes trailed to Morgan. "Maybe."

Whether it was at Morgan's order or Shiloh's, the mustang turned in a tight circle, walking backward. Her head wouldn't stop. It was going up and down, and her back hooves started to stomp the ground.

Morgan said to me, "I gotta run her. Too many people around."

I nodded, but she didn't wait. She made one soft clicking sound, and Shiloh tore out of there.

No one spoke. We all watched. How could we not?

Shiloh's mane was flying behind her, making her look like she was soaring. Morgan was bent forward, her head buried in the hair and her arms wrapped around Shiloh's neck. She rode her with no reins, no saddle or stirrups, nothing to anchor her to the horse except her body and the connection they both shared.

That feeling began to expand inside me again. It had been there, rooted deep, just waiting for the right person. Waiting for Morgan.

The emotion began to fill me.

I still didn't name it, but I knew I couldn't stop it either.

# CHAPTER THIRTY-FOUR

*Brody*

Shanna and Gayle followed me to my cabin.

Abby and Jen went to the main lodge, but Finn came with us too. Once Shanna and Gayle were inside, he stopped me, asking, "You need backup?"

I shook my head before nodding toward the lodge's patio where Matthew and Peter were sitting. They had a perfect view of my place. "I'm worried about them."

"Them?" He turned to see. "Oh." When his attention came back to me, his eyes were troubled, and his own frown gave him away. "My brother was creepy with the videos, but I honestly feel if he has to choose between who to protect—Morgan or our father—he'll choose Morgan. We'll all choose Morgan."

"Why?"

"What?"

"Why choose a stepsister you never see over the man who's giving you a livelihood?" Peter held the keys to all of their empires. He was powerful.

Finn shrugged. "Our birth mother died after having Abby and me, so when we got Karen, she became our mother. We also got a father during that time. Sure, before then he paid our bills and provided for us, but he wasn't around until he fell in love with Karen. She anchored him in a way, and we actually had a loving family for four years. Morgan was a part of that. We grieved when Karen died, but it was more than that. We didn't only lose her and Morgan——we lost him. He shipped us all off to our private schools, hired nannies, and pretty much moved to New York. Now, the only one who sees him regularly is Matthew, and it's always in business meetings. I'd love to have a father. I would, but that'll never happen. We thought for a moment, after Matt brought us the script, maybe we could get him back. He seemed excited about the whole process, but once we got here, yeah." His voice faded, then a decrepit laugh left him. "You can see how that worked out. There's no trying to get him back, but Morgan. She's different." He turned to look at the mountains behind us. "She stays out there so she doesn't get hurt anymore. And it's terrifying her that she can't pull completely away again." He studied me a moment. "You love her."

He named what I was unwilling to.

"Yes. I do."

He held his hand up. "Then know that I'm always in your corner. I'm proud to have met you."

I shook his hand, and it felt as if something more were being solidified in that moment. I knew there would be problems moving forward. I felt it first with Matthew, and it had only gotten exponentially stronger with the appearance of Peter Kellerman.

I didn't know what it would be or how it would come about, but I knew it would affect Morgan, and I wouldn't allow that.

"Thank you. You too." I meant those words. I would need his help. The premonition was weighing heavily on me. After a second, I added, "If you hurt Jen, I'll beat you up." I smirked. "Again."

He laughed, releasing my hand. "Same if you hurt my sister." He clapped me on the arm.

"If I hurt your sister, I'll *let* you beat me up."

"Let?" He began walking back to the main house. "Let, huh?"

"Yes. Let."

He waved, turning around. "We'll see, Golden Boy. We'll see."

"Golden Boy?" The door had opened behind me. Gayle stood there. "I thought it was Bad Boy Brody this whole time."

"Nah." I raked a hand over my face. I was suddenly so tired. My whole body was beginning to ache. "I think the bad boy is gone." Then I thought of Peter and Matthew Kellerman. "Well, maybe not."

I followed her inside.

Shanna was making herself a drink in the kitchen.

"Hey." There was a whole bottle of rum on the counter. "Where'd that come from?"

"My purse." She poured some in a second glass and passed it to Gayle. The two clinked their drinks together before Shanna turned to me. "This is a time that I need to drink."

She downed half the liquid in one gulp.

Gayle winced after her sip and set it down. "That's a bit strong for my taste."

Shanna asked, "You want one?"

"Thought I had a drinking problem?"

She snorted, rolling her eyes and picking her glass up again. "You aren't an alcoholic. We all know that, and you're better now." She motioned outside my patio door. "Your time of rest was really a time of sex, right? Goddamn. I would've loved to have tricked my boss into giving me vacation if that were the case."

I sat at the kitchen table, watching Shanna finish her drink and pour a second one. Gayle took her glass, joining me at the table.

"I didn't plan that. You decided to give me the time off."

"You were supposed to be resting and healing." Shanna grabbed the bottle and took a seat too.

"I was grieving my brother's death."

She eyed me skeptically. "How are you handling that? You seem like you've found your purpose in life."

Shit. Maybe I had.

I didn't want to think about that, so I waved it off. "I'm distracting myself."

"With Wild Horse Woman out there?"

"Maybe."

Gayle snorted. "Come on. How long has this been going on?" She leaned forward, her arms going flat on the table. "You need to tell me everything."

So I did.

When we first arrived.

The night I saw her running from the house.

When the herd first made their appearance.

Gayle asked, "How did you two start talking?"

I hesitated.

"Brody!"

I relented. "I went on a walk, and she was at the river. That was our first conversation."

"And how did you go from having a conversation to sticking your prick inside her?" Her eyes flashed. She wasn't messing around.

I told her about the cabin visit.

She frowned, deep in thought. "That was why Abby Kellerman was here?"

"She said she heard Morgan talking to me. She wanted to know about her sister."

Shanna sighed heavily. "None of this is in the script. None of it!"

Gayle handed over her drink. "Take mine."

"Gladly." Shanna picked it up and took a long drag from it.

Gayle focused on me again. "You still haven't told me when you started sleeping with her."

"The first night of my week off."

That was it. She wasn't going to get the details from me, and when my mouth remained clamped shut, Gayle realized it.

She nodded, leaning back in her seat. "You love her?"

That was also none of her business. "I care for her."

She scoffed, her eyes flicking to the ceiling. She could read between the lines. "So what does this mean? We don't know about her. What do we need to know?"

"What do you mean?"

"You were ready for trouble out there. I know you, Brody. I saw how you reacted to Kellerman Senior showing up. You expecting trouble?"

"Yes, but I don't know what it will be."

Shanna threw her hands in the air. "Why isn't any of this in the script? It should be in the goddamn script. This girl should be in there. It's a happily-ever-after ending right now. Karen Kellerman was murdered, but they wanted the end shot to be Peter and Karen riding off into the distance. Credits. Fucking credits. That's how I'm supposed to tell the real ending, but this girl—she has a daughter! A daughter, who is like this mythical freak creature, and gorgeous, and she lives with fucking mustangs." She was yelling. "It's a much better fucking movie than what I have now."

"Can you put her in?" Gayle asked, making my attention whip to her.

"No!" I jerked forward on my seat. "The contract is for the script how it was written. You can't change it."

"No. That isn't true. I do have creative license, but I would have to do more research and look into how her presence would alter the plotline. If it alters it too much, you're right. There might be areas that they would fight me on."

Gayle leaned forward again. "The movie will still happen. Finding out about this girl won't change that unless Shanna decides to start that fight."

Shanna rounded on her, her chest puffing up. "I don't—"

"They didn't put her in for a reason, Shanna." Gayle clipped her head from side to side. "They're going to fight you on it, and you know it. They'll take you to court, and they have the money to do it."

"Aren't they also the producers?"

Shanna groaned at my question as her hands flew into the air. "She's a gold mine. She is drop-dead gorgeous. Her whole story is captivating. She's sleeping with Hollywood's bad boy, and she's a Kellerman! A Kellerman. A movie needs to be made just about her."

"But not this movie. This one is about her mother."

"Oh my God, her mother." Shanna's head fell back at Gayle's reminder. "Was she there when her mom was murdered?"

Both women waited, watching me.

I scowled. "None of your business."

"Brody—"

"No!" My voice rose over Gayle's. I stared hard at Shanna. "She is not a part of the movie, and it is not my job to divulge anything. My job is to act in this movie. I will do that, but I *won't* do that."

Problem number one just uncovered itself.

I was staring into the faces of two women I respected and wanted to keep working with, but they both had agendas. I shot Gayle a look. "You'll have my back on this. There is no leeway on this subject matter."

Her eye twitched once, then twice, before she glanced sideways to Shanna.

My director's pupils were dilated. There was a sloppy, mad quality to her, but her eyes were still locked on me. Hard. Her mouth was set in a fierce line. "Brody."

"I mean it." I skewered both of them. "When it comes to her, there's no negotiation on my part. None."

"I can replace you."

And threat number one was just thrown out.

I waited a beat, choosing my words, but not fast enough.

Gayle shoved back her chair and folded her arms over her chest. "His job is to be an actor, not an informant. Your argument is not with him for that one."

"With who then?" Shanna's head swung a little more than it needed to. She almost fell off the chair. "With the girl? She took off on a freaking wild horse. Let me go round up one of my own to find her! Are you kidding me?"

Gayle's chest rose and fell a few times. When she spoke again, she was a little calmer. "I *suggest* you ask the appropriate people, like her stepfather or any one of her stepsiblings—not my client."

Shanna's gaze switched, settling directly on me before she slowly pushed back and stood. She took a breath, smoothing her hands down her shirt and pants and then patting her hair into place. "I see. If you'll excuse me both, I have a few Kellermans to pin down."

The room was thick with tension, and neither Gayle nor I spoke a word as Shanna walked across the room, opened the door, and went outside.

Once the door clicked shut, Gayle slumped back into her chair. "For fuck's sake, Brody." Her eyes sparkled in anger. "Goddamn warn me when you have a secret like this, would you?"

I swallowed. "It wasn't supposed to come out."

"Secrets like this always come out! That's golden rule number one." She leaned forward and jammed her finger against the table as she continued, "They always come out. You plan for when they do. Got it?"

I nodded. "Got it."

"Now"—she waved in the direction Shanna just disappeared—"that problem is resolved, for now, but she'll come back. Trust me. Shanna isn't called a pit bull when it comes to her movies. She's a great white fucking shark. She'll be back." She motioned out toward the mountainside next. "I have to know about your girlfriend. I don't care if you're in love with her. I have to know how to protect you as well as how to protect her."

"No."

"Brody!"

"No." I didn't yell, but I made sure she knew I meant it when I said, "I will not violate her trust."

"Brody!" Gayle yelled again.

"Brody."

We both swung around at the second name spoken. It was soft but clear, and like the ghost she constantly embodied, Morgan appeared just inside the patio doors. She had climbed up over the patio and came inside. Gayle and I hadn't heard her at all.

Her hands were flat against her legs as she stepped farther inside, eyes fixed on Gayle. "I'll tell you what you need to know if it means you'll protect him."

Gayle blinked a few times, and she looked taken aback. Then she nodded, her eyebrows pulling together. She cleared her throat. "I'd like that. Thank you."

We were all off balance. The tension was still in the air, and for a moment, Gayle and I didn't move. The only one who seemed calm was Morgan.

She took Shanna's vacated seat and gestured to Gayle's. "If you'd like to sit for all of this?"

# CHAPTER THIRTY-FIVE

*Brody*

It was three hours later when Morgan left to find her sister. Gayle had stayed behind longer to collect herself, and she was still shaking her head when I pulled the cabin door shut behind us. "That girl . . ." She wrapped her arms around herself. The air had gotten noticeably colder, but I didn't mind it. "That girl is special, Brody."

"I know."

"No." She turned around and placed her hand on my arm. "You aren't fully understanding me. Yes, she's special in the way that she's remarkable, and I can see why Shanna is going to do everything she can to get that girl into the movie, but she's special in a way that not even you can compete with. I can see the bond between you two. I can tell you think you love her."

Think?

I wish I hadn't. It was deeper than she could possibly realize.

Picking her words carefully, she went on. "She is wild in her heart. You cannot tame her. You will never be able to take her with you on your next acting gig. You travel constantly. You go everywhere, all over the world. You're from two completely opposite worlds. You'll never fully fit in with hers, and she'll never fully fit in with yours. I watched her in there as she told me about her mother, about everything. She looked out that window no fewer than twenty times in three hours. Twenty times, Brody. Did you watch her body language? She kept rubbing her arms. She kept moving in her seat. She kept tapping her leg. She was restless because she wanted to go back out there. I saw how she took off before. Her mare was responding to her. She wanted to run, not the mare. The mare would've stayed beside her through a fire. It was her. Not the mustang."

Anger burned my throat. "Why are you telling me this? To keep me from falling for her? Too fucking late. I fell. I'm in. I'm *all* in."

A sadness fell over her face, and she patted my arm. "Then I am here for you not just as a manager, but as a friend." Her hand fell from my arm. The sadness deepened. A tear formed in her eye.

She reached up to wipe away it away, but I caught her hand. She looked at me in surprise.

"I have to try. I'm so far gone that I'll regret it more if I walk. Can you understand?"

She nodded. The tear slipped down her cheek. "I do."

This was the mother side of her, the part that started to extend towards me. I'd gotten glimpses of it before, but a tear—that was new. I couldn't remember my own mother crying for me.

It calmed me, slightly.

She pulled her hand free, going back to hugging herself as she looked toward the main house. "You say the whole estate is in her name?"

"Yes."

"You're worried about the father, aren't you?"

I looked too.

The main house stood high up on the cliff's hill, nestled into the side. It took on an imposing air, as if it were daring someone to challenge it. Authority clung to it tighter than it had before, and I knew it was Peter Kellerman's effect. He had everyone on edge, whether they realized it or not.

Yeah, to answer her question. I was worried. I was more than worried, but I didn't know what problems his presence would bring. I just knew they would.

A soft sigh left me.

It'd been a long night of shooting. An even longer few hours until I found Morgan, and all I wanted to do was hold her.

"Is everyone still here?" I moved around Gayle, going toward the house. There were more cars in the driveway than there should have been.

She fell into step beside me. "I suppose they're all just waiting to be told what to do."

No. They would've gone to the hotel or to a bar to do that. No one slept last night. They would've been tired.

My pace quickened.

If they were inside, there was a reason.

They were gathered in the main living room. Shanna was at the front, standing on the fireplace's hearth and holding up the movie script. Everyone else was gathered inside, so tight all the chairs were filled. People were sitting on the floor. Others were lined against the walls, a few spilling out to the entryway and even in the kitchen behind.

"It is the right thing to do, so I apologize for the mess up in your schedules."

I looked for the Kellermans, Jen, or Morgan, but none of them were there.

They weren't on the back patio, which left Matthew's office maybe?

"I realize you might have projects lined up after this, so we'll be in touch to work out the new schedule. But, guys. I really think this will make the movie better. It's the truth too."

Shanna's words got my attention, and I went back.

Her eyes were shining. Her neck was straining, and she was waving that movie script around. "This story is no longer about Karen Kellerman. It's no longer the story the Kellermans have told us. It's about Morgan—"

"What are you doing?" I was pushing forward into the room before Gayle could stop me.

That anger was back. He was pushing from the dark regions inside me, knowing he might have to be let loose soon.

Shanna's hand went down to her side and she squared off to me. "I'm changing the script, Brody."

I looked at Gayle in the doorway. She didn't give me any nod to keep going or to shut up. She was as surprised as I was.

"You don't have the right."

"I do, actually." Shanna pulled out the packet of papers that had been rolled up in her back pocket. It was her contract. "This gives me the creative license. I can change the script if I decide to do so. I'm sorry. I am. I know you want to protect your girlfriend, but this *is* going to happen."

"They'll fight you."

"No." She shook her head. "I talked to my lawyers before I had a meeting with Peter and Matthew Kellerman. They all agreed. I can do the changes, and I'm going to. I'll need time to have the script rewritten." She gestured around the room. "That's what I was telling everyone. Everything is on hold for now. The rewrites and a new ending will completely change the entire scope of the movie, for the better, though. This will *all* be for the better."

"For whom?"

I could see Morgan's face in my mind. She would be so terrified. She'd go back to Shiloh.

*"She is wild in her heart . . ."*

*"You're from two completely opposite worlds."*

Gayle met my gaze, both of us remembering her words. Her face twisted in regret, a pitying expression pulled at her mouth. She tilted her head to the side as if to tell me she was sorry.

I didn't want to see it, hear it, take it.

Shanna answered my question, "This is better for everyone."

"Not for Morgan. She won't want this."

"You don't know that. Everyone wants to be famous."

Not her. Not Morgan. I shook my head. "That's her worst nightmare."

A step creaked behind me, and I whirled. Matthew Kellerman was on the stairs. His father behind him. Matthew paused on the last step before stepping all the way down.

"You did this?"

His eyes widened. "I—"

It took one second, one single breath, for me to be across the room and have him up against the wall. I had him pinned, and he didn't fight me. "You sold her out? You're her stepbrother. You're supposed to protect her. You said you would protect her!"

*"Yo. This is Kyle. Do your thing."*

I slammed him against the wall again. "You're supposed to be there for her. You aren't supposed to sell her out."

*"Kyle, fucking call me. Where the hell—"*

I saw the guilt in his eyes. He'd done what I said. He wasn't even trying to hide it.

"You're supposed to love her. How is this loving her?" But the fight was leaving me.

*"Kyle, where are you?"*

He wasn't struggling.

I was just beating him up. That was all.

*"Listen, Brody—I'm damn proud of you . . ."*

I swallowed hard. My throat was burning.

I felt gentle hands on top of mine, and someone was saying, "Let him go, Brody. Let him go." I let him slide back down until his feet touched the ground, but I didn't let him go. My hands were still curled around his shirt as I leaned closer to him, spitting the words into his traitorous face.

"How could you tell Shanna about Morgan?"

"Brody. Stop. Please."

Kara was trying to pull my hands away from Kellerman.

*"I can't wait to get there."*

And I blinked.

How had my hands gotten around his throat? Disgust rose up, but I didn't know who it was for: him or myself.

I lowered him back to the floor.

When had I done this?

"Kyle," I whispered, finally releasing Kellerman.

*"Kyle!"*

*"9-1-1. What is your emergency?"*

"Brody!" Someone slapped me across the face.

I came back to reality. Kara was winding up to slap me again. I gently caught her hand and moved out of the way. "Don't hit me." It was a hoarse whisper, nothing more.

"You spaced out." She let out a huff, gesturing to Matthew, who was holding his throat and gasping for air. "You assaulted your boss. You're whack-o in the head, you know that?"

Matthew kept rubbing his neck, but he gasped out, "No, no. It's okay. I asked for it." He was watching me, and I saw the fear there. I rolled my eyes. He didn't want me to tell anyone about the security footage.

I turned around, knowing Morgan's father would be there.

He was watching me; his face was impassive. He was tan, abnormally so, but everything but the lines of age were the same as what I noted before.

He stood like he could handle himself well in a fight. He wouldn't back down like the weasel shit behind me.

Then he spoke, "You're in love with my daughter?"

I looked beyond him, out to the patio and even farther. I saw Morgan there. She had returned to the fields and was standing on top of Shiloh, but she was watching me. I knew she was. I could *feel* her gaze.

I said, "No, sir. I'm in love with your *step*daughter."

"Brody."

Shanna had come into the hallway where we were standing. My eyes fell to her hand. She was still holding that damned script. "They gave me the okay, not that I needed it. There's no fighting this. It *is* going to happen. Your girlfriend is going to be written into the movie. It might be in her and your best interests if I get the true story." She paused, biting her lip. "I'll need to talk to her to get that."

I laughed in disbelief.

This was why they were all okay with me putting my hands on Matthew Kellerman. They weren't even balking at that.

They wanted my help with Morgan.

I shook my head. "You gotta be kidding me."

"Brody."

I held out my hand. "Not another goddamn step, Shanna."

I was watching out that patio. She was still there, still standing on top of Shiloh, and still watching me. No. She was waiting for me.

"We can talk later, Brody? How about that?"

I tuned her out. I was at a loss as to how to handle the amount of betrayal that happened in this room.

I lifted my gaze to Peter Kellerman. "You just did a very stupid and careless thing."

Laughter filled the house, coming in from outside.

It died sharply a second later, and I heard Abby ask, "What's going on?"

I didn't take my eyes away from the Senior Kellerman. "You left her when she was a child. You paid for strangers to raise her and then pulled them when she was eighteen. You think audiences are going to care that you financially took care of her? Created a bank account for her with her inheritance, but your son had to show her how to get the money?" I felt the air in the room shift. People were waking up and realizing there was maybe a whole other story to be told than what they originally thought. "I don't know about your love story with Morgan's mother. I heard it was a good one. You must've really loved her, but you're going to sell out Morgan for what? You're going to become the villain of the story, not the guy who murdered Karen. If the truth is going to come out, they're going to know how you abandoned your children once Karen Kellerman was in the ground."

"Brody!"

Someone gasped.

I didn't know who. I didn't care.

A storm was raging within Peter Kellerman, and his impassive guard slipped. He took a step toward me, trying to loom over me. He didn't. We were the exact same height. He jerked his hands up. I didn't flinch.

I wanted him to hit me. I could hit back.

But it was just an intimidation trick. He wanted me to cower in front of all these people.

I grinned and lifted an eyebrow mockingly. "My father used to do the same thing. It stopped working long ago."

A vein popped out from the side of his neck. He ground out, "Get the fuck off my lands, *boy*."

I didn't move. "This is Morgan's land, Morgan's house."

"I goddamn know whose land this is." He almost spit on me. "I want you out of this house or I won't give a shit about lawyers and courts. I will pound your face into the ground. You hear me?"

I held my hands up. I got what I wanted. *The monster.* Everyone goddamn knew who it was now.

No one said a word as I walked out of that house.

# CHAPTER THIRTY-SIX

## Morgan

Brody was hurting.

I hopped off Shiloh and scrambled over the patio as he walked up the front steps.

"What happened?"

I knew what was said in the house. I heard it. I wasn't asking about that.

He shook his head, going to the bedroom and lying on the bed.

I stood in the doorway, staring down at him. "Brody." I felt his pain. It sliced through me, along with a lot of anger. A ton of anger. "Brody. What happened?"

He let out a sigh, gazing at the ceiling. "They approved the new storyline. Peter and Matthew. Both of them. You're being written into the movie."

I sat next to him on the bed and touched his leg. "What *else* is going on?"

"What?"

He still wouldn't look at me, so I scraped my nails lightly down his leg. It got his attention. "What aren't you telling me?"

"Aren't you pissed at them?"

There. I looked at him closely. I saw the shadows in his eyes. There was anger for me, pain for me, but that wasn't what was wrong. I climbed up over him on the bed. He leaned back, frowning as he watched me move to straddle him.

Slowly, I was stretched on top of him. Chest to chest. Groin to groin. I let my feet fall between his legs, and I propped my head up, resting on my hands.

I peered right down to him. "What's going on with you?"

He groaned, closing his eyes. "I just went to bat for you, and you're in here trying to slide into my thoughts."

I didn't hide my grin. I let it fully show.

Despite his arguing, he was enjoying this as much as I was.

I caught his hand in mine, lifting my head. "I like that you fought for me. I like that you hurt for me." I caressed my finger up the middle of his palm.

His hand jerked, but I felt some of his tension starting to wane.

"But I can tell there's other stuff." I stretched over him, sensually moving my body until I had scooted farther up. I tapped him softly on the side of the head. "What is going on in there that has to do with you?"

He looked the other way. "You sound like a goddamn counselor."

I took his chin and turned him back to me. "They sent me to a bunch of them. I'm glad something stuck."

"Did you feel your privacy was intruded on too?"

I grinned again. "You're like a wounded lion that is trying to be all growly at your own cub."

That got a small laugh, and his hands went to my waist.

A tingle shot through me at the touch.

"You are not a cub. That's for damned sure." His thumb began to rub back and forth, and he trailed his other hand up and down my side, pushing underneath my shirt. "Your family stuff is bringing up my family shit. It gives me whiplash sometimes."

"Kyle is haunting you?"

"No." His hand kept moving, and the tingles were making me warm all over. "Yes."

He let out another soft sigh as he stopped and then just hugged me to him. I rested my head on his chest, and his hand moved to smooth down my hair. It was another caress, but one from comfort, one that was soothing.

I closed my eyes, savoring the feeling.

He was lulling me, drawing me to him just from that touch.

Every time he held me, it made me never want to leave.

Still smoothing down my hair, he said, "He's not haunting me, but the grief comes at me."

I frowned slightly, feeling his heartbeat speed up.

Then it went back down, he murmured, "He called me before he died." He stopped. His chest rose, and he held the deep breath.

I did the same. Waiting.

His chest lowered once more. "I keep hearing it, over and over. I keep reliving it." He stopped smoothing down my hair, and I lifted my head.

I needed to see his eyes. I needed to see into him.

Raw torment looked back at me. I didn't even see Brody. The anguish coated all of him, and my own emotions swelled to mirror his. Needing to distract myself from the pain that was too overwhelming, I chewed on the inside of my cheek. The physical pain cleared enough of the emotional pain that I could hear him again.

"Sometimes I can't help but wonder if he killed himself." His eyes focused on me.

My heart was hurting, hanging so heavily in my own chest I couldn't be sure it wouldn't drop to the floor.

I buried my head into his shoulder, wrapping my arms around him. I felt his come around me in return. "I'm so sorry." God, I was.

I was aching right alongside him.

"He was coming to see me." His voice choked up. "He told me how proud he was of me, and they think . . ."

I lifted my head once again. "What about his wife?"

"I can't bring myself to ask her." He shifted to his side. Our legs were still tangled, and he used the position to pull me flush against his body.

"Then you have to." I breathed out, knowing he could feel my air.

His hands tightened on my waist. "You'd come with me?"

I hesitated before shaking my head. "You know I can't leave Shiloh."

He let out a soft curse, moving to his back.

I sat up, and I gazed down at him. "This is the right time. They're postponing the movie." I began to trace circles on his chest. "You can go, talk to her, get some closure, and then come back to me."

His hands went back to my waist, and suddenly, he lifted me. He held me above him like I was a doll, as if I weighed nothing. And he smiled up at me. My hair fell down, forming a curtain around us.

He said, "You heard everything, didn't you?"

I smiled down at him. "Good hearing, remember?"

He grew somber, his eyes studying every inch of my face, and then he murmured, "You heard what I said to your stepfather?"

My throat went tight, my heart thumped in an uneven pitter-patter rhythm against my chest, and an odd giggle threatened to break free. I ignored all of that, just feeling my face heating up. I blamed the angle he was holding me.

"Yes," I whispered my answer.

"It's true," he whispered back.

Lowering me back down until I was lying on top of him again, he looked up. His hand caught the side of my face, and his fingers slid through my hair. He was staring so hard at me. He repeated, "It's true."

He still hadn't said the words to me.

My own words were caught in my throat, but I moved until my lips touched his.

Slowly. Tenderly. A soft graze.

My heart was thundering like the herd in me.

I moved up and applied pressure, trying to tell him I felt the same. I wanted to show him how much I felt the same, but his hand tightened around my face, and his lips opened over mine. His tongue slid inside, and after that, I was lost.

We made love through the rest of the day.

Once. Twice.

Later in the evening, we were still lying in bed when someone knocked on his door. Reluctantly, he got up to answer, and even though he shut the door behind him when he stepped outside, I could still hear their conversation. It was his manager. He told her he'd fly out with everyone else.

"Really?"

I curled on my side, hugging his pillow to me and smiling as I eavesdropped.

Brody laughed. "You sound surprised."

"I just thought . . . I thought you'd put up more of a fight. That's all."

"It's decided. I can't fight it."

"Really?"

He laughed again. "I'm not happy about it. Trust me, but I'll go and come back when I need to."

"Ah. I see. She's inside waiting for you, isn't she?"

There was silence.

"Just try to protect yourself, Brody. You're unpredictable. You can be a hothead at times. You're a rakish flirt other days, and today, I saw how much you can love someone. Please don't get hurt, any more than you already have been."

I sat up, suspending my breath.

There was silence again, and then I heard a very soft, "Too late." And my lungs depleted themselves.

A single tear slipped down my cheek.

I didn't want to hurt him. I didn't want to get hurt either, but I knew what he wanted. It might not be the same thing Matthew wanted, but it was similar. He wanted me with him, and that meant wherever he would go after this.

As if sensing my pain, Shiloh whinnied in the distance.

I moved over, looking out his bedroom window.

She was at the edge of the fence, staring right back at me.

She wanted me to go to her, and she was waiting as she swished her tail back and forth.

I couldn't, not that night.

I placed my hand against the window, trying to let her know.

I had to be his tonight.

The outside door opened, and I settled back against the pillows, snuggling under his blanket and closing my eyes. When he came into the room, I pretended to be asleep.

He snorted, sat on the bed, and ran a hand down my arm. "You're a horrible actor."

I laughed, rolling to my back and then closing my eyes when his hand went to my breast. "How'd you know?"

"Because I saw Shiloh out there, and I saw her leave so I know you did something to tell her to go. That's how I knew." His thumb tweaked over my nipple, then back again. They were hardening under his touch, and the ache was forming for him again.

I wanted to pull him down with me, but I waited.

I liked this torture when he would run his hand down my stomach and then linger at my entrance, playing with me there.

I wasn't disappointed. He did exactly that, building the throb even higher before he said, "I fly out in the morning with the rest of the crew."

"Yeah?" I began to pant, opening my legs wider for him.

His finger went around me and then dipped inside.

I gasped silently, and then a second finger went in, which had my back arching off the bed an inch.

"But I have till then."

I opened my eyes.

He added a third finger, and he was watching me, his eyes dark with hunger and lust. Then he began to move his fingers, thrusting into me in a slow and steady rhythm, and I lay there, never wanting him to stop, never wanting him to leave.

I tried to relay that as he settled himself between my thighs and slid into me. I tried to relay that many times throughout the night, and when he got up to shower and pack in the morning, neither of us had slept at all.

Then the knock came, and we both knew our time was up.

It was his ride to the airport.

I stood, pulled on his shorts and sweatshirt that I hadn't let him pack, and followed him to the door.

His manager stood there, and she blinked a few times when she saw me. "Oh." She moved back a step and offered a small wave. "I'll . . . uh—" She gestured to the car that had two other people sitting in it. "I'll wait by the car for you."

The passengers were both gaping at me.

Gayle was halfway to the car, when she pivoted and came back. She pointed to his suitcase. "I'll help grab this one."

He nodded. He had another bag over his shoulder, and he also handed that one over. "Thanks, Gayle." Brody's hand came to my waist. He said to her, "I'll be there in a second."

She went back, putting his things into the trunk and getting behind the wheel.

They were still watching, but Brody turned so his back shielded us. He pulled me to him, his head burrowing in the crook of my neck and shoulder. He ran a hand down my back.

I waited, wondering what he might say. Would he say the words? When he was going to go? *Was* he going to?

He didn't. He just kissed up my neck and moved his mouth to find mine.

I poured everything into that kiss, my arms around his neck, and I rose all the way up to my tiptoes.

When he pulled back, his eyes were hooded, but they cleared for a bit. He only said, "I'll be back," before he pressed one last kiss to my forehead and pulled away.

He descended the steps, got into the passenger seat, and only looked back once when the car turned away.

I didn't know if he watched me in the rearview mirror, but I stayed there just in case. When the car was in the driveway and no longer within sight because of the trees, I took off. I had to go as far with them as possible.

Running barefoot through the fields, I called for Shiloh.

I whinnied. I neighed. I yelled her name in panic.

She came galloping through the trees a moment later. She must not have been far away, and like so many times before, I ran to meet her. She veered over, and I swung up onto her back. She barely paused.

I didn't have to give her much guidance.

She knew the other weird smelling horse that I'd grown attached to was in that car, and I wanted to run next to him. It was a minute later when we broke through the brush and the tree line. The car was ahead of us, so I leaned forward on Shiloh and urged her to go faster.

She did.

Then, as we were catching up, the car moved to the side, and we were able to run next to it.

I looked over to Brody, who was watching me, but then he pointed beyond me to my other side.

I looked over.

The entire herd was running beside us, like heads of smoke wafting through the trees.

We went with them until they turned onto the main road, and I pulled Shiloh back. The herd switched, moving to the next mountain valley, and after a moment of watching the car, I let Shiloh pull me away.

We joined the herd.

# CHAPTER THIRTY-SEVEN

## *Brody*

"Brody."

Gayle was tapping my arm, so I reluctantly opened my eyes. "We're landing."

Just like the last time we'd flown together, she thought I'd been asleep the whole flight home, but unlike the last time, I hadn't been. Dark sunglasses kept the illusion and kept prying questions from coming my way. We took over almost the entire plane, but I had to give Shanna some credit. She stashed a few of us in first class. I was by the window, Kara next to me, and Gayle behind me. Shanna was across the aisle, but she seemed as much in a non-talkative mood as I was. Once she sat, she ordered a merlot and kept the drinks coming.

Everyone in first class had been drinking, except Kara and me. Even Gayle had two glasses of bourbon. The flight attendants had been nervous, with reason, but they seemed to relax since we were close to landing. No fights between the passengers had broken out.

"Is there anything you need, Mr. Asher?"

I glanced up, hearing the slightly warmer than necessary voice. The flight attendant was there, her smile warm and alluring.

Kara snorted next to me, rolling her eyes.

"No. I'm good. Thank you."

"Okay." Her eyes were inviting. "Just let me know."

As the attendant left, Kara muttered, "I might need some help, Miss. A washcloth to wipe away the drool you dribbled on my lap, perhaps?" She snorted. "If only they knew how taken you are with your current paramour." The seatbelt lights went on, and everyone began straightening up, readying for landing. Chairs were put in the normal place. Tray tables were put away. Drinks and trash were collected. One of the flight attendants went to hand out any coats that had been hung up when we boarded.

Gayle leaned forward again. "Watch it, Kara. Green doesn't look becoming on you."

I expected a cutting remark back, but my colleague remained silent, only pressing her lips together. She sat back, and everyone was quiet until we fully landed and the hatch door was opened.

I collected my carry-on, slung it over my shoulder, and waited my turn. Shanna and two others were in front of us.

She looked back, stepping into the main aisle and meeting my gaze. Remorse flashed in her eyes, but she only asked, "Did you sleep well, Brody?"

Everyone within hearing distance looked to me.

"Oh no," someone said behind me.

I looked back. Gayle was checking her phone. She was scrolling over her screen, her frown burrowing deeper and deeper. She looked up, some of color draining from her face.

"It's been leaked. The press knows about Morgan."

Goddamn!

I turned to Shanna. "You're fucking with her life. Don't you get that?"

She didn't respond. Her hand tightened around her bag, and she moved forward, heading off the plane.

Kara muttered under her breath, "Whereas you're just fucking her, in general."

"That's what you're pissed about? That I'm not fucking you?"

She'd started to go forward but stopped and twisted around to glare at me.

I met her look head-on.

No response came, but her face filled with color before she turned and followed Shanna off the plane.

Once I hit the airport corridor, people were waiting with their phones ready. I heard the continuous clicks of shutters and tried to avoid looking directly into the flashes. The questions didn't come right away. I was on the normal walkway and heading for the baggage claim before people started asking what movie I was shooting. If they could take a picture of me, a selfie with me. Once I stopped for those, the autographs started.

Gayle waited beside me, and when a small crowd formed, airport security showed up. They helped move us along, finally offering a cart to drive us to the baggage claim. Normally, I didn't take them up on the offer, but I wasn't in a mood to be a celebrity that day.

Gayle had a car waiting for us outside, and I got in, ignoring the small group of paparazzi that seemed to always know when we'd be there. I ducked inside to wait while Gayle remained inside to collect our suitcases.

Someone knocked on the window. I ignored it until the door opened again. The driver leaned down. "A Miss Kara Stone is wondering if she could get a ride with you?"

I almost rolled my eyes because the girl had some balls after the comment she made on the plane, but I waved her in. "Yeah. That's fine."

She didn't need to be told. She darted around the driver and scrambled in, taking one of the front seats away from me. She only had one bag on her lap. I asked, "Where's your suitcase?"

"One of the assistants is getting it."

"Watch it, Kara. Your diva side is coming out already."

She narrowed her eyes at me. "Like you're one to talk."

I narrowed mine right back, though she still couldn't see through my sunglasses. "I'm not in there because I didn't want to deal with the paparazzi. That's the only reason."

"You've been a diva the whole time, not just today."

"Excuse me?"

"Come on, Brody. You had your own cabin the whole time. You had time off. Then you think you can threaten our bosses and get away with it." Her fist pounded into the seat by her leg. "And you know what really pisses me off? You *will* get away with it."

I was silent a moment and then asked in a low voice, "Do you have a sister or a brother?"

She was quiet, too, picking at her shirt. "A sister."

"Are you close?"

"Sometimes. It's a hate-love relationship."

"Well, I hope for your sake you're never on the phone with her when she dies. Trust me. It's something that fucks with you."

Her shoulders lowered. She gathered her hands together in her lap and refused to look up from them. "I'm sorry. I am. I just . . . this movie was supposed to be my big break. But it's not. It's all about you."

I frowned. "What do you mean?"

"Everyone worries about you. Everyone talks about you. Shanna leaked your girlfriend, and she's using you to draw up the hype. I heard your manager. You know it's leaked, right?"

I clenched my jaw. "She said Morgan was leaked, not the two of us."

"Nope. It's out." She pulled her phone out, pulled up her browser, and handed it over, and there in big, bold letters at the top of article was *Hollywood Bad Boy Falls Hard!*

I couldn't—no, I could.

Anger started inside, rolling right into rage.

I knew it.

"Shanna did that?"

"Or someone else, but it was approved by her. If not, heads would be rolling so she could find the leak." She put her phone away. "I know you're probably livid about this, but you falling in love with that girl is going to sell gold. You were riding the line between the bad boy everyone loves to love and the bad boy who's just disgusting. You were going into the disgusting category. There's a short video of you squaring off against Peter Kellerman. It's obvious how much you love her. The press is going to go nuts once Shanna leaks footage of Morgan, and she will."

Goddamn.

I felt sucker punched, but I shouldn't have. I should've been prepared for this. I should've been ready to strike back.

I had nothing.

I was scrambling for cover in a situation everyone around me was saying would help me.

The door opened again, and Gayle climbed in. The bags were put in the trunk, and when the driver got behind the wheel, I turned to my manager.

"Did you know Shanna was going to use my connection to Morgan?"

She'd been reaching for the seat belt, but she paused, her eyes shifting between Kara and me. "What?"

She was so still, though.

Too still.

I knew then. "You knew, didn't you?"

Kara said, "I showed him *Persons'* headline."

Gayle swore under her breath, her hand letting go of the belt as she leaned back against the seat. "Why did you do that? He wouldn't have noticed."

Betrayal settled right next to the sick feeling. All of it was rolling around and around with my fury. I was keeping it in because I didn't trust myself.

God, I needed Morgan.

She would've known what to say, how to calm me.

A touch. A smile. A joke about Shiloh was all it would take to make everything right with me again.

I focused on breathing through my nose. I didn't dare open my mouth. I didn't know what I would say.

Kara was rolling her eyes again. "At least you aren't hiding it. Did you plant the story?"

Gayle went completely still again. Her eyes rounded and she blanched. "God no!" She looked at me. "After your outburst, I knew Shanna would use your relationship with Morgan. I just didn't think she'd do it so quickly. She's hungry, Brody. She wants this movie to launch her next one, and it's going to have a blockbuster budget. She will leak everything she can to get people salivating." Her hand rested on mine.

I pulled away.

It didn't deter her. "You and that horse prodigy girl are her ticket. And there's nothing we can do about it."

"Have you even tried?" I bit out.

"Yes."

I looked at her. Waiting.

"I looked over your contract. There's nothing we can do to stop it. This is all in her right as the movie director, especially since Peter and Matthew Kellerman okayed everything."

"My God, sit down and realize this is all helping you." Kara flung her hands in the air. "Why do you think I'm so jealous? I'm sitting in it up to my chest, and it isn't because you're sleeping with her and not me. I'm jealous of *you*, Brody. And you're so pissed and worried about your girl, that you can't even see how all of this is benefitting you."

I sat back, and I was quiet as the car left the airport.

Kara was dropped off first and then Gayle.

She lingered in her seat and asked, "Are you okay?" She reached for my hand and squeezed it.

I was tempted to pull away, but I was wrestling with so many demons inside.

Kara's words hit hard, and I knew from their perspective I was being idiotic. They didn't understand. Then again, I thought back to Morgan's reaction. She hadn't even been so worked up about it, but it was because she didn't realize what this meant. The world wouldn't be content to let her remain hiding. The world would go to her.

The press would be nuts.

They'd camp out around the land.

They would go and get long-distance zoom lenses, and images of her would be sold left and right.

Her life was going to change, and she had no idea how much. And it was her loved ones who had shoved her over the cliff's edge.

I didn't give one shit that this might erase any last concerns about my career.

"They're going to destroy her."

"This was going to happen whether you were doing the movie or not. You know that, right?"

"What do you mean?"

"As soon as the script was written, as soon as they got Morgan to sign off on it, the world was coming to her front door. No one could've stopped that, you included. You were captivated the first moment you saw her, right?"

I gave a begrudging nod.

"It was no different for the rest of us. Even last night when she was standing on that horse. I saw her out there. She defies gravity. She's what movies are written about, and once Shanna gets ahold of some pictures of her to leak, everyone else will fall in love with her too." She leaned forward, ignoring the open car door and driver waiting for her to exit. "She has you, though. Kellerman didn't plan for *you*."

My head whipped to hers. "You're saying Kellerman wanted this?"

She hesitated. "I don't know, but I saw the look in his eyes. I think he's been hoping something like this would happen since the beginning."

My mouth dried. "He wanted her kept secret."

"Some of the photos leaked couldn't have come from the movie crew. He played all of us."

"What are you talking about?"

She leaned forward. "Ask yourself this one question. If he wanted her secret kept, why did he have the damn script written in the first place?"

# CHAPTER THIRTY-EIGHT

*Brody*

I wanted to feel the wind whipping past me. I blamed Morgan's influence and was driving through the hills on my Harley two hours later. I called my brother's widow and asked to talk. Cheryl agreed.

I picked a hole-in-the-wall kind of place. The walls were littered with signatures, graffiti, and old images of customers who wanted to feel as if they left some memory there hung on the walls. The booths were covered in old black leather, and when I walked in, the hostess didn't blink an eye.

"Mr. Asher." A professional smile greeted me as she grabbed a few menus. "How many?"

"Just two. Somewhere private."

"Of course."

The interior was cast in low lights. Only a few candles on the tables and some lights lining the walkways gave us any indication where to go and sit in the place. She showed me to a back booth, and there only two others in our section. Both were empty.

She extended a hand toward one side of the booth. "Will this suit you?"

"It's perfect." I slid in one side, and she placed the drink menu in front of me. "I have one other joining me. Cheryl Asher."

She straightened. "Of course. I'll show Ms. Conway to your booth when she arrives."

"She's using her maiden name?"

She nodded. "She is, Mr. Asher."

Fuck.

I sat back as she left. What did that mean? I'd only been gone five weeks, maybe longer.

The server came once, took my order, and then Cheryl slipped into the side across from me.

My sister-in-law kept to the background whenever I was around their family. I spent time with Kyle first and foremost, then my nieces when they came along. The number of times Cheryl and I had a conversation could be counted on one hand, and most of those times had been because of his funeral.

I leaned forward, resting my arms on the table. "I wasn't sure if you'd come." I looked her over, noting the bags under her eyes through her sunglasses. "You look tired."

She wore a white scarf around her neck and a black dress. As she got comfortable, she took the glasses off and pulled the scarf off her head so it fell down her front, resting behind her neck. A sad smile graced her face. She folded the glasses, positioning them in perfect alignment with her napkin. "That isn't usually thought of as a compliment, but I'll take it. It's better than being told I look like death."

I raised an eyebrow. "Someone said that to you?"

She met my gaze briefly, that sad smile still in place. "You'd be surprised how many people have told me that and pretend as if they just realized how insensitive the comment was." Her grin went flat. "Assholes, the lot of them."

I laughed shortly. This was more personality from my sister-in-law than I'd ever seen before.

She showed more, saying, "Thank you for calling."

Right to business.

Okay.

I went with it.

"We had a break in shooting the movie."

The server came back, my soda and water in hand. She skimmed a look over us both before turning to my sister-in-law. "Ms. Conway? Something to drink?"

"Beer. Please. Tall."

This was new. Cheryl never drank before. She left that for Kyle and me.

The server nodded again.

Cheryl kept fiddling with her sunglasses. She didn't look like she was going to stay long.

"Cheryl." I gestured in the direction the server disappeared. "They're calling you by your maiden name?"

She didn't answer right away, taking a moment and looking at her lap. "This wasn't just your spot before. It was yours and Kyle's."

He and I had spent many nights in this bar, getting falling over wasted while we played pool. We were so sloppy, I could only imagine what names the staff must've called us, but we were regulars.

She added, "I started coming here after the accident. I wanted to . . ." She reached up, flicking a finger over her cheek. "He's everywhere, but I just remember the fights at home. I don't feel that when I come here. He loved coming here. He loved spending time with you here."

I sank back against my seat. My own head went low.

We'd drink.

We'd laugh.

We'd be stupid together.

No one cared who we were back then.

My throat was thick when I rasped out, "I asked you to come today because I needed to talk to you about something. I haven't been able to shake it—"

"It was ruled an accident." She was looking at me with a knowing look, like she was privy to the mess in my head. "He didn't kill himself."

I just looked at her. She said the words I wanted to hear, the words I'd been too chickenshit to ask, but all I could do in that moment was stare at my sister-in-law.

The thought that he had . . .

I eyed the bottle of bourbon on the wall behind the bar. That'd go down real smooth.

Her head lifted. She looked so tired, but she'd never looked so strong. I could see why my brother fell in love with her. She'd been the rock of their relationship, not him.

She said, "I know that's why you called today. Or, I guessed. Your old publicist was a bitch. She never said anything outright, but she hinted that he took his own life. I saw the same interviews you did, and I know you sent her a cease and desist, but she still put that out there."

A few interviews too late. A few phone calls too late.

Shelby shouldn't have even had the opportunity to do any interviews, but I hadn't been thinking. I'd been wallowing. I'd been drinking.

I was mourning.

"About that, I'm sorr—"

"No." She leaned forward, her hand resting on mine. "It's not true. I want you to know that. I didn't know for sure if that's what you were questioning, but when you called earlier, I just had this certainty. Your brother did not kill himself. He loved you. He loved us. He loved life, and he was so goddamn proud of you. You have no idea how much life was bursting out of him when he left to go to your premiere."

I didn't have any words. The relief inside—I believed her.

I could almost imagine Kyle snorting, saying, *"About fucking time. Ass."*

"Thank you, Cheryl." I drew in a ragged breath. I felt some of the storm in me start to settle, and just like that, I wanted Morgan here. I wanted her next to me. She would've held my hand under the table. She would've realized it was too hard for me to speak, and she would've started a conversation with Cheryl for me, because that's what my sister-in-law needed.

She needed to hear the words back, that I believed her. That Kyle wouldn't have done what some greedy bitch had insinuated, but she didn't understand.

I was ashamed.

As soon as I accepted her words, a new wave of guilt came with it. I should've believed it from the day one, from when the accident happened.

I hadn't. I let the doubt sink in.

Cheryl didn't make a sound, not one whimper, but her hand lifted to wipe at a tear.

Fuck's sake.

I should've been around more. I should've called more, stopped by her house to check in, helped more with the actual funeral instead of just paying for everything. Kyle had money. I knew Cheryl and the girls would be taken care of, but I had more. It was one way I could help without having to see the evidence that he was really gone.

I felt daggers sliding down my throat.

This was why he'd been haunting me. I hadn't stepped up.

"I'm sorry for not being here more."

Her head moved left to right, but she didn't look up. "No, it's fine. We grieve differently."

I reached over and grasped her hand. "My brother loved you, and he *was* loved. He was happy with you. You made him happy."

Morgan was right.

This was why I came back to Los Angeles. I needed closure, and I needed to step up, be there for Cheryl and his family now that he was gone.

Fuck Shanna and her script change, but I was thankful in this small moment.

After that, we talked. I was told everything amazing that happened to Alisma and Ambrea. They were in gymnastics, but now they wanted to play tennis. Cheryl smiled so wide as she talked about their tennis games. Alisma wouldn't sit still at the events, and Ambrea kept wanting to bring their pet rabbit with them.

By the end of the night, my stomach hurt from laughing. My cheeks hurt from smiling.

It felt good to talk about him. Damned good.

"Last call, folks." The server paused, looking between us.

Cheryl shook her head. "Goodness. I'm drunk. I haven't been like this for a long time."

I said to the server, "I'll take the bill."

"No, no, Bro—" Cheryl started protesting.

The server walked away, already knowing it was pointless. I was paying, and that was it.

"It's my job to help you guys out."

Cheryl started to shake her head.

"I mean it, Cheryl. I'll feel like I'm still helping Kyle in some way."

Knowing she couldn't argue with that, the fight left her.

After paying the bill, we were walking out as I asked, "You want a ride home?" I started to gesture to where my bike was when the camera flashes started.

"Brody!"

"Brody, smile!"

Paparazzi.

They were everywhere, swarming us around the sidewalk.

I didn't think. I threw an arm around Cheryl's shoulders and pulled her with me to my bike. I had parked it down the road.

"Brody, isn't that your brother's widow?"

"Are you two together now?"

"Brody, are you cheating on Morgan?"

That stopped me, and I whirled around.

The fucker was right behind me and raised his camera, blinding me with the flash of his camera.

Fuck. That'd be in all the papers tomorrow.

"Brody." Cheryl tugged on my arm. "Come on."

We got to my bike. I handed Cheryl the helmet and then swung my leg over the seat. After I knocked the kickstand back with my heel, I held the bike steady as she climbed on behind me.

"Do you talk to Morgan regularly?" Some guy was recording this. He got in front of the bike. "Was it love at first sight?"

"Move!" I barked out, turning the engine on.

He didn't, but I started edging out. When I was two feet from hitting him, he finally moved.

The cameras were still rolling. The flashes kept going. So did the questions. They were talking to me as if they knew me, as if I were their best friend, as if they knew who Morgan was. They knew nothing, and I leaned forward, zooming down the street.

Cheryl had her hands tight around my waist, but I wasn't thinking of my sister-in-law or even my brother.

I understood Morgan in that moment, when she would kick Shiloh into a dead sprint.

She was racing away from the world.

—

Cheryl was quiet when I pulled up to her parents' house. She climbed off, handing me the helmet. I thought she'd go in right away, and I moved to start the bike again, but she didn't. She half-hugged herself with one arm and tilted her head to the side.

"I stopped watching television after Kyle died, because . . . well, you know." She glanced at her house, tugging on her scarf. "When you left for that movie, it faded away and my mom told me I could start watching television again. It was on *EGossip Tonight*. It's on all the blog sites too."

There it was again. Morgan and me.

I started to feel the same irritation I felt with anyone trying to pry into my business, it was gut instinct. But this was Cheryl. She had no angle. She just cared.

I forced my hands off the handles but kept them in my lap.

Cheryl could take an hour or two or three to say whatever she wanted. I would wait.

"I know how you hate being told your own gossip." A fleeting smile flared and vanished behind a cough. "I just wanted to let you know that if you wanted to talk, I'm here if you need me too."

"Thank you."

She was studying my face and laughing a bit nervously. "And I can tell you don't want to talk about her at all." She gestured to me. "I forget sometimes how much you and Kyle look alike. He always got the same expression." She quieted and then gestured behind her. "I should head in." She started to edge backward, stopping halfway to her door to say, "I mean it, Brody. If you need something, I'm here. I really am."

I nodded. "Thank you, Cheryl."

She gave me a small wave before unlocking the door and ducking inside.

I got back on my bike and raced away feeling something fixed inside me, and because I was missing my woman, I imagined her running next to me on Shiloh.

# CHAPTER THIRTY-NINE

## Morgan

From where I was lying on the rock, I could hear the engine of a motorcycle driving along the road beneath me.

One, no—two.

Wait.

More engines sounded.

I rolled over and saw a whole train of motorcycles weaving through the mountains.

I was high enough that I doubted they could see me, but I recognized that these guys came through the mountains once a year. I rolled over and propped my head up, resting my chin on my hands.

I counted thirty before there was a small break and another group sped into view.

I swung my legs around so they were hanging off the edge and sat there comfortably perched. The wind rose and slid across the back of my neck, picking my hair up. When an eagle flew below me, a thrill skittered over me.

Halfway across the nation was Brody. He'd be in his home or some building surrounded by similar houses or other buildings. I didn't understand it, but I knew people enjoyed city living. They enjoyed living near other people.

Other people brought problems.

They brought hurts and aches and eternal sadness.

I tipped my head back and drank in the mountain air.

A movement caught my attention, and I looked down.

The motorcycles had pulled over. People were running on the street, some running in the middle of the road even. Then a few began waving their arms in the air.

I frowned, looking farther down the road, but there was nothing there. Reactions like this usually meant they saw a moose or bear. But no, the herd would've sensed another animal like that. And the horses were hidden from the road, so it wasn't that.

I stood, walking closer to the edge. Maybe I wasn't seeing the animal, but they began waving their arms faster and more franticly.

They were waving to me.

I cocked my head to the side, and it clicked. They thought I was going to jump.

Oh!

I shook my head and waved as I backed away. I didn't want to attract attention. They would break off from the road and start through the woods. They'd get hurt or lost. I had to leave before they did any of that, but as I climbed back down to where the herd was, I heard their shouting. It was growing. I heard tree branches breaking.

They had moved into the woods.

The stallion's head lifted, but there was no decision to be made. He began off, and the rest of the herd slowly followed. A few mares had foaled late, so the small colts were jumping all around. One saw me and started to charge. He was only a day old, so his feet folded underneath him and his head took a nosedive.

I just laughed, stepping over him and walking to meet Shiloh. She was already coming over to meet me. Shoal was right next to her, and after I climbed up on Shiloh, she started toward rest of the herd.

When we couldn't hear those people anymore, all seemed right again.

The only thing that would have made it better was if Brody were with me.

But I didn't want to think of him or the way his arms felt around me. That brought feelings I never used to experience before. They filled my head, gave me confusing thoughts, so instead, I bent forward and rested my cheek against Shiloh's neck. I let her steady everything for me like she always did.

—

When I walked to the main house, I didn't know how much time had passed since I'd last been there. I didn't think it was a month, that felt too long, but the nights were getting chillier. The days were beginning to shorten, so I knew we were nearing to a new season.

"Well, look what the cat dragged in."

I gave Finn a look. "You're still here?"

He was just leaving the barn and fell into step next to me. Shoving his hands into his light sweatshirt's pockets, he let his elbows flap around, nudging me with one. "It's been over a while. I'm surprised you held out this long." He looked behind us for a moment. "How do you handle it out there for so long?"

I shrugged. "It's second nature." He didn't know I had clothes and blankets stashed in places out there or that I only came back when I needed things like food or water if I couldn't find it. I tried sleeping in the barn apartment, but it didn't feel how it used to. It was cold. It wasn't mine any longer.

I'd watched the house a few days after Brody left. Peter took off the same afternoon and Matthew went later in the week. Once they were gone, I stopped worrying so much.

But that brought a different question to mind. I looked at Finn. He, Abby, and Jen remained at the house. "Don't you guys have to work?"

"Ah." He laughed again. "Yes, we do, but Matthew asked us to remain here in case the movie crew came back. Lucky for us, we can do most of our work online for the company."

"My life wouldn't be that different if I had to work."

"What?" He drew to a stop, turning to face me. "You lie."

I fought against a grin. "I thought about it before, about working. I would've worked with horses somewhere. And if I was poor, I would've made enough to buy a camper and park it somewhere and live off the land still." I tapped him on the nose. "See. I thought of everything."

"You're so lucky Matthew set up all your bills. You have no idea what the rest of the world is like."

Heartache. Harsh. Cold.

I shrugged, starting for the house again. "Does it matter?"

"Do you realize how big your boy toy is?"

"Huh?"

"Brody. Bad Boy Brody. You remember him? I am pretty sure he was proclaiming his love for you four weeks ago."

His elbow was coming in to nudge me again, but I slapped it away. "I know who you're talking about. What do you mean about how 'big' he is?"

He stopped, clasping his eyes tightly closed. "Oh, shit. Wrong choice of words."

I frowned. "What?"

"Yes." His eyes opened again, and he patted me on the shoulder. "Sometimes I'm glad you aren't jaded by society."

"Are you referring to the size of his penis?"

He choked and then bent over to cough it out.

I patted him on the shoulder. "Yes. Sometimes I'm glad you forget I'm not completely stupid." I paused. "Like the rest of society."

He laughed.

We were crossing the driveway to the house when we both heard the crunch of tires on gravel.

As one, we turned.

It was a black van, and Finn started cursing right away. Before I could move, he was striding toward them, and when they stopped and the doors opened, he yelled over his shoulder, "Get in the house, Morgan! Now!"

"But—" There were men running at him.

I froze.

I was ten years old again.

They raised their phones and cameras toward me.

*Flash!*

*Flash!*

One guy held up a recorder to videotape.

"Morgan!" one yelled, holding out his phone. "Were you just with the horses? Do you and Brody talk every night?"

A second one pushed ahead of the first, his phone out too. "Are you missing Brody? What do you think about the rumors that he's having an affair with his late brother's widow? Are you two still together?"

They were moving past Finn, but he struck a hand out.

One reporter ran right into it, clotheslined. He fell to the ground.

The other managed to duck, but Finn rounded, grabbed his shoulders, and threw him on the ground next to his friend.

The guy holding the camera gave Finn a wide berth, and while he didn't stop videotaping me, he didn't come any closer either.

Beat red, Finn pointed at him and screamed. "Get the fuck off our property! NOW!"

The clotheslined guy was getting back to his feet, scowling and brushing off his pants. "You don't have any signs posted. This could be considered a regular road to us."

"Bullshit." Finn got in his way, blocking me, but the other two could see. "Get out! Now!"

The door opened behind me, and Abby rushed out. "Finn!"

Jen followed at a slower pace, the landline phone in her hand. She waved it in the air. "I just called the cops, assholes. And we do have a sign posted. No trespassing!" She walked down the steps, still shouting.

"Get off our lands!" Abby put her two cents in as she and Jen both stepped in front of me.

When the reporters and camera guy didn't have their shot anymore, they grumbled but got back into the van and left.

Finn walked after them, literally escorting them off the land.

Once they were out of eyesight, both Jen and Abby dissolved into uneasy laughter.

"Man." Abby was shaking her head. "You have no idea the crazy shit we've had lately."

"Stuff like that?"

What did they mean about Brody? He was having an affair?

I knew it wasn't true, or it probably wasn't true, but the words burned in my memory.

Finn rejoined us, brushing his hands down his pants like he'd gotten dirt on them. "This has been happening regularly since the movie crew left, but that was the worst so far."

"They've never driven up the driveway before," Jen added.

"I thought there was a sign down there."

Finn grunted, eyeing Abby. "I didn't walk it, but I bet you anything they moved it."

Jen frowned. "They wouldn't.'"

He nodded. "Bet you twenty bucks." He wiggled his eyebrows. "Should we walk down and see?"

"No way." Abby wrinkled her nose and then remembered I was there. "Oh, Morgan!"

They all stopped and turned to me.

I pointed at the driveway. "What was that about?"

Finn slid his arm around my shoulders, drawing me against his side so he could walk me to the house. "That, my little sister, was the cost of being in a relationship with your celebrity."

"What?"

Abby, who was walking with Jen behind us, laughed. "Some bikers spotted you a week ago, and it's been insane ever since. They weren't looking for you, but with the tabloids and everything, they guessed who you were."

Finn led the way to the kitchen, taking his arm from my shoulders and pulling out a bottle of wine. He went to the cupboard and pulled out four wine glasses. "It wouldn't be a big deal, but some of those bikers hang out locally. They got to blabbing at a few bars."

Jen took the corkscrew from Finn and began to open the bottle. "The press started showing up a few days after the movie crew left. It's mostly just the gossip sites."

Finn nodded to me, pulling out a second bottle. "You're becoming big news. They all want a shot of you."

"And they just got some." Abby's lips pressed into a disapproving line.

"We have people coming tomorrow." Finn switched to me. "I figured you would be okay with it, but I ordered a big gate to be built at the end of the driveway. No fence will go up, but the gate will be big, and we'll have cameras installed and more signs posted. If they trespass again, we'll have proof. We can prosecute."

Gates.

Signs.

Trespassers.

I swallowed a hard knot, feeling it travel to my stomach.

This was what Brody had been talking about.

He said things would change. He said they would come to me. I laughed him off, thinking no one could find me. I'd been wrong.

They quieted, watching me.

Finn asked quietly, "You okay, Morgan?"

Fear pooled in my chest. "That was it? I mean, no one else will come on our land. Right?"

No one answered, and they all shared a look.

It was worse than I thought.

I shook my head, murmuring to myself, "But why? I don't get this. Why do they care?"

"Because of Brody."

I looked up at Jen.

Her eyes were so solemn. "You haven't been to the outside, but they're insane about him. It was starting up before Kyle died. Brody had a major movie coming out, and it all hit at the same time. His brother died the night of the movie premiere. That movie hit number one at the box office for six weeks in a row. To be fair, I don't think Brody even realizes how insane his celebrity status is. He really did become tabloid gold after that. He was sleeping with all these different people. Partying every night. He was getting into fights. When he came here for the movie, it *did* stop. That was why Gayle got him to do the movie, or part of the reason. She got him out of L.A., but now? After the leaks?" She frowned, looking to Finn, who nodded as if encouraging her. She added, "I'm assuming Shanna leaked everything. There are pictures of you on websites and in gossip magazines. You and Brody are the next *it* couple."

I wanted to run.

"No." I raked my hands through my hair. "This makes no sense. At all."

"Well." Jen bypassed her wineglass and picked up the bottle.

"No, no."

She ignored Abby, taking a long drag from the bottle. "Get used to it. As long Brody is crazy about you, you're the next big thing."

Finn took the bottle from his fiancée, shooting her a look. "She's the next big thing until this movie is done."

"Finn."

He handed the bottle to Abby, and she capped off her glass. There were two glasses left on the counter, both filled to the top.

Jen took one.

I could only stare at the last one.

Okay.

There'd been terror and panic in the beginning.

Yes. Brody was a big deal. I knew that. And I was missing him at that moment so much, but in the end, none of this mattered. The movie people, the press, those assholes with the cameras— they'd come back. The movie would get done. And they'd leave after that.

There'd be pictures of me, but eventually, it would all die down.

My life wasn't that world.

It was here. It was with Shiloh.

No matter what anyone said, they could not trap me.

Finn had been watching me. "What are you thinking, Morgan?"

Abby moved to my side. "Are you okay?"

None of this mattered to me.

I looked up. "I own the land the herd runs on, right?"

Slowly, Finn nodded. "Yeah."

"Then why should I care about any of this?" I could hide from anyone.

"Morgan, I don't think you're understanding what we're saying."

I held up a hand, stopping my brother. "No. I get it. I do. They want to take pictures of me. Right?"

"Well, that, and . . ." He shared looks with the other two, and his eyebrows pinching together. He tugged at his collar, looking back to me. "They want to know you."

"Why?"

"What do you mean, why?"

"Why do they care?"

"Because you're . . ." His lips pressed together as he chose his words carefully. "Jen? I'm shit at explaining this stuff."

Jen stepped forward. She stared at me steadily and put it bluntly, "You defy people's expectations of life just by you being who you are. They want to know what it's like to be so in tune with a mustang that she turns at the slightest touch from you. They want to know how you got Brody to fall in love with you and what it's like to be in bed with him. They want to daydream about you and use the idea of you to escape their lives. That's why people are going to go crazy over you, and if you give them what they want . . . if you let them in, there will be a time when they turn on you. My advice—"

"Jen." Finn stepped next to her.

"—run."

"Jen!"

She turned on my brother, raising her chin in defiance. "I've been in that world enough. They'll destroy her. Brody knows how to handle them. She doesn't."

"Stop, Jen." He dropped his voice low.

"I'm supposed to hide?"

They turned to me again.

I lifted a shoulder. "You guys are acting as if that's a novelty to me. It isn't." I cracked a half-grin. "Trust me, I have no problem hiding."

A tear fell from one of Abby's eyes. Her lip began to tremble. "But don't hide from us. That's what we want. You're here. You're in the house again." She stepped close, her hand trailing down my arm to hold mine. "Please don't go."

I squeezed her hand. She was as much a sister to me as Shiloh. I moved close and rested my forehead against hers.

Her eyes drifted shut. Her shoulders slumped. "That's all we want."

I lifted my head back.

Finn was smiling as he reached for me. "We just don't want to lose you. We don't want them to chase you away. That's all."

I went into his arms, and he hugged me tight. I hugged him back, but I didn't say anything. I couldn't. They wanted promises I didn't know I could keep.

Jen coughed. "Now, on to more important matters." She held up a bottle. "Like drinking. I don't know about you guys, but I could down two of these myself."

A few more bottles were brought out, and we moved our small group to the back patio for the rest of the night. I sipped a glass of wine. Jen and Abby both had four. Finn had a bottle just himself, which he told me was only two glasses.

I laughed. I smiled. I heard how Finn and Jen first started dating, how she thought he was a pansy-ass at first, and how he hit on her the entire night until she finally began laughing with him. I heard about their whirlwind romance and then how he proposed to her.

Abby, who had been mostly quiet, perked up as soon as we started talking about the wedding. I saw the wistfulness in her eyes when they talked about loving each other, about the wedding, and their hopes for a future.

Yes. The whole night felt alien to me, as if I had on someone else's skin or had stepped into someone else's world, but it was a good world.

At least for the night.

# CHAPTER FORTY

*Brody*

Two months of meetings, negotiations, and planning passed.

Not all of it was for *Unbroke*. Some of those meetings were for the next superhero franchise of movies. They had promised me a role, and the good word from Shanna sealed it. I had gotten the part, and they didn't care about the leaked stories about Morgan or about my relationship with Morgan. They weren't told how I fought against the director and some of the producers. That wasn't the type of publicity Shanna wanted—it was too messy.

We were also sent new scheduling contracts to finish the shooting for *Unbroke*, and I'd gone home to start packing.

My television was on, but I heard my door buzzer over the din of the talking heads.

"Just in time," I said to Gayle, who was standing patiently on my doorstep.

Just as I shut the door, the journalist cut to a new segment, drawing my and Gayle's attention. "And we have new images of Morgan Kellerman, the rumored new love interest of Brody Asher." She turned to her co-anchor. "What do you think, Josh? Sizzling or not?"

"Not just sizzling, Julia." The guy crooned to the television camera. "But hot, hot, hot sizzling! I have to say, I totally get how this mystery woman trapped our own Brody Asher."

"You think Bad Boy Brody is no longer? You think this vixen has tamed our bad boy?"

"I don't know, Julia." The co-anchor laughed.

I was disgusted, so I tuned out their continued gossip and went to turn off the television.

Gayle came in, shutting the door.

She trailed behind me as I returned to the bedroom to finish packing.

She lingered in the doorway. "You're leaving?"

"Are you surprised?" I stopped and turned back. "My next project is lined up. Schedules are booked, and we start shooting next week. Why wouldn't I go back?"

She looked at a loss and then sputtered out, crossing her arms over chest. "You run everything by me first."

I shook my head. "I run everything work-related by you first. My going back now, going early, isn't business. It's personal."

"But—"

I waited for her to finish her thought, and then I waited some more. Eventually, I raised an eyebrow. "Yeah?"

"I don't think you should be attached to Morgan Kellerman."

Ah. There it was.

Gayle hadn't said much on the topic in the beginning, but it'd been two months since we left. Finn connected Morgan and I on the phone a few times, but it wasn't enough. I knew about the bikers who spotted her on the hill. I knew the press had been pushing to get more shots of her. I knew they had to install a gate at the end of the driveway, but I knew the rumors hadn't gone away. They only intensified. There were reporters, bloggers, and radio hosts all vying to get information. I told myself I should stay away to keep the attention away from her as much as possible, but the fact that I hadn't been at Morgan's side these last two months astonished even myself.

I was supposed to be there, not here.

I sighed, turning back to my packing. "I'm doing the superhero movie."

"That isn't what this is about." She came to my side. "Please, Brody. Think about this."

"What's the issue?"

"It's her." She flung a hand toward me. "It's you. Forget this media storm that you tried to stop. It's coming. I told you that before we left the estate, and I stand by my feelings. Matthew Kellerman wanted this. I guarantee it."

"It doesn't matter anymore. It's happening. I'm going back. I'm doing the movie, we are going to finish shooting, and then I'm going to New Zealand for the next project."

"And then to Iceland for the project after that."

They hadn't booked me for just one superhero movie. They hired me for two. It was what every actor dreamed of landing. The franchise was a moneymaker, and it would ensure my career for years.

I was going to do it. And I was happy about it. But I couldn't ignore the bittersweetness of it all.

As if sensing my thoughts, Gayle murmured, "She'll never go with you. She'll never leave those horses or those mountains."

"I'll bring her horse."

She snorted. "You'll bring a mustang with you to every place you shoot?" She chided me softly. "It would be traumatic for the horse *and* the girl, and you know it."

"What do you want me to do, Gayle?" I clipped out.

"I want you to go to Montana. I want you to find her, be with her. I want you to love her because you already do, and when you're done with *Unbroke*, I want you to get on that plane for New Zealand, and I want you to forget her."

Forget her.

Forget someone I loved, but I hadn't said the words to her.

I'd been apart from her and had been aching every minute of the day because she wasn't by my side.

"That's easy," I murmured back.

She looked relieved.

"It's just like losing Kyle all over again, only worse."

She tensed, her eyes closing.

"She's in me *already*, Gayle. I forget her, and that means I rip a part of myself out when I go."

235

I scanned my room. I was mostly packed. Grabbing the last of my things, I put them in the bag, slung it over my shoulder, and then grabbed a baseball hat and sunglasses. It wasn't a great camouflage, but I'd be in first class, so I just had to make it through the airport.

"You'll send the rest of my stuff? What I'll need for the movie?"

She nodded, her head hanging low. "Yeah. I will."

She had a key to my home. She used it when I wasn't there, and I did trust her, but I placed my hand on her shoulder when the doorbell rang again. That was the driver.

I squeezed her shoulder lightly. "I came back to L.A. to find peace about Kyle's death. I met with Cheryl, and I did that. I stayed because I knew you needed me here for all of the meetings." But those were done. I bent and brushed a kiss to her cheek. "I'll see you in a week."

She grabbed for my hand on her shoulder and squeezed it back. "I was there for you after Kyle. I'll be there for you after . . ." She cleared her throat. "After you finish shooting *Unbroke*."

I put on my hat, pulled it low, and then put on the sunglasses. I had one bag and was wearing jeans that were ripped at the knees and a T-shirt. I had my wallet, my phone, and my keys. If Morgan could live in the woods for weeks with almost nothing, I could fly over a few states with the same.

I flashed Gayle a grin. "I know you will." I caught her hand once more and then went to open the door.

I left Gayle in the house because I trusted her. She was still one of my people.

The driver was there, the same one I always used. He took my bag for me as we went to the car.

"Thank you, Conlin."

He nodded to me, and I got into the car.

# CHAPTER FORTY-ONE

## *Morgan*

I was returning from seeing Shiloh and riding with the herd and had decided to take a detour through the now-empty barn. They had sent the horses back to their original ranch once the movie crew left, but I still enjoyed walking through it versus going through the normal gate. I was reaching to open the barn door when I heard cars approaching.

Finn always wanted me to stay hidden when people arrived. He checked them out first. So, when the door was open just enough for me to slip through, I did and shut it quickly behind me. I remained in the barn, following his wishes and waiting for whoever it was to either leave once they realized no one was home. Minutes ticked by slowly, and eventually I heard Matthew's voice, which drove me deeper into the shadows.

"I thought Finley and Abigail were still here."

I shrank farther back. That was Peter as well.

"No. They're in town for a meeting with a few other developers I had flown in. They think they're going to start looking for new projects in the area."

"Well, you never know. They might be."

"True."

They laughed together, drawing closer to the barn.

"Are you sure Morgan isn't here?"

"Are you serious? Morgan's always out there with the herd. I promise."

I tried to make out if there were any others with them, but there were only two sets of footsteps. They went to the gate, and I waited to see if they would free the latch.

"So this was your brain child. The movie people are coming back. Are you ready to pull the trigger?"

Matthew laughed uneasily. "There was a problem with the initial paperwork Morgan signed."

"What?"

Peter sounded angry and harsh.

"It'll be fine. I promise. I'll get her to sign another. I'll just say it's paperwork to allow the movie to finish filming here. It'll be like an addendum or something. She'll have no idea."

"What if she doesn't sign?"

"She will."

"What if she sees it as a way to keep the movie from happening? Her lover boy was adamant about that."

"I talked to Finn. Asher hasn't been in contact with Morgan, and we know he's been in Los Angeles, lining up his next projects. We're good. And Morgan *will* sign. I'll tell her she has to or her lover won't be coming back."

"You underestimate her."

"No." Matthew's reproach was swift and firm. "You underestimated Karen."

"I didn't know she would put in that clause. The land and inheritance should've gone to me."

"You're the one who sent *him*."

"He was supposed to take the kid with him. He wanted Morgan." Peter's tone was hard. "I never told him to kill Karen. I'd have time to get her to put me in the will, not leave everything to her kid."

I sucked in my breath. My heart was beating too fast.

No.

I wasn't hearing this.

"I would never want my own wife dead."

*I heard car tires on the drive, and I wanted to see who was coming home. It could be Matt or Finley, maybe even Abby.*

"But you were okay with him taking Morgan?" Matthew's voice broke.

There was silence.

Then a quiet, "You're still hung up on the girl? She's a freak of nature, Matthew. Let her go. She'll move on. She'll be fine."

*My mother knelt before me. She held a finger to her mouth and whispered as tears fell down her face. "We're going to play hide-and-go-seek, okay? Okay, Morgan?"*

"She'll have no home. You want to sell this land out from underneath her."

"You're in this too, *pup*. Don't stand there all self-righteous. The movie was your goddamn brainchild. Slip an extra piece of paper in with her contracts so she thinks she's signing her approval for the movie when she's really signing away her rights to the land."

*Someone was knocking on the door. This person was knocking harder and harder on the door. They began yelling. It wasn't Matt or Finley or Abby.*

More silence.

Then a more subdued Matthew said, "Let's just take the specs we came to get and go."

"Fine with me." Peter paused a beat. "She will be fine, Matthew. You can take care of her if the actor doesn't. She's a survivor."

*"I love you so much, Morgan. So much." My mother ran her hands down my head, smoothing my hair and pulling me close to press a kiss to my forehead. "You're such a good hider. I know you can hide for days if you needed to, right? You can hide so good that it would take me days to find you."*

*I nodded. She knew I was good at that. I'd just go with the horses. Shoal would take care of me. She always did.*

*"Okay, Morgan. I need you to hide like that."*

*The man was kicking at the door.*

*I began to shake, my hands trembling. I didn't want to go.*

*"Go, honey. Go." She stood and went to the door.*

*I didn't dare move.*

*I feared a piece of straw would crinkle under my foot, and they would know I was there. They would know I knew their plan.*

Peter sent the monster.

My legs were shaking. My arms were trembling.

And Matthew—he plotted to take my home from me, *my home*. It had always been mine. I might not use it as often as a normal person would, but it was mine.

I heard the thundering of hooves in the distance. The herd was stampeding. Shiloh would be with them. I looked out the barn window, but I couldn't see them. I could only hear them.

"Damn horses," Peter cursed. "They were a plague back then and still are. They'll get shoved off the land."

"Where will they go?"

"Do you really care?"

"Where they go, she goes."

"They'll probably be shot if people are smart." Peter laughed crudely to himself. "The national park isn't too far for them to travel. Maybe they'll go there. The rangers can deal with the herd."

Tears welled in my eyes and lingered on my eyelashes. They pooled there, growing larger.

"I care about Morgan. I don't want you here when I handle all of this and she finds out."

Peter grunted, cursing again. "You're wasting your time on the girl. She's as much a mustang as those four-legged fucks out there. Let go of your idea of this cozy family. It'll never happen."

I waited to hear Matthew's response, but it didn't come.

They left after that.

I heard them walking around the land, taking their specs, whatever that meant. When they came into the barn, I moved to the apartment above.

As they were leaving the property two hours later, I went to stand in the driveway. If either of them turned, they would see me, but they just climbed back into their car and drove away. I just watched their taillights fade into the distance.

Run and hide.

That was what Peter expected me to do.

*"Hide, Morgan. Hide."* I heard my mother's whisper.

I lifted my chin in defiance. *Not this time, Mom.*

# CHAPTER FORTY-TWO

## Morgan

I was on Matthew's new computer when Finn and Abby returned. They came in, talking like normal. It was an hour before they noticed the light was on in Matthew's office.

"Holy shit!"

Abby screamed.

"What?" Finn came running.

But Abby was frozen in the doorway, just staring at me.

"What?" Finn asked again, sounding cross as he stopped behind her.

Both gaped at me, blinking like shocked owls.

"Wha—" Finn raked a hand through his hair, coming inside. "Morgan?"

I smiled at them over the computer screen. "What? How do you guys think I got my college degree?" I snorted. "You didn't think I actually went to the college, did you?"

"You—I—" Abby closed her mouth and sank into one of the chairs across from me. "I forgot."

"Me too." Then Finn narrowed his eyes. "What are you doing?"

"Sending people emails and printing out the contract Matthew had me sign before." I pushed print and waited till the document was done. I pushed it across the desk toward Finn. "According to a conversation I overheard between Matthew and *your* father, they tried to trick me. Matthew said there was something wrong with the original paperwork and he was going to try to get me to sign

241

something again." I leaned back in my chair. "They want to sell my lands."

"What?" Abby jerked forward.

Finn cursed under his breath. He reached for the contract and began reading it. Once he was done, he handed it to his sister. "There's nothing in there about you giving anyone power to sell the lands. There's only one clause that states the movie has to be filmed on the property, but that's it."

I nodded. "I know. I didn't read what I signed, and I think he snuck in an extra piece of paper, knowing I didn't know."

"There was no piece of paper."

Matthew was standing in the doorway. His torn eyes held mine before he pinched at his forehead as if combatting a headache. "You weren't supposed to hear us. You weren't supposed to hear any of that."

Abby jerked out of her chair.

Finn did, too, his hands in the air. "You should leave, brother."

I didn't think that was a good idea. Matthew had answers. I wanted them, and for once, I wasn't leaving until I got them. He owed me that much.

Matthew only gave Finn a scornful look, his lips pressing together a moment before he straightened from the doorframe. He had his suit jacket thrown over one shoulder, but as he moved, he pulled it forward and folded it over one of his arms. "You're all right. I should leave, but you don't know the truth. Any of it."

He produced a folder of papers and tossed it on the desk in front of me.

He pointed at them, walking toward the windows, but he only turned his back to the window. He faced us. "Those were the papers I was going to ask you to sign, Morgan."

I didn't hesitate. I grabbed them, and then thrust my arm toward Finn. "Lighter."

He handed it over, glaring at Matthew the whole time.

I had the papers on fire within a few seconds, and I walked around the desk, taking them into the bathroom. I held the file as long as I could before letting them fall into the toilet. The fire was immediately snuffed out. A column of white smoke filled the room, and I went back to the office.

The smoke was drifting in there as well.

I met Matthew's gaze. "You have my answer."

He was watching me, and I swore I saw a fleeting grin tug at the corner of his mouth. He nodded before asking, "Did you have fun hanging out in the barn earlier?"

"You knew?"

He gestured to Finn. "When your boy toy had Finn take all the cameras down, they missed some. I still have two up, the entrance and exit of the barn."

"But—" My mind was racing.

Abby and Finn didn't know what else was said at that meeting. They didn't know most of it.

Matthew sighed, pointing to the bathroom. "I never snuck in an extra piece of paper where you would've signed your rights away to the land. He thinks I did because that is what he wants." He gestured to the bathroom. "You just set fire to the movie crew's amended contract for when they come back to finish filming the movie."

"Oh." Abby cocked her head to the side. "Didn't see that coming."

Finn winced. "What are you saying?"

"Dad thinks the movie's a ploy, a way to showcase our land to a very select clientele that would want to buy it. He doesn't want any general buyer. He wants the best buyer he can get." Matthew looked at me. "I found a recording at the main office in New York." His eyes grew hooded, but I caught a flash of sympathy. "I know what he did." So did I. "I know what happened that day."

I looked down.

No one knew.

Matthew continued, "He doesn't know I know about the recording, but then he started pitching plans on how to sell the land to the best buyer." His voice broke into a whisper, "I couldn't let him hurt you again."

"Say what?"

I looked up. Finn was skirting between Matthew and me, his eyebrows arched high. "What is going on here? I'm not following any of this."

Matthew paid him no attention. "The movie idea was mine. I told him it'd get the land publicity that we couldn't buy, and that we could trick you into signing papers that you'd never question. I told him I could get you to sign your home away." His voice grew thick again. "I'm sorry, Morgan. For everything." He reached inside his suit jacket and pulled out a small device. He tossed it onto the desk.

Finn gripped the back of his neck. "What the hell is that?"

"A listening device." Matthew regarded his brother for the first time. "I've been working with the FBI to help build a case against our father."

Abby could only gape at the device. "I'm not understanding any of this. Matt." Her bottom lip started trembling. "What is going on?"

I stood. It was my turn. "Your father sent my father here." And I waited.

Silence.

No one moved. No one made a sound.

And then, "What?" from Abby.

*"Hide, Morgan. Hide."*

I stood taller. "She died because of me. Your father wanted me gone."

*I ran toward the barn.*

*Run.*

*Hide.*

*I was doing both.*

*I could feel my own tears falling. I was so scared, but I did what she said.*

*Under the fence.*

*I kept going.*

*Down the hill, through the fields.*

*"Morgan!"*

"I was in the house when he came." I couldn't tell them how I thought it'd been them at first, how happy I had been. "She knew it was my father. He was pounding at the door, and she told me we were going to play a game."

"Oh my God." Abby stumbled backward, but Finn caught her. He turned her into his chest, his arm coming around her.

I could hear her crying, and a part of me was thankful. I should be the one crying, but I couldn't. I turned off like I always did. There were no tears, not from me anyway.

*Our house was high on the mountain. I was over the first slope in the hill. But—no. I got back up and looked behind me.*

*He could follow my footsteps.*

*Mama . . .*

*I wanted to go back, but she said to hide.*

*I had to get to Shoal. He wouldn't be able to find me if I were with her.*

*I kept going as fast as I could.*

*Under the next fence, and then I was free into the terrain.*

*There were woods. The river. I kept going and going. I was getting so cold. She said to hide for days. I'd need Shoal.*

"Morgan!"

I couldn't form words. It took a moment for me to choke out, "I could hear her screaming." But then he started screaming. "He came after me."

The room was completely silent, only breaking up for Abby's crying.

The back of my neck started tingling. I didn't understand it, but I looked anyway. There was no sound. No movement to announce his presence, but I felt him anyway. And standing in the doorway, like Matthew had been moments earlier, was Brody.

My eyes met his, and he said it for me. "Her mom told her to run. She never stopped."

I wanted to go to him. I wanted to wrap my arms around him, tell him everything that happened, and let Brody fight for me, but I had made a promise. I was staying. If I went to him and let him touch me, I'd crumble. I had to hold firm, for now.

Finn sighed in relief, getting up and shaking Brody's hand. "Perfect timing, buddy."

Brody nodded. Abby went to him, giving him a hug, but Brody was back to looking at me.

He saw my torment.

He nodded, just slightly, and then focused on Matthew.

The two stared at each other.

Both clenched their jaws.

Matthew narrowed his eyes. "This is a family meeting."

Brody smirked. "I think I have more reason to be here than you do."

"He stays."

Matthew swung his head to mine. He wanted to challenge me, but I stared him down. When his chest rose and fell, I knew I won.

I murmured, "I shared. Now you share. Tell us everything."

Abby asked, "You said you've been working with the FBI?"

He pointed to Finn. "I took that recording to the cops, but they wanted more, so I told them I would get it. And in all our meetings, he never once said what really happened back then. We talked about the movie, about tricking Morgan, and he made a lot of statements about how Karen wasn't supposed to bequeath her land and money to Morgan. He was her husband, so he was supposed to inherit it. He was angry about that, but he never confessed that he was the one who sent Morgan's father to the house." He looked at his brother. "Because you forgot to take those two cameras down, we have what we need on tape."

Abby gasped, jumping to her feet. "You have video of him talking about it?"

Matthew jerked his head in an abrupt nod. "Yes," he rasped out. "The police already have a copy."

My knees gave out. I almost fell back onto the desk chair.

"You turned Dad in?"

Matthew nodded at Finn, smiling. "I'm sorry for not looping you in."

"He may be a bastard, but he's still your father."

That came from Brody.

Matthew looked up, and the two shared a look. Whatever passed between them had Matthew's shoulders rolling back. His voice was a bit clearer than before when he continued, "They're arresting him right now. I came to tell you before it's all over the news."

"Fuck." Brody shook his head. "Shanna must be shitting herself in gold right now."

"Yeah, well." Matthew cleared his throat, lines of pain forming around his mouth and eyes. He tugged at his collar. "I actually *can* shut down the movie." He looked at me. "If you want. There's a clause in the contract, but I want you to make the decision. I don't think anyone has the right to make it for you."

There was no question.

"I want it made. For her."

# CHAPTER FORTY-THREE

*Brody*

I held Morgan that whole night through.

There'd been no words I could use to express how I felt when I walked down that hallway and heard what they were talking about. It was perfect timing in some ways, but my arms had been itching to take her, hold her, and carry her away. Once Matthew, Finn, and Abby left the room, Morgan leapt at me at the same time I was going to her.

Her arms and legs wrapped around me, and it was all the permission I needed to carry her from the house and down to my cabin.

When I realized she'd been sleeping in my bed, a wave of tenderness filled me. But again, there'd been no words.

I set her down, and our lips found each other's. I showed her how I felt that night, and she showed me.

After only a few hours of sleep, the police were knocking on the door. They questioned Morgan, and once they were done, they assured us they had enough to press official charges against Peter Kellerman, who was already in custody.

The gossip already swirling about Morgan and me went up a whole other level with Peter Kellerman's arrest. So, when the news broke, I wasn't surprised when ABC, CBS, and CNN picked up the story as well.

We were all in the living room at the main lodge watching the press release when Gayle called.

Morgan was on my lap and looked down. She saw the name, and without saying a word, she shifted to the side so I could stand. She snuggled into where I'd been sitting as I crossed the room and went out to the patio, shutting the door behind me.

"Is it true?"

"Hello to you too, Gayle."

"It's true then."

I sighed. Some days we didn't need to use actual words to communicate. "When are you coming?"

"Now. Shanna's with me."

I looked back. Morgan was watching me, not the television screen.

I'd have to use a car and pick them up or send someone. "When?"

"We're arriving in an hour."

I barked out a laugh. "That's the real reason you're calling."

"You'll pick us up?"

"I'll be incognito and everything."

She laughed from her side. "How are you?"

She wasn't asking about me. "She's strong. So I'm strong."

"You picked a good one then."

I heard her begrudging respect, and my smile grew. I nodded to myself. "I know. See you in an hour."

Morgan shut the television off when I came back. "That was your manager?"

I nodded, saying to the whole room, "She's arriving in an hour with Shanna."

Matthew cursed but was smiling at the same time. "She's coming to make sure the movie is still a go."

"Yeah." I glanced to Morgan and then Finn. "I was going to go and pick them up."

"You have a car?"

I rented a motorcycle. I hadn't been able to help myself, so I asked, "Could I borrow a car?"

Abby laughed, the sound filling the entire room and hall. She stood and gestured to Finn. "I think they'll go crazy if they see you, even if you wear a baseball cap and sunglasses. They'll still recognize you."

Probably. They all saw my disguise yesterday.

"We'll go." She and Finn both started for the door. "We'll get food and—"

"We're out of wine."

"—we'll get some booze too."

Both Abby and Finn laughed.

I warned, "They'll want to stay here."

Abby turned around at the door. She glanced to Morgan. "Is that what you want?"

Morgan shook her head. "It's Brody's call."

They all waited for my decision.

They'd want to stay here. I wanted them at the hotel. I sigh before saying, "They should stay here. They'll be swarmed in the hotel lobby every time they leave otherwise."

"Decision made." Abby followed her twin outside and waved over her shoulder. "Be back in an hour and a half with two more if all goes accordingly."

Once they were gone, the room became awkward.

Matthew laughed to himself. "And on that note, I have some business to take care of."

He was halfway to his office when Morgan called to him, "You'll kick him out?"

Matthew stopped. His shoulders tensed, and he took a breath before he turned back around. His face was fully guarded as he nodded. "Yes. I already have the board of directors working on removing him. He's been arrested. His position will be stripped from him."

Morgan's head cocked to the side. "Another item you've been planning." Her tone was knowing.

"I started planning this the day I found out what he'd done. Yes."

"You'll promote Finn and Abby?"

Matthew's eyes narrowed a bit, studying Morgan. "I had already planned on it." His eyes flicked to me and then back to her.

"If you wish to come to the company, you could have a position there."

"Do you know who my grandfather was?"

I didn't know if it was the sudden jump in topic or the question itself that surprised Matthew more, but his eyes went wide as he shook his head.

"My mom never talked about him, but the money I have is from him." Morgan shifted on her feet. "I've never looked for him."

"And you want to know now?"

"Do I have other family? Do you know why she was estranged from her family?"

Matthew hesitated again. I could see his reluctance, but his head lifted again. "Your grandfather died and left most of his estate to Karen, but not all of it. The rest of your family didn't like that she got the majority, and they fought her. They took her to court to try to get more of the inheritance, but they didn't win, and she left after that. I don't know all of it, but I did overhear her telling my father that she feared her family would come for you and also your money one day. She took up with *your* father because she thought he would protect her. She took up with *my* father to help protect against him. In some ways, it was a sad cycle."

As he spoke, Morgan's head lowered a centimeter at a time. By the time he was done, she was fully looking at the floor.

I stepped forward, my hand going to her shoulder. I drew her against my side.

He added, "I wish I could say they were people worth knowing, but if Karen was scared of them, I doubt they would be."

I nodded to him. "Thank you for telling her."

Morgan didn't say anything. She turned and moved into me as I wrapped both my arms around her.

As Matthew left, with some reluctance again, I just held her close to me as we walked back to my cabin.

An hour later, I shifted to my back and pulled her against me. I skimmed a hand down her arm. "You were hoping to find more of your family?"

She rolled her head to look at me as her free hand caught mine. She laced our fingers together, gently kissing my hand before resting them on her stomach. She settled more against me, getting comfortable.

She murmured, almost too quiet for me to hear, "I think I'd always hoped."

I traced a hand down the side of her face, lingering over her cheek and lips before I skimmed down her knee and leg.

She closed her eyes at the touch, as if it helped to steady her. "It's a sobering thought to think you're completely alone. Creatures aren't meant to be alone."

I sat up in bed and grinned at her. "Creatures?"

"Four-legged or two-legged. We aren't supposed to be on our own." She bit down on her lip. "I think I might look for my mother's family, and judge for myself if I should stay away."

A strand of her hair fell forward, coming to a rest on her cheek.

I lifted it, tucking it back in place, before moving to tug her lower free from between her teeth. "How will you know if they're good people or not?"

"They probably are not, but I have to see myself. I'll know." She grinned. "I have horse instincts, remember? We can tell who are good and who are not."

I grunted. That was true enough.

I traced my finger over her face again, down her chin, resting in the cleft there before falling back to my side. "I worry about you."

"Why?"

"Because I care about you." It was more. We both still hadn't said the words.

She smiled. "I'm fine. I've always been fine." She laughed, poking me in the chest. "It's you I worry about. You aren't fine, unlike me."

I started to laugh and then thought about it. "Shit. You're right." I slid my hand against hers, lacing our fingers again. "You're more stable than I am." I couldn't help myself. She was an inch away, an inch too far. I tugged her onto my lap, and she squealed until she straddled me.

I was tired. I wasn't hard, but he would rise again. It wouldn't be long. I ran my hand down her back, around her ass, and cupped her there. I couldn't stop running my hands over her. I felt my dick stirring. It wouldn't be long at all.

I rocked her over me, and she let out a full-body sigh, tipping backward.

She let go of the sheet, but it didn't fall all the way. It fell open, letting me see her. I tugged it down and then cupped one of her perfect breasts.

I could watch as the sun bathed her through the window for hours. I felt her hair on my legs. Both her breasts free for me to touch, lick, taste. They were there for me to hold on to, every inch of her was. She was soft but toned.

I let go of her breast and ran a hand down her waist, rubbing over her stomach and then lower, lingering on her nub. She shuddered slightly, breathing heavier, as she always did when I touched her there. And while she remained like that, literally a buffet for me to touch and taste, I leaned forward and caught one of her nipples in my mouth.

She surged alive, straightening and sliding her hands through my hair. She moved higher on my lap, and I held her tight to me, my teeth biting her gently. I licked around her breast, loving the taste of her, loving how I could almost touch her anywhere and she would gasp in pleasure.

"Brody," she said on another sigh.

I let go of her breast, tipping my head back so her lips could find mine.

I could die touching her like this.

Her mouth on mine. Her legs straddling me. My dick rising to her entrance.

I caught her bottom lip with my teeth, and she gasped lightly and slid down onto me.

I opened my eyes and looked up. She was gazing down at me, a look of wonder in them, and her hands found my face. Her thumb rubbed over my lip in a familiar gesture that I hadn't known how much I'd missed until right then. I felt her body tighten, then that look of wonder melted into something more, something warm, something kind, something overwhelming. I felt it surge through me, and I wanted to say it first. I didn't know why, but I knew I had to.

I leaned back so I could see her, making sure I had her full attention.

"I love you."

At my words, that emotion was named.

It was something loving in her, but her lips found mine. That was her response, and I couldn't do anything except savor the touch. I held her hips and began to move her up and down on me. She rolled them with me, riding me, but I wasn't content this way. I laid her down, my lips never moving from her, and I bracketed her between my arms, thrusting in slow, deep strokes. I rode her this time. Her legs lifted, her ankles hooking around my back, and I began to thrust harder and faster.

I skimmed a hand down her side, rubbing against her breast as we kissed.

I kept moving in her. She kept moving with me.

We were synced. Maybe we always had been. It was something deeper than us. I felt it when I first saw her on that horse, crossing in front of my car. It'd been there the whole time, like we were literal soul mates.

And as I thought that word, it clicked in place for me. Everything flooded loose.

We were.

I just hadn't realized.

I stopped moving and lifted my head.

My eyes found hers, and she twisted her head to the side. "What's wrong?" she asked, touching my mouth.

I caught her fingertip, kissing it before releasing it. "I have never felt like this with someone before."

I lowered my lips to hers.

It wasn't the first time I made love to her, but it was the first time I was in awe of it.

# CHAPTER FORTY-FOUR

*Brody*

Gayle was glaring at me.

I was sitting across the dinner table from my manager and raised an eyebrow. "What's with the look?"

Her eyes flicked to the ceiling and then she leaned close to me. She dropped her voice so no one else could hear, but she didn't need to worry. Finn was having a lively debate with Shanna about the stock market. The two were fanatics, who would've guessed that? But I knew it served a purpose. No one wanted to talk about the elephant in the room, and at the moment, I didn't know if it was Morgan or if it was the reason my manager and director both flew out a week early. I went with the latter because Gayle hissed at me, "You goddamn glow after sex. You know that?"

I almost choked on a piece of steak. I started laughing. I didn't expect that from her. "What's the problem with that?"

"Nothing." Her eyes cut to Morgan. She didn't say any more, but I knew her worries.

"So." Shanna called a halt to the other conversation, clearing her throat.

The air suddenly shifted, growing somber. Tense.

She looked from me to Morgan and then settled on Matthew. "We saw the press release."

Matthew nodded, wiping a cloth napkin over his mouth. He folded it and then set it on his lap, resting his arms back on the table. "Yes. I'm sure you did."

"Is it true? He aided in Karen Kellerman's murder then?"

The Kellermans all looked at Morgan, who didn't respond.

Matthew glanced to Morgan as he answered, "Are you asking for the movie? Or . . ."

"I need to be prepared for how it might impact the movie."

Matthew seemed at a loss.

I understood where Shanna was coming from.

I leaned forward. "The evidence is good, even if he gets off." I looked right at the director. "Put it in the movie."

Morgan's hand found mine under the table.

"I need to know what to put in. It could change the scope of the movie. Again. I have to know what it is."

Matthew's attention shifted to me, and I narrowed my eyes at him. "If you're waiting for me to heel, you're going to be waiting till you die, Kellerman."

Matthew cleared his throat. His gaze went back to Shanna. "Put in the movie that he told Karen's murderer where she was. You can leave it at that."

Her mouth fell open. She shared a shocked look with Gayle.

"Okay." She clamped her mouth shut. "Okay. I'll do that then. That's helpful, and I have everything planned and sorted. We'll have to do some new scenes from the beginning, but Brody"—she turned to me—"I don't think those reshoots will take long. We have two months before you go to New Zealand, right?"

I straightened in my seat. I hadn't shared that with Morgan yet. My eyes fell to her, but she was looking down at her lap and still holding my hand. She hadn't pulled that away . . . yet.

"Yes. I'll be in New Zealand."

"He goes to Iceland right after that one too."

Gayle was adding that for Shanna's benefit in case she went into editing and found more reshoots were needed.

Shanna nodded. "That's helpful, yes. We'll get it all worked out. I'll have my assistant catch up with you during one of those projects if I need to. Hopefully it'll just be about the promotion schedule."

"That sounds fine."

I looked at Gayle. "It does?"

"I've talked to the other franchise. They'll work with us on the promotion schedule for *Unbroke* if it conflicts with their shooting schedule. Everything will have to be planned far in advance, though." She sent the last sentence to Shanna as a warning. Everything took time. Everything had to be planned.

My gaze fell to Morgan again.

She didn't understand that world. Contracts, agreements, itineraries. Those were words she knew, but their concepts didn't have a place in her life. Her days were open. She could wake when she wanted, go for a walk in the woods, a ride on Shiloh.

A knot rose in my chest and burrowed there.

Gayle was right.

I was under contract for the next two years. There'd be another project after another, and that was what every successful actor wanted. Being busy meant more work would come, more money would come, but it was about riding the wave.

My wave started with the movie Kyle died trying to get to. It started there, and it seemed it would keep going.

*"She'll never go with you. She'll never leave those horses or those lands."*

Gayle was watching me.

*"I want you to forget her."*

Her words echoed in my head.

# CHAPTER FORTY-FIVE

*Brody*

Everything moved quickly after that dinner.

The movie was back in business.

To keep from any leaks being released—ones that weren't from Shanna's people, anyway—the cast and crew filled the estate again and more trailers were brought onto the land. If I wasn't shooting, I was with Morgan. We were usually in bed or sitting on my patio. There were a few times I went with her into the wilderness because she missed Shiloh. On the days I was working long hours, I knew I could look up and find Morgan watching from astride the mare. When we weren't doing any of those, we spent the evenings with her siblings. Gayle joined us a few times, and even Shanna once. I think both started to enjoy the bond that was evident between the siblings. Finn and Abby were the closest, but they doted on Morgan. Matthew's relationship was a little shaky among them all, but he seemed to be making an effort. There was no more shadiness or secrets from him, or so he claimed. He and I weren't chums, but he didn't protest my presence and I didn't beat him up.

Progress.

There was the usual buzz among the crew. People were like that. They talked. They gossiped. The only times they fell silent were when they were working.

And one other time.

I was running lines with Kara by the river, but the crew wasn't being quiet. The cameras were off at that moment. Shanna wanted to get a look at some of what we'd already shot in case she needed to redo it, so it was a normal day.

People were laughing.

Even Kara and I were joking with each other. Then a hush fell over everyone.

I looked over, and saw Morgan across the opposite bank. She was sitting on Shiloh, who was pawing at the ground.

"Oh wow," Kara said under her breath, lowering her script.

I looked from Morgan to everyone else before going to her side.

Shanna's assistant was tapping her on the arm, and she pulled her attention away from the tablet she was reviewing film on. "What?"

The assistant pointed at Morgan, and Shanna said, "Oh."

She looked at me, too, before standing. There were plenty of yards before she got to the river, and even more before she got down to where Kara and I were standing, but we were immediately across from Morgan.

I was eyeing Shiloh. "She wants to bolt."

Morgan leaned forward a little. I saw how she tightened her legs around the mare, signaling her for to hold. She said, "She'll wait for me." Morgan was watching Shanna coming toward us at a slow but steady pace. "Can I be here?"

Should she be there was a better question.

I wasn't given the chance to answer because Shanna arrived almost in a huff. She forced herself back, her body almost swaying from the abrupt change in motion. Her mouth was hanging open, but she tucked some of her frizzing hair behind her ear and crossed her arms over her chest.

"Morgan."

Morgan nodded back. "Can I be here?"

Shanna had been around Morgan on a few occasions, but Morgan was either sitting by me or on my lap. If she wasn't with me, she was with Finn or Abby. She was shielded from the burning questions everyone knew Shanna had for her. But this occasion was the second time she saw her on Shiloh, and I could tell Shanna's director's eye was going crazy.

She wanted to shoot Shiloh, but she wanted to shoot Morgan on Shiloh even more. No extra or horse handler would have the ease Morgan had on that horse, or the magic.

She forced out a breath, and I heard her counting to three under her breath before she managed a bright smile. "Of course, of course, Morgan." She cleared her throat, her head inclining a little. "And this is your horse? That famous Shoal?"

"This is Shiloh."

Shiloh backed up a few steps, throwing her head back at the mention of her name.

Shanna was almost drooling. I saw how she tightened her grip on her arm. She was literally holding herself back.

She blinked rapidly a few times. "Shiloh. Not Shoal."

"She's Shoal's daughter. Shoal's with the herd."

"Yes. The herd." Shanna was almost preening from excitement. "Where's the herd? Not close, right?" Her head suddenly popped high up from her neck.

Morgan was hiding her own grin. "They're on the other ridge." She nodded toward the next mountain. "Everyone's safe."

"Yes. Yes."

Kara, who was watching the exchange with the rest of the crew, cracked a grin at Shanna's mannerisms.

Shanna began patting her chest repeatedly. I didn't think she knew what she was doing.

"Could I—um—" She shot me a look.

I raised an eyebrow.

"Could you—" She faltered again but took a firm step forward. Her arms fell from her chest. "Could I ask you to run your horse up and down that bank for me?" Her voice was awestruck. She gestured to one of the cameras. "It would be amazing if we could get some footage of you and especially on your horse. I'd love to capture this. In a way, this movie is just as much about you as your mother, and you're in your natural element." The excitement and gushing faded, and her voice grew concise. "I don't think you realize the effect you have on that horse. It isn't something I could ever produce in a studio or with another actor."

Morgan cocked her head to the side. Her eyes found mine.

I held up a hand. "It's your call, not mine."

She nodded. "You just want me to run up and down the bank?"

"Yes, yes!" Shanna's eyes got big as she began backing away toward the camera. "Just run back and forth. Do whatever you feel comfortable with. The more you run, the better."

Morgan frowned, but Shanna was running back to the camera and missed it. She was barking orders and everyone was scrambling.

Shiloh reared back from the sudden commotion, lifting straight up so she was standing only on her hind legs.

Kara grabbed my hand and gripped it hard.

The only one not alarmed was Morgan.

Shanna snapped her fingers at the camera guy, and he swung the lens around. Whether Morgan knew it or not, she was already being recorded.

She bent forward, running her hand over Shiloh's neck and crooning to her. She was soothing her. After a second rearing, Shiloh's feet landed on the ground and stayed, but she was pawing there. She wanted to run. That was obvious.

Making a clicking sound, Morgan had Shiloh turn and she let her do what she wanted.

Morgan bent low, and Shiloh took off at a canter.

Her mane and tail flew behind her, fanning out, and it really was magical to watch. I'd witnessed this first hand, and so much more, but I was as much awestruck as the rest.

Morgan let Shiloh go as fast as she wanted before reining her in and having her gallop just as fast back to where we were. She kept doing it, and there was one time Morgan sat up, arching her back and letting her head fall back. Her hair looked like an extension of Shiloh's mane, flying free behind her as she let her arms fall out like she was flying.

"Wow."

I heard Kara's soft word and glanced down. Her eyes were glued to Morgan, as were everyone else's.

After Shiloh's need to run waned, the mustang faltered to a stop, and Morgan had her just walk around.

Shanna's assistant appeared at my side. "Shanna wants to know if she would stand on her horse?"

I looked down at her. The assistant looked away for a moment, saying, "She knows she can. She saw it one time but didn't catch it on camera."

They wanted Morgan to be a show horse for them? Where she would perform tricks and acts on command?

I growled. "No!"

The assistant flinched and then ran back to Shanna.

I didn't watch her relay my message. I was pissed, beyond pissed.

Morgan wasn't a circus performer. I got that they wanted to capture some of her magic because that was truly what it was, magic, but she was precious and invaluable and she wasn't there to be treated like an event at a goddamn festival.

Morgan stopped after a while. She and Shiloh cantered back over to where we stood, and Kara seemed braver. She stepped forward, her toes dipping into the river. She wasn't scared of the mustang like she had been moments before.

Sensing my anger, Morgan narrowed her eyes at me in a questioning manner. Her head tilted to the side, just a slight bit.

But Shanna was at my side, and she was just as breathless as before. "That was amazing, Morgan. Truly amazing." She stopped, gulped, and looked at me.

I knew what she wanted to ask.

I shook my head. Don't do it—

She did, "Could you stand on her? For just a moment?"

"What?"

"You know, I saw you that night outside the estate. We were all in the living room and you were out there. I saw you standing on your horse. Could you do it again?" She was so excited, her hand jerking toward the cameras. "It would be really amazing for the movie."

"Let it go, Shanna," I said. "She already gave you more than enough." And she knew it. She turned and looked at me, her eyes telling me she did. But she wanted more. I saw her hunger. She wanted as much from Morgan as she could take.

It would be like trying to get water from a rock. Eventually, she would throw the rock away in disgust.

I moved in front of her, physically standing in her way. "She's done enough."

Kara stood next to me, shoulder to shoulder.

I was surprised but thankful.

She said, "She's done enough, Shanna."

We were both protecting Morgan, but it wasn't entirely about that.

We'd both been used at one point. We were pushed to the extreme, having demands placed on us that we wanted to fulfill because we wanted to please others. We wanted to do as much as we could for our directors, agents, producers, and fans, but there was a price. There was always a price. And if we kept trying, we became hollow inside.

In that moment, Kara was with me.

We were protecting Morgan from becoming like us. We were doing this because we wished someone had done it for us.

I said quietly, inclining my head, "You have enough, Shanna."

There was a splash of hooves cutting through water, and then Morgan and Shiloh were on our bank, and she was approaching where we stood.

Shiloh moved forward, and Shanna was backing away.

She was looking from Morgan's face, to Shiloh's hooves, and then to me. She repeated the gesture, going around and around until I was convinced she would make herself dizzy, "What are you doing?"

Morgan had no words for herself. She cracked a grin. "You're upsetting Brody. Shiloh's grown somewhat fond of him."

Shanna looked perplexed.

Kara started laughing. She poked me in the side. "Good thing the stallion doesn't see you as a threat. He must take pity on you."

I looked up to Morgan. "You should maybe go. Shiloh's going to hurt someone."

She was watching the rest of the crew. They were all watching us back, and the braver ones were starting to move closer. They wanted to pet the mustang, but Shiloh wasn't an animal in a petting zoo. She was wild and dangerous and the only one allowed to ride her was Morgan.

Her entire body was alert and tense. Power rippled from the mustang, and Morgan was immune to it. I looked up and gazed at her in a new light. She wasn't immune to it. She was *included* in it.

As she sat on top of that horse, she was every bit as powerful as the mustang. The bond was so clear and evident that I wouldn't have been surprised to see invisible strings attaching the two.

But Morgan made a decision then.

She slid off Shiloh, and as soon as Morgan's feet touched the ground, the mustang sprang away. It was like they had rehearsed it or had a conversation ahead of time, but Shiloh didn't hesitate. She crashed through the river and then was gone into the trees. It took three seconds to happen.

It was as she had never been there in the first place.

But Morgan stayed.

# CHAPTER FORTY-SIX

*Brody*

For the rest of our shooting, Morgan was at my side. She waited on the sidelines while I was working and was there while I waited for my time. She even began to help Kara, running lines with her.

There were moments when she noticed a discrepancy in the script and told Shanna. She became an asset for Shanna. When we would arrive on site, Shanna would pull Morgan aside, and they would consult together. I knew Morgan's input was invaluable, and Shanna grew more and more excited as the shooting drew to a close.

I couldn't say that people started to forget who Morgan was. They just grew more accustomed to her.

We had two scenes left to do that week and then we were done. Completely done.

There was an excited buzz with everyone. People had already started packing up, but most people were sticking around for the wrap party. The Kellermans were planning it, and there were rumors of kegs, wine, face painting, a DJ. Tents were put on the lawn.

They wanted to take advantage of the abnormal warm weather. Morgan insisted it wouldn't last.

The new scene we were shooting wasn't a hard one. I was supposed to be on a walk with my "sister," and she was supposed to be telling me how much of a mistake it was to marry Karen.

The sister was walking with me. The cameras were moving ahead of us.

I was just about to deliver the line about how she was wrong, when someone screamed, ruining the scene.

One of the assistants was helping the horse handlers, but the horse was rearing up. Her hooves were flailing, and the handler was thrown off.

The actress by me screamed.

Everyone froze for a second.

Then, suddenly, there was a streak running past everyone.

Morgan weaved around those in her way.

I started forward, "Mor—"

The actress's hand clamped on my arm, stopping me. "Look!"

The horse kept rearing up and down, and the rope had been released. The handler rolled to safety, stood, and started pulling the other horse away.

Morgan darted around the last person.

The horse saw her coming, swinging her head around, and even I could see the wild panic in her eye.

A wheelbarrow had been abandoned in the path, but Morgan jumped, used it as a springboard, and launched herself onto the horse's back.

It happened so quickly.

The horse jumped around, trying unsuccessfully to buck Morgan off. She clambered forward, grabbing onto the reins and sliding into the saddle as her feet found the stirrups. She looked a little awkward in the saddle, but that was because I rarely saw her use one.

The horse stopped trying to buck her off, only lifting her head in the air and flaring her nostrils. Her ears were twitching all around, then finally settled straight up and alert.

When the horse stopped completely and lowered her head back down, Morgan kicked it into a soft trot. She looped around, going through the river, and letting her run in some figure eights on the opposite bank. She was letting her run some of her tension out.

"A snake!" someone shouted.

The shout broke everyone from their reverie. People started scrambling for safety, but the person laughed, waving his hands. "No. No. It *was* a snake. Taffy killed it."

"Who's Taffy?" the actress asked next to me.

And that was when I recognized the horse. I gestured to her. "The horse Morgan's soothing." I moved forward, walking next to Shanna toward where the handler was standing.

The guy had scooped it up and dumped it into the wheelbarrow.

A few girls ran the opposite direction, but he just shook his head. "It's already dead."

"Are you okay?" Shanna asked the handler who'd been bucked off.

She nodded. "Yeah, just shook up still. The snake startled Taffy, and then when I fell off, it almost got me. Taffy killed it." She gestured toward where Morgan was still loping Taffy in circles. "She's shook up too."

Shanna didn't say anything, but she turned to watch Morgan as the rest of us did.

I glanced at her from the corner of my eye. Her gaze darted to one of the cameramen, and he nodded, already swinging the lens around to zoom in on Morgan.

I stifled a growl. "Morgan!" I moved toward the river.

She looked over, wheeling Taffy back around. "Everyone okay?"

"Yeah." And because I knew it would grate on Shanna's nerves, I waved down the river. "Why don't you run her back to the barn and bring a different one for the last scene?"

I heard Shanna let out a sigh of frustration.

Morgan looked to the handlers. "Is that okay? Do you need her still?"

The male handler shook his head. "Nah. Run her back. Saves us time from loading her in the trailer." He gestured to the snake. "I gotta get rid of this anyway. You're saving me some work."

Morgan nodded. She looked at the other female handler. "You're okay? She didn't get you?"

"No. I'm good. She saved me actually."

"Okay." Morgan grinned at me. "See you in a bit." I heard the excitement in her voice. She loved Shiloh first, but she loved horses in general, and it wasn't long before she had Taffy turned toward the barn.

The horse kicked up dirt, speeding away.

"It's almost as if you don't want me to get the extra shots that'll make this movie a masterpiece."

I turned to Shanna. She had remained while everyone else went back to working.

"I am trying to keep you from using Morgan. There's no contract saying you can use the footage you take of her. If she gets hurt, are you going to compensate her? She isn't protected by a union or insurance."

Shanna paused, studying me. "I don't understand you. She's going to be fine. She'll stay here. She'll live out there with her horse. She's never going to fully know her own fame, but if she has a kid, maybe they will. Maybe it'll be good for them. I don't get why you want to protect her so much unless . . ." A different thought moved in the back of her mind, coming forward until she actually stepped back. She gazed at me with new awareness. "You're hoping she'll go with you, aren't you?"

Goddamn.

I turned away.

"That's it, isn't it? You're hoping to get her to leave with you. *Then* it'll be a problem. Then it'll be too much for her, but Brody . . ." She was shaking her head in pity. It made me grit my teeth. I didn't need her sympathy. "You can't force her to leave, and you can't change her. You know that, don't you?"

I didn't say a word.

Her hand came to my arm, but I moved out of her reach. I didn't need to be soothed.

"Brody, this is going to end badly if you don't accept her for who she is."

I didn't need to hear that.

I walked away and did the last two scenes until Shanna called a wrap, and then I went home to where I knew Morgan was waiting for me.

# CHAPTER FORTY-SEVEN

## Morgan

"You aren't celebrating like the rest of us?"

The whole crew was partying and had been since seven that night.

I glanced down to my lap. I was sitting on the edge of the deck, and I had my hands wedged under my legs. Others had looked up to where I sat, all wearing mixed expressions of fear and awe. It was the same every time I was around them. I was not one of them. They would never forget that, no matter what I did. For weeks, I tried to blend in. I wanted to be in the back scenery. I didn't want attention. I only wanted to be near Brody. I wanted to watch him do his work.

I turned around from my perch on the back patio of the house and saw Matthew shutting the door behind him, a glass of wine in hand.

I smiled. "I feel like Brody would make some remark about you having wine tonight."

My oldest stepbrother stifled a small laugh, leaning against the railing that I sat on. "I'm sure of it." He found Brody where he was sitting by the bonfire, laughing with Finn, Abby, and a few of his colleagues. "Is he drinking tonight?"

There was a glass beside him, but he had only been sipping it. "A little."

Matthew turned his focus on me. I could feel his gaze on my side profile.

We hadn't talked about Peter's part in my mother's death, but I knew that was a conversation that had to happen.

"We can't go back to what we all had, Matthew." I felt more than saw him go still beside me. "You were a brother to me for four years, but my mother died." I felt knives in my lungs. "I learned what a person could do to another that day, and I suppose you were right in some ways. I turned off my humanity, and I never really turned it back on." I gazed around the backyard, seeing them laughing, seeing them enjoying each other's company. I shook my head. "I don't understand them. I care for Finn. I care for Abby. I care for you, but it's more like a trickle of emotion."

The corner of his mouth twitched, but he remained silent.

"Not with Brody, though." I remembered seeing him in that car. I remembered feeling him in his cabin as I ran back to Shiloh. I remembered feeling pulled to him, as if I had no say about the matter.

I looked at my brother, or someone who I used to consider a brother.

He was watching me steadily. There was no shock or anger at my words. He was merely letting me speak.

"I feel alive when I am with Brody or with Shiloh."

"Morgan." He leaned toward me.

"Don't!" I spoke harsh, and he moved back again. "You need to hear this, and understand what I'm saying to you. I didn't want the movie people here, but I *am* glad they came. My mom was a good mom. She loved me, and she loved you guys. She had horrible taste in men, but she still loved them." One killed her while the other helped. "I will never be my mother. I will never let a man do to me what was done to her. No one will have that power over me." My voice grew hoarse. "All I see when I go on the computer is people hurting people. All I see when I watch television is people hurting people. It's useless and senseless." I searched the woods, but I knew the herd was long gone. They would've heard the humans celebrating. "There are rules and hierarchies in that world, too, but they don't kill for sport. They don't hunt each other down. If another stallion comes into the herd, he gets chased away unless he fights. He may die, but that was his choice to stay and fight as long as he could. It's the way for most of the animals, and I don't understand why humans hate as they do."

There were tears rolling down my cheeks.

"Before you came, I never cried."

"Morgan." He edged closer an inch. "Can you . . . can you come down from that ledge? Please."

I looked at him fully, twisting my body around.

He didn't get it.

I could jump from the patio and land safely.

I could climb to the top of the barn and sit there as long as I wanted. There were cliff edges I laid on for my naps.

I could walk miles barefoot in the wilderness and not feel a sliver.

I could run amongst pounding hooves and embrace the beat that I felt through my feet.

But more than any of that, I could survive in a land that would kill even the best hunters or campers. They grew up soft, which was why they thought of me as strange.

"You still look at me like that little kid I was when she died."

That was their mistake.

I was hard in ways they were not.

They just didn't want to admit it.

I looked back to Brody. "He loves me, but he wants to change me. He wants to tame me." I could not. I would not. If I did, I would die. "He wants me to go away with him, and he won't accept that I can never leave."

Shiloh was like air for me. These lands were like my food.

"He just loves you, Morgan."

That was the problem.

I said, "He shouldn't."

I had suddenly lost my desire to be around these humans. Without a word, I dropped from the patio. One person gasped, but Matthew didn't say a word. I felt his eyes as I darted around the crowd and slipped through the barn.

Tonight, I wanted to be with Shiloh.

# CHAPTER FORTY-EIGHT

*Brody*

I spent an hour searching for Morgan.

I tried to keep track of where she was, and the last I saw, she was on the deck with Matthew. The next time I looked, they were both gone. I found him later in his office.

"Have you seen Morgan?"

He looked up over the computer screen to me. The light illuminated his face, but a shadow crossed his eyes. He stared a second and then shook his head. "I haven't. No."

My eyes narrowed. "She was talking to you last. You know where she went."

He rubbed a hand over his face, scooted his chair back, and gestured to one of the chairs across from him. "Would you like to sit?"

"No."

He sighed. "Brody."

I relented, giving a grudging grunt. "Fine."

I sat, and he continued to stare at me.

I inclined my head, lifting a hand. "If you have words of wisdom you'd like to impart on me, have at it."

"Brody, I—"

"I meant about where your sister is."

That caught his attention. "So you *do* think of her as my sister now."

"I think I have no option. You're not going anywhere."

I was testing him, baiting him. I knew he talked to her. I knew she was gone, and I had a feeling he knew why she left. I wanted him to spill it, and to do it as soon as possible. I was tired, and I wanted to feel Morgan underneath me so badly I was almost aching for her.

"Brody." He bowed his head a second.

No.

I could hear his sympathy.

He was going to say words I didn't want to hear, not from him. No way in fucking hell.

I started to stand. "I'm not going to hear this. I don't give a shit what it is. I'm not listening." I started to go.

He shoved his chair back, and as it crashed into the wall behind him, his fist slammed down on his desk. "You will sit, and you will listen to what I have to say."

"Why?" I rounded on him, raising my chin in a challenge. "Why the hell should I listen to whatever you have to say? You might've known her the longest, but you don't know her the best. I do. Me. Not you! A few weeks ago, you were the enemy."

"You will listen to me because I'm the one she opened up to! That's why!" His chest was heaving.

And from deeper inside the house, we heard someone ask about who was yelling.

His eyes jerked to the door, and a muscle pulsed in his neck. "Can you please shut the door?"

I didn't move.

"Please!" He spat the word this time.

I folded my arms over my chest.

I was being an asshole and probably looked like a spoiled, selfish brat, but I didn't care. I loved Morgan. I knew Morgan. I was the one who brought her back to them. She fell for me, and she grew anchored to me. He wouldn't even have her in his life if it weren't for me.

"Shut the goddamn door!"

I took two strides, slammed it shut, and then turned around. "Yeah?"

He let out a curse, raking a hand over his face. He pointed to the chair again. "Fuck's sake, Asher. You're almost as stubborn as Morgan herself." He tried to gentle his tone. "Sit." He righted his own chair and then sat.

I followed suit, but slowly.

My stomach was in knots, and every instinct in me was telling me I didn't want to hear what he was going to say and it was going to hurt threefold because it was coming from *him*.

His hand raked through his hair. "Trust me. This is not something I want to be a part of, but she confided in me just now. Not you."

I clenched my jaw. "What'd she say?"

"She doesn't feel."

"What?" I lifted my head and sat forward. "What do you mean she doesn't feel?"

"I mean exactly what I said. She told me that she turned her humanity off when her mother died. She turned it off, Brody."

That wasn't true. I felt her shiver under my touch. She laughed with me.

Then I remembered how she recounted the events of the day her mother died. How she didn't cry or get angry. Even her reaction when she found out Matthew had been recording us was off. It wasn't a reaction at all, as if . . . she had turned off her humanity.

I sank back in the chair.

"She told me that she doesn't understand us. Those were her words." His mouth twisted into a grimace as if he thought he should laugh at that but couldn't. "She felt a tickle of humanity when it came to Finn, Abby, me. She said the only ones who made her feel alive were you, and Shiloh." A sad smile lingered on his face. "Congratulations. You're competing with a goddamn horse for her."

He was right.

And just like that, I knew where she went.

"She has to be out there to survive. She won't live if you take her away from here."

I closed my eyes and lowered my head.

Another fucking person telling me that.

Fuck. I was telling myself that, but . . .

I looked up at him. "I can't imagine life without her."

"And you have a blooming career that will take you all over the world."

I nodded. My head felt so fucking heavy. "And a goddamn horse will keep her from coming with me."

"I'm sorry." He actually sounded as if he meant it. "I truly am."

I nodded, my chin falling to my chest. "Yeah."

My insides were being seared.

I stood and cleared my throat, and even that goddamn hurt.

Matthew watched me, then stood with me. "What are you going to do? You fly out tomorrow, don't you?"

"I have another day here." After that, I was headed right to New Zealand to start filming my next movie.

"Then take it."

"What?"

Matthew looked fierce as he said, "Take it. Take the day. Go find her. Make her need you as much as she needs that horse. Maybe then you'll have a chance." His voice went to a whisper. "Maybe then, but you're going to have to fight for her."

I was sure if I did a poll, everyone would tell me to leave her. Love her tonight, but then leave and forget her. As I left the house and continued past the barn to the wilderness beyond, I knew I wasn't going to do any of that.

I couldn't let her go. That was all I knew.

So, I went to find her.

# CHAPTER FORTY-NINE

## Morgan

The herd left as soon as they heard him coming.

Shiloh waited, but finally, I motioned for her to go, and she did, just not before letting out a soft neigh and giving me a nip on my shoulders. She wasn't happy, but neither was I.

How could someone be so torn? Be content in two different places but always be yearning for the other?

It wasn't normal.

I wasn't normal.

"Morgan!"

I was sitting on a rock, my knees pulled up with my elbows resting on them. I looked up and waited, and a few seconds and several suspicious crashes later, he fell through some foliage and landed on the grass clearing before my rock.

He looked up, saw my shoes, and craned his neck farther back.

His eyes found mine. "Oh. Hey." He sat back and combed his fingers through his hair. "Fancy meeting you here."

I rolled my eyes. "I wanted to be with the herd toni—"

"I'm leaving tomorrow."

I stopped, looked at him a moment, and then blinked. "What?"

"We're done shooting. My plane leaves tomorrow night at midnight."

I swallowed over a knot. "For New Zealand?"

He nodded slowly, his eyes never leaving mine. "Yeah."

"Why didn't you tell me?"

"I was going to tonight. You dipped out before I could."

The knot was still lodged smack dab in my throat. I should've realized. I should've been prepared.

I felt like someone slapped me in the face.

"I see."

I looked down at the rock but had to close my eyes. My head was swimming.

"Thought you said you wanted to be with the herd."

I didn't look up as I waved in their general direction. "You scared them off."

"Oh."

I opened my eyes but still couldn't look. My throat shouldn't be burning, but it was.

I knew he was going, but I hadn't thought about it. I hadn't allowed myself to.

*Why do I suddenly feel like I'm ten years old again?*

"Hey." Brody's voice dropped to a husky whisper. He scooted closer, his legs extending out by the rock as he peered up at me. He tugged on one of my hands. "What's going on?"

I shook my head.

I didn't cry, but this was the second time I felt tears that night. I didn't cry, right?

"You knew I'd be going." He pulled back, resting his hands behind him to help prop him up. He kept his legs by the rock. One foot was pulled toward him.

I did.

I should've nodded at this part.

I couldn't.

I didn't want him to go, so I hadn't let myself think about it. I croaked, "I know."

I was a fool.

"Morgan. Hey." He sat back up, but he didn't reach for my hand. His voice went back to an intimate whisper.

It sent tingles through me, and that wasn't fair. He was manipulating me.

No. No, he wasn't.

My head hung lower as I admitted that.

This was Brody being Brody. He was being amazing. Kind. Wonderful. Loving. He was being the guy thousands of women wanted and I got, and I was making him sit in the middle of a woods while I . . . sulked on a goddamn rock.

I jerked my head up. The words were out before I knew I was going to ask them. "Why are you with me?"

"What?" He looked taken aback.

"Why?" I gestured to myself. "I would rather spend time with a horse over a person any day of the week."

Brody remarked, "Uh . . . most would. Have you met people? They can be monsters."

I kept going as if he hadn't spoken. "The only person who's pulled me away from Shiloh is you, and you're leaving, and I . . ." My heart was racing. My chest felt tight. It was hurting.

I was hurting.

Someone was squeezing my heart, and I had no clue what was going on. "Brody, I—you're leaving tomorrow. What are you doing with me?" I scrambled to my feet and jumped over him. I thought about running. I looked at the brush. I could go. I could crash through that foliage and be gone in an instant. He found his way there. He could find his way home.

What was I doing still standing there?

I loved him.

My heart thumped—literally.

I loved him.

I hadn't loved anyone since my mother. I cared. I could care, but not love.

And I loved Brody.

That was why I couldn't leave his side. That was why I'd been ignoring Shiloh for him. I blinked rapidly, forcing tears away. I had no idea what any of that meant.

"I can't leave."

I paused after saying those words.

The silence was palpable.

I turned and looked at him. He was standing, but his eyes were wide and his hands were flat against his sides. He looked as if I just kicked him.

"Okay." He frowned.

That was it?

I frowned too. "You don't have anything to say?"

"I—" He held his hands up and shrugged. "I already knew that."

"Why aren't you pissed?"

"Because I already knew you wouldn't come with me." He gestured over my shoulder. "You replaced your mom with a horse. What'd I expect?" He seemed strained as he said that, his eyes closing and lines forming around his mouth.

"What?"

"Shiloh. Or Shoal. Or whoever else. You replaced your mom with a horse, with someone who can't talk, who can't walk on two legs." He waited. "Who can't leave you."

I sucked in a breath.

My pulse was still racing, but it took on a whole different feel.

Anger was rising.

"Fuck you."

He smirked, shaking his head. "There she is. There's the girl that you want to hide."

His words were almost mean as his mouth twisted into a snarl, but I saw how his hands trembled, felt the mixed emotions pouring off him. "I got your message via your brother. Two thumbs-up, Morgan. Way to deliver a punch. Tell the brother who's obsessed with you your real secrets. You wanted to stick a knife in me? That was the way to go. Or"—he reached into his back pocket and pulled out a pocket knife before flipping open the blade—"here's the real thing. Here you go." He pretended to hand it to me. "Stick it in me. Turn it a few times. That's what you did by telling Matthew your deepest darkest secrets."

I flinched with the first harsh message, and I kept flinching.

He was being so mean, almost cruel.

My eyes began to water again. "Stop it," I croaked out. It wasn't even a raspy whisper. It was really a croak. That was all I could manage.

I just wanted him to stop it.

"Why?" He surged closer, his eyes blazing. "You don't have feelings? Right? That's the message you sent. You couldn't love me because you can't feel anymore. You shut it all off. You don't understand humanity, how we're so mean to each other." He clapped and then pointed his hands to me. "But hey. You just learned your own lesson. You were cruel to me. Going to Matthew, telling him why you couldn't be with me, and then darting off to Wilderness Land. That's what humans do. We're cowards. We hurt. We get pissed. We say shit to hurt other people. That's what we do, and that's what *you* did. You hurt *me*."

He stopped, biting off those words.

I flinched again, my entire body jerking to the side as if his words physically struck me.

He was right.

Goddamn.

He was right.

I blinked a few times, wiped the last of the tears away, and faced him.

I had hurt him, and I think I did it on purpose. No. I know I did.

"You have to leave me."

He advanced on me. "Fuck you."

I stayed put. I barely heard his retort as I raised my chin. "I will be a cancer to you."

"Shut up."

He still advanced.

I tuned him out. He wanted to hurt me, but we both knew I was the one who was really hurting him.

I lowered my head and said, "My mom was murdered, and my family abandoned me. I'm toxic. I'll never be what you want."

He was right in front of me. His eyes were still blazing, and his nostrils were flaring.

I didn't move or retreat. The urge was there, but I just looked up and met his gaze, holding his eyes as fiercely as I was holding my ground.

"You think you're fucked up?" His eyes were smoldering.

"I know I am."

"Well, get in line, honey." He bent, and his hands found my waist. "I listened to my brother die. Think that was a piece of cake? My publicist/manager betrayed me. Then I had to go and identify his body. Also another piece of cake, right?"

I didn't react, but shivers of pleasure shot through me at his touch.

He straightened, lifting me with him.

I closed my eyes. What was I doing?

He was carrying me away, and somehow he seemed to know exactly where to go. We were just outside the hot spring. He stepped through the tree line, into the clearing, and he kept going. He went all the way into the water, clothes and all, and I was shivering, but it wasn't from the cold.

My teeth were almost rattling together.

My limbs were shaking.

I had no idea what was going on with me.

I glanced down at myself, and it was like looking at a stranger's body.

A single beam from the moon fell onto the water, and I could see how my nipples were erect. My legs had wound themselves around his waist. When he shifted so my back was resting over a rock, he didn't move to retreat. He leaned over me, his eyes glittering from the moonlight, and his hand caught the side of my face.

His thumb rubbed over my cheek. "Your eyes are dilated. What are you thinking right now?"

That I had no idea what was happening.

I always wanted him. I understood that feeling, but there were others swirling around in me—feelings I had never experienced before. It was as if he pulled down the divider inside me, and the other half I thought dead was spilling free.

I shook my head, only able to gasp in sound.

He ran his hand down my throat, circling, and moving down my chest until it lay flat between my breasts.

My heart drummed stronger, trying to press against his hand. A soft smile lit up his face and he looked back to me. "You feel that?"

I was feeling too much. That was the problem.

I could still only gurgle out a sound.

I felt like I was dying.

I started to shake my head. I didn't want this. It was too much, too overwhelming, too powerful.

It made me feel weak.

It made me feel vulnerable.

I hated this.

I began to push him away.

He tightened his hold on me. "Morgan. What's wro—" He was frowning as he stepped back, but his hands were still on me.

My legs were still wound around his waist.

I was thrashing.

I had to get away from him, and I began to pound on his chest.

"Morgan!" He caught my wrists and pushed them down until my hands were pinned to my sides. His head was right above mine. There were only a few inches of space between our lips.

But I was raging on the inside.

I was panicked, but I knew my legs were still locked around him, my anchor. I couldn't let go of him, but I wanted to be away. My insides were tearing in half—ripping and shredding and sending quakes through my whole body. I couldn't even form words.

My mom was there. I was seeing flashes of her.

*"Morgan, honey."*

*Her voice was so soft, so warm, so loving.*

*She knelt in front of me, pulling me to her while he pounding against the door.*

*I felt her fear. She was shaking as badly as I was.*

*I felt her tears on my shoulders as she whispered, "I want you to grow up and be strong. Be bold. Be loving. Be fierce. I want you to have children of your own, and they will make you proud." She pulled back, framing my face with her hands.*

She knew she was going to die.

I had forgotten this memory.

*The tears were coating her face. "You have already made me so proud. You're so intelligent. You're beautiful. You're a leader. You will do amazing things one day." She tapped my forehead, more tears sliding free. "And I can't wait to see what you do."*

*The guy at the door wouldn't go away.*

*She hugged me again, burrowing her head into the crook of my neck and shoulder. "I love you so much, Morgan. And I will always, always be with you." She pressed her hand right over my heart. "I'm right here. I'm in there with you."*

I returned to that rock, with Brody looking at me with such concern.

"Morgan?"

I pulled my hands from his and framed his face like my mother had done to me. "I'm here."

He collapsed on top of me, his head falling to where hers had been. "God." His body shook with fervor. "I was freaking out. You looked like you were having a seizure or something." He lifted his head back up and smoothed my hair back. He kept repeating that movement to calm himself. "What just happened?"

"I . . ." I saw her again.

*Her hand on my chest. "I'm right here. I'm in there with you."*

"I remembered something. It came back to me just now."

I reached up and brushed some of his hair back.

It felt right, whatever happened to me. I didn't feel half-dead anymore. I didn't have words for it, but it was almost as if I'd been in pieces before and somehow was just put back together.

Instead of trying to explain that, I just said, "I love you."

His eyes softened. His thumb went to my mouth and traced my lips. "I love you too."

I nodded. "I know."

His lips curved up. "You know?"

"You told me, but I've known this whole time. You're almost obsessed with me."

He let out a laugh. The rest of his mouth formed a full smile, but it was tender, and it was filled with love. "Really? I'm obsessed with you?"

I nodded again. "It's easy to do. I've heard I'm pretty spectacular at things like climbing. I know a lot of horse tricks."

"Horse tricks?" More laughter, but it ended on a soft sigh. His hand cupped the side of my face, and he leaned close. "Maybe the tables are turned here. Maybe you're obsessed with me?"

"Maybe." I was smiling. "I heard you're hot stuff. You're famous too."

"I am. I'm very famous."

"And rich."

His laughter softened. "Yeah, but so are you."

"I had a rich grandfather, I hear."

"You still want to find your biological family?"

I tilted my head to the side. Did I?

"No. I have siblings who love me. They don't care that we aren't biological, so I won't either." I traced a finger down his shoulder and over his bicep to his wrist before going back up and lingering over his chest. "I trust my mom. She stayed away for a reason." I traced small circles over him, loving how his muscles shifted under my touch. "You leave tomorrow?"

His hand went around to the back of my neck. "I leave tomorrow night."

The angry words were spent between us. My explosion was gone. It left behind a trail of too much, but I felt an urgency push to the forefront. We had tonight and tomorrow. That was it. My eyes lifted to his, and I saw the same anguish there.

He let out a breath of air, letting his forehead fall to rest on mine gently. "You won't come with me?"

That ripping apart feeling started in me again. I shook my head, just an inch. "I don't know how I can."

"You pack a bag and then get on a plane with me. That's how you do it."

I didn't respond to his joke that wasn't really a joke.

"I will die if I can't be out here."

He lifted his head again, and I already felt him pulling away, though that was his only movement. His body still was on top of me.

I caught his face, not letting him look away. I held it firmly and tried to implore him. "You opened something inside me, and I thank you for that. I didn't know it was still there, but . . ." How could I explain it? No words seemed appropriate. "But I'm still not enough."

His eyebrows pushed together. "What do you mean?"

"I'm not human enough to be with you."

His shirt molded to his back, showing every muscle and how perfect he was.

I wanted him, but I had to let him go.

I may love him, dream of him, yearn for him, but I could never be what he needed.

Softly, I said, "You have the world at your fingertips. You can't give it up by staying in one place."

"And you can't come with me."

It'd been the problem from the beginning. He reached for my hand and laced our fingers together. "This sucks."

I squeezed his hand back because, really, there was nothing else I could do. When he looked at me, I said, "We have tonight."

His eyes grew hooded in the moonlight, but he nodded. "Yeah." He slid back into the water and turned to me. Like so many other times, he fit between my legs as if he was meant to be there, and his hands found my waist. He leaned down to me, slowly sliding my shirt up and then pulling it from my body. "Tonight, then I go tomorrow."

I wanted the lust to push away everything else, but as he made love to me that night, I couldn't stop the tears from falling.

He was saying goodbye to me.

# CHAPTER FIFTY

*Brody*

I flew the next night to New Zealand.

Gayle flew in a few days after, and she stayed with me most of the time.

I did my scenes. I had everything memorized. I was never late to set, and they didn't need any retakes because of me.

I was professional. I was calm. I was sober. I was abstinent, and every night in my hotel, I debated leaving and going to her.

Every goddamn night.

I would sit on the edge of my bed, cradling my head in my hands and debating the pros and cons. The phone was within reach. I could call. I could make an excuse. I could get a few days off, fly back, hold her again, but I'd always have to leave.

I'd feel that sensation of having my insides scooped out every time I had to fly back.

It wouldn't be enough.

I would decide against it, only to have a new debate start in my head.

I could fly her to me. She could stay a few days and then go back to Shiloh. But I always knew she wouldn't come.

Finn called a few times, but after I shot the first movie and flew to Iceland to begin shooting the next one, it was too hard to hear how she was. He always said the same. She was good. She was spending the day with Shiloh and the herd, and she would be with them for the evenings. Matthew relocated Finn and Abigail to

Montana permanently. She was supposed to start building a huge resort that was half a waterpark. Finn was proud, boasting about how it would get national attention.

I could only think about how much more attention it would bring to Morgan, which wasn't a comment I made. I held it back, and eventually those phone calls to Finn stopped.

Just like the attention of our relationship.

I didn't ask Gayle if the paparazzi and blog sites were still talking about Morgan, but I knew a few still were. I got the alerts on my phone, and at first, they had been hard to read, but eventually, they became like everything else—nothing but a blur.

They couldn't get up-close shots of her, and I wondered if Morgan was doing it on purpose to piss them off. If it had become a game to her. There was one where she held up a middle finger, but she was grinning toward the camera.

I had to think it was a game.

She could've easily disappeared, evading even the long-distance zoom lens. I told Finn to educate her on the distance they used for those cameras, and he insisted he had.

My phone pinged again, as if it knew I was thinking of her, and I pulled it up.

It was another shot of her, but this time she was running on the side of a cliff.

I sat up straight.

In all the other shots, she'd been staring at the person who took the pictures. She was either standing or sitting. She was never shot when she was on Shiloh, which told me she knew what she was doing, but this shot was different.

I touched the picture on my screen as if I could touch her again.

I was a fool.

I had to let her go. It would never work.

An incoming call replaced the picture, and I grimaced. It was as if Gayle knew I was considering going AWOL and she needed to crush the plan before it got off the ground.

I answered it. "I got your email from Shanna."

Gayle had forwarded me an email from Shanna that morning. She told about the updated promotion schedule, which was more extensive than the first time I had seen it. The more press the movie got, the higher her allocated budget was for pushing the movie. I had to finish this last movie, and then the plan was to fly back to L.A. for a week before I had to start the press tour.

"That isn't what this is about."

*Morgan . . .*

Dread sank in me. Gayle was serious. "What's wrong?"

"Okay. You're going to get pissed at me, but you have to get over that for now."

"What is it?" I raised my voice.

"Your sister-in-law got in touch with me."

"Cheryl?"

"Yeah." Gayle hesitated a moment, but I didn't have the patience for that crap right then.

"Gayle!" I clipped out. "Spit it out."

"Okay. Okay. Look, you must've talked to her about Morgan. Right?"

That dread was back and doubling.

"Gayle, what the hell happened?"

"Cheryl knows you're miserable without Morgan. She said she wanted to meet Morgan, maybe see if there was anything she could do to help get you two together, but she was going to wait until you got back from your last movie. But then—"

She was hesitating again. She was on my last goddamn nerve.

"Gayle!"

"But then she saw a picture of Morgan, where she looked scared, running."

I knew exactly what image she was talking about.

I checked the time stamp. It was an old alert that hadn't come through right away.

Gayle kept going, dropping her voice lower, "She asked if I'd make the introductions. She saw that picture and didn't want to wait anymore. I don't know why, but she was adamant. She felt something was wrong and didn't want you to lose *your* soulmate."

Like she lost Kyle.

I felt the impending doom coming, though. She was leading up to something bad, and I bit out, "Tell me what's wrong. Now."

"Cheryl took your nieces to Montana. They're missing."

"What?" Cheryl was there? Cheryl took my nieces there? "What do you mean they're *missing*?"

"Right. Okay. They got there. Cheryl was tired, and took a nap, and the girls were gone when she woke up. We don't know what happened, but Finn called a local tracker. He could track them into the wilderness, but then he lost them. He lost their trail."

She kept explaining, but I couldn't hear her words anymore.

My heart was pounding.

A buzz was in the air, filling my ears and making my skin crawl. It was growing louder and louder. It was blurring my vision.

I felt myself slipping.

Felt the way the phone cut into my hand.

The way I slid to the ground . . .

I couldn't talk as everything slammed back into place, came back into focus, and I heard myself saying, "I have to leave."

I wasn't slipping anymore. I was back in command.

Gayle's voice came back to me. "Finn wanted to find Morgan, said she could find the girls, but we can't find her."

"What do you mean you can't find Morgan?"

"She's been missing for a week."

That picture. It came back to mind. I had sensed something was different . . . wrong.

"What happened?"

"Nothing. I mean, no one knows. Finn said she had been sleeping at the house every day, but in the last few weeks, she went back to staying out there again. Temps are higher than normal, so maybe that's why?"

"Are you there now?"

"I just got off the plane."

"When did my nieces go missing?"

She didn't reply.

Oh God no.

"Gayle." I shouldn't have to prompt this. This was more torture. "How long, Gayle?"

"They've been out there for eighteen hours."

Eighteen goddamn hours.

Sweet Ambrea. Bubbly Alisma.

They were missing, and so was Morgan.

"I'm coming."

# CHAPTER FIFTY-ONE

*Brody*

I left immediately. I was on the next available flight, and a car was waiting for me when I landed in Montana almost a full day later. I hadn't slept. My eyes were bloodshot, and I wasn't prepared for the frenzy waiting for me outside the airport.

"Brody!"

Flash!

Flash!

"Are you here for Morgan?"

"Is it true that your nieces are missing?"

I stopped at that question and whirled on the reporter who asked it. She hadn't expected a sudden response, and her eyes went wide. She began to pull back her microphone, but at the last second, she caught herself and thrust it closer in my face. She asked, "If your nieces were here to visit Morgan, does that mean your relationship is back on?"

Another reporter jostled for attention, pushing his phone in front of me. "We heard a search party is being organized. Is that for Morgan or your nieces?"

I looked at him and then took my sunglasses off. I didn't care that the cameras were flashing non-stop or this clip would be on the news that night. "Does it goddamn matter? People are missing and you're asking about my supposed love life?"

"Mr. Asher."

The driver prompted me. I went past the rest of them and slid into the backseat.

No one was waiting for me, not that I had expected anyone to be. A part of me was glad Gayle wasn't there. I didn't want to hear her apologies for connecting Cheryl with the Kellermans, and I didn't want to feel her sympathy.

I had to find Morgan.

I would find Morgan, and she would find my nieces.

It was that easy to me.

I just had to find her first.

# CHAPTER FIFTY-TWO

*Brody*

The entire front yard was a sea of red and orange vests. Red and white tents were being set up, and people were milling all around the Kellerman estate. When the car stopped, a group of people came out of the house.

Cheryl ran into my arms, and I held her for a long moment.

She was crying and hiccupping at the same time. "I only meant to nap for an hour. I didn't think the jet lag would hit me that hard, but I hadn't slept the night before, and they're gone, Brody. They're gone."

She kept crying into my shoulder. I looked over her head to Gayle, nodding to her. Finn, Abby, and Jen were with her. Shanna joined the group, and I frowned. "What are you doing here?"

Her eyes darted over my shoulder, but she folded her hands behind her back. "I came to help."

I looked back, spotted the camera set up on a pedestal, and turned to glare at her.

"Is there press here?"

"No." Finn shook his head firmly. "No press allowed."

Shanna gestured to the camera. "It'll all work out in the end, Brody. I have no doubt."

She was filming for the movie.

I swore at her. "Are you serious?"

She didn't respond, slinking away this time.

A man in a red vest approached the group. He was holding a clipboard, and he cleared his throat to announce his presence. He nodded to Finn. "We're ready to start again."

"Again?"

He looked at me, and when the recognition hit him, his eyes rounded slightly. "Mr. Asher, my name's Alfred." He held out his hand for me to shake and then continued, "I'm the search organizer and tracker. These are your nieces, I'm told?"

"They are."

Cheryl pulled back from my chest, tears still wet on her face. She wiped them away with her hands and rolled her shoulders back. "I want to go this time."

"No, Cheryl."

"Cheryl, no."

Gayle and Finn both spoke at the same time.

My manager reached out and touched her shoulder. "You went on the first search, and I know how exhausted you are." Her eyes met mine as she continued speaking to my sister-in-law, "Besides, I have a feeling Brody will be too concerned about you to fully do a thorough search himself."

"How many searches have you done?" I asked the man.

"This will be our fourth. We've been trying to hit certain sections at the same time so we can ensure no one in the search party goes missing themselves." He gestured beyond the field and fence. "We're doing an arm's length stretch between people, all moving in a straight line." He glanced back to Cheryl, who was sniffling into a ball of tissues someone had handed her.

He seemed to want to say more, but stayed silent.

I said to Gayle, "Maybe you want to help Cheryl inside?"

"Of course."

I gathered her shoulders and gently shifted her toward Gayle, who stepped up and wrapped her arm around Cheryl.

"Go with Gayle now."

"Brody, find them. Find her too."

That was the plan.

As soon as they were gone, Alfred started back in, "Uh, Finn said you have a relationship with his sister. He mentioned it's normal for her to be out there, and you could find her?"

He coughed as he spoke, and I knew the elephant in the room was the paparazzi. He knew full well what Morgan could do and how I knew her. He also didn't care, and that made me damned peachy.

"Yeah." I gazed out over the search party. They had around sixty volunteers. "I'll try."

Alfred frowned and his brow pinching together in thought. "We've been pretty loud. You think there's a shot she's heard us, just hasn't come to help?"

"There's no way Morgan would hear you guys and ignore you. I need to know all of the sections you've covered, because she isn't in any of those. She's somewhere else."

"You think something happened to Morgan?" It was the first trace of fear I heard from Finn since I got here.

I met his eyes once. "I don't know." I asked the man, "Have you seen the herd?"

He shook his head. "No, no horses. We were warned about them, but nothing."

"That might be good."

Finn said, "Morgan would be by the herd."

"If they aren't here, then she might be okay after all. She might just not be within hearing distance." I turned to Finn. "There was a lot of press at the airport." I recognized two of those reporters. "Reputable channels were there. Is there anything else going on?"

"Ah." He scratched at his forehead, thinking.

"Yes." His hand fell away. "My dad's trial started today. I hadn't even considered that with this going on." He waved behind me. "Today was jury selection. That's where Matthew is. He told us to handle this, and he'd handle Dad." He turned to Abby and Jen. "I totally forgot."

Jen reached for his hand but tried to put on a brave front as she turned to me. "Brody, find Morgan. If anyone can, it's you."

No more time was wasted after that.

I took my bag to the cabin I used before, and I felt Morgan's presence as soon as the door swung open. It wasn't that she was staying out in the wilderness like they thought; she had been using my place. I could smell her everywhere. She didn't wear perfumes or lotions. She would've bathed out there so she wouldn't smell like a human. She wouldn't have wanted the herd to start wondering if she wasn't one of them. I knew all that, but I still wasn't ready for the impact. Her presence felt like a punch, even in her absence, and I shoved down the fear that I wouldn't see her or my nieces again.

It wouldn't come to that.

I changed into jeans, hiking boots, a shirt with a thermal pack, and a coat. A water bottle was hooked to my pack, and I had the essentials in there. If I had to stay out past a night, I could survive. Aside for the two times I took a walk and accidentally on purpose got lost so she would find me, Morgan and I spent a handful of days out there. Hopefully, some of the things she showed me stuck, and I could find my way back to the little spots she liked.

I made one more side trip to talk to the organizer and have him fill me in on the areas they had already covered.

She could hear better and see better than anyone I knew, but there were still some of her places that would've been beyond hearing distance.

I was clinging to that hope.

She was there, somewhere, and I would find her . . . or vice versa.

"You sure you can do this?" Alfred asked, the same worry in his voice that was just in Finn's.

I grinned briefly. "Think I'm just a pansy-ass Hollywood boy?"

He grunted. "We're searching for three bodies right now. I don't want to add a fourth."

Bodies.

He saw the look and corrected, "We say bodies. We're always hoping to find them warm and kicking, if you get my drift."

I did. I still didn't like hearing it that way.

I nodded toward where the search party was congregating. "You guys are hitting the southwest section now?" More than half had recognized me and were watching us back, but I was grateful none pulled out phones. They weren't turning this into a different situation than what it was.

Morgan, then my nieces. They were my only priorities.

"We hit the southwest section with the first search, but we'll go past it now. There's still a lot of land out there."

And animals.

And ravines.

And sinkholes.

And so many other dangerous elements.

He asked, "You really think you might know where your girl is?"

"If she was in most of her spots, she would've heard you and come to see what was going on. She would've helped, but there are a few spots where she wouldn't have heard you. I'm going to go there first."

He was looking past me and into the thick forest. "You know enough of the land not to die?"

I was asking myself the same question. "We'll see, huh?"

He didn't laugh.

Neither did I.

# CHAPTER FIFTY-THREE

## Morgan

I was in the river when Shiloh found me.

I ignored her. It wasn't that I didn't want to pay her attention, but it wasn't weird for her to suddenly come to my side and stare at me. She usually did it when she thought I pocketed a treat for her while I was in the barn or if she wanted a scratch.

I didn't want to. Not then and there.

I was lying in the river, floating with one hand holding on to a rock that stuck out from the bank. It was the best of both worlds. I didn't have to worry about floating away and I was cool. It would get dark in a few hours, and the temperature was starting to drop.

She continued to stand above me, and when I still didn't pay her attention, she stomped her hoof on the ground.

"What?" I looked up.

Her head was lowered. She was staring right at me.

A different awareness began through my body.

Something was wrong.

I stood and scrambled onto the bank, not taking my eyes away from Shiloh's. "What?" I knew she couldn't answer, but sometimes she showed me somehow.

She did neither.

She didn't stop staring.

"What?"

Her nostrils flared, and she moved her body closer.

And she just stood there again.

I frowned but got onto her back. We'd gone for a run that day, and the herd was there. We'd been sticking closer to the other mountain during the last week. Something told me Shiloh didn't want me on her back for shits and giggles.

Some of the other herd lifted their heads from drinking or grazing. Their ears were going all around.

They were sensing something, but I couldn't make out if it was Shiloh's weird behavior or another thing.

A few dropped their heads and went back to drinking. Their ears relaxed.

Only Shoal kept her ears perked up, and she swung her head to us.

"Okay." I patted Shiloh. "You're trying to tell me something, so just show me instead."

As if she understood, she turned and left.

She carried me away from the herd and toward the lands closer to the house. I was still confused, but after she crossed another river, I heard him. Then I could smell him. It was the same body wash he used, but it had mixed with his own scent.

Brody was there.

Brody was close.

Brody was—

"Morgan!"

—searching for me.

I sat up straighter and made a clicking sound. Shiloh picked up her pace, and we were soon loping down a path toward him.

"Morgan!"

He was thrashing again.

I couldn't help a smile because this is what he always did. He showed up, made a nuisance of himself in the woods, and needed to be rescued by me.

Shiloh stopped in the middle of our path, waiting for him to find us.

Sticks were breaking.

He was pushing branches out of the way, and sometimes the force would move half a tree. All sound traveled far, but so did his cursing, which he was doing a lot of.

"Fucking hell." *Whack!* "Are you serious? I don't remember the trees being so damn dense before." Another *whack! Crack.* A roar. "Goddamn! Get away from my face."

He broke through the last of the foliage and half fell onto the trail. It wasn't a big trail, more like a game trail, and he hauled himself to his feet, stumbling forward as if he didn't even notice he actually found the path he was probably looking for.

He was waving his hands around his face, swatting away gnats, and then Shiloh moved a hoof and his gaze jerked to us.

"Morgan!" He flung his hands in the air. "Morgan!" A wide smile was spreading.

He was coming to me. I could slide off Shiloh's back and go to him. I should run to him as he ran to me. We would meet each other halfway and fall into each other's arms, but then what?

I didn't know.

So, I remained on her back.

I was drinking in the sight of him.

His eyes were alert and sober. They were just as dark as I remembered them. His hair was shorter. There wasn't enough to grab a handful anymore, but it suited him. He had a little stubble of a beard showing, just a slight stubble. He could shave it, and his face would be smooth and clean like he kept it for the movie.

He was dressed in a long-sleeve shirt, jeans that molded to his form but were baggy enough to hike in. My gaze traveled to his shoes, which were sturdy hiking boots.

I noted the pack on his back and the baseball hat swinging from it.

He came prepared.

And he was just as gorgeous as he had ever been.

He'd put on some weight, but not fluff. I saw how his arms had swung and how the shirt clung to his muscles. It was all muscle. Finn would have said Brody needed to "bulk up."

To me, he just looked mouth-wateringly gorgeous.

I wasn't prepared for the sight of him.

I felt joy when I heard him before, and then the old stirrings started again.

I'd slept in the bed he used, smelling him and trying to lie to myself that the sheets still held his warmth. They did not. It was my warmth, and after two months, his smell was gone too. That was when I stopped returning to the cabin.

I gazed at him, wondering why he wasn't coming any closer. Then I realized he wasn't approaching because of Shiloh.

She would kick him. She knew him, knew he was mine, but she wouldn't allow him next to her without my restraint, and I couldn't give it. I hadn't yet.

I was still staring at him and experiencing all the emotions I tried to suppress for so long. It was why I stayed away. I had to forget him. I had to move on or I was going to do something drastic.

"What are you doing here?" My voice was hoarse, and Shiloh reacted to the thick emotion there. She danced to the side, her head flaring up.

I patted her absentmindedly, and she settled, but Brody backed another good distance away.

He held his hands up slowly, speaking low and fast, "My nieces are missing. I need your help to find them."

"What?" They were *here*?

Shiloh shifted again, her anxiety rising with my own.

"I can explain everything later, but hey're somewhere on your land."

My mouth dried. "Are there search parties?"

He nodded.

"They tried to find you first but couldn't, so by the time they called me, eighteen hours had already passed." He pointed behind him toward the southwest section. "They haven't swept the east side at all. I have no idea where the girls went. No one does, but they would go past the fields. They wouldn't have gone to the north side of the house. Everything slopes south. That's where they would've gone."

"How old are your nieces?"

"Nine and eleven years old. They're smart, but they're only . . ."

His voice rasped in barely contained desperation.

"Okay." I began edging Shiloh toward him. My legs tightened. I was telling her to remain calm, and I was running a hand over her neck to further soothe her because she was going to hate me in a moment.

"What are you doing?" He eyed Shiloh as she eyed him right back.

I scooted forward on her and drew her body to the side of him. "You need to get on."

"What?" His eyes almost bulged out. "No. She'll kill me."

"She's never bucked me off. If you're coming up, she knows it's because I want you up here. She'll allow it for now." She would have to. Going on foot wasn't an option.

He was still watching her, his jaw clenching.

Shiloh kept shifting around. She wasn't happy about this, but she wasn't bolting. Not yet.

"You have to get on. We can't waste time. I can't ride to get a horse for you from the barn, and I wouldn't waste the time even if there were horses there. I can't leave you out here alone."

"I can find my way back."

I snorted. "How?" I gestured to the side. "Which direction would you go?"

He pulled out a compass and smirked at me. "I'd go north."

"That works if you're in a straight line from the house. You aren't."

"I'm not?"

"You're southeast, and you're close to the next mountain. You go north, and you'll walk right by the house. You won't even see it." I leaned down, my arm extended. "I love that you came, and I love seeing you right now, but enough's enough. Get the fuck up so I can save the day."

He started to reach for my hand but drew back at the end of my words.

His eyes met mine.

A bolt spread through both of us.

I needed him. That was all I knew in that moment, and he answered the look. He needed me too.

It was dark, deep, and almost desperate. They were all the same feelings I'd been tortured with since he left, but I was different. I had become different in his absence, and I wanted to tell him, but those words—like everything else—needed to wait.

He nodded and then his hand touched mine, and I felt the tingle like I knew I would.

I pulled at the same time as he jumped, and then we had a wild mustang beneath us. He was firmly settled behind me, and Shiloh was jumping all around. She was trying to buck us both off, but I held firm. Brody's arms were wrapped around my waist, and if we'd both been naked, he could've been inside me already. But I was bent forward, whispering and crooning to Shiloh. I was asking her not to leave us, telling her we needed her help.

I spoke to her as if she were a human. "There are two little girls who need our help. We have to take him back. I can't leave him out here. I love him, Shiloh. I can't lose him." Not again. She was still darting around, kicking her hind legs.

I began begging, "Please, Shiloh. I need your help. I will give you a whole bag of apples after this, but we need to find the babies. Two little girls. They're the same age I was when your mother helped me."

I didn't know what did the trick—if it was my pleading, if she somehow magically understood me, or if she felt the desperation in me.

For all I knew, it was the promise of treats.

But in the next second, she swung around and bolted to the house.

I almost fell off from the abrupt change in her, but I grabbed her neck and held tight. Brody was plastered to my back, and I think maybe she realized the only way to get him off was to deliver him to the place he always went.

She tore through the woods at a breakneck speed.

She wasn't smooth. She almost hit a few trees. She jumped a few times when I didn't think she should've. She could've gone down, broken an ankle, but she kept going with sheer will. Her face was sideways at times, her body too. She was neighing and whinnying, and sounding terrified as we lumbered to an awkward stop a few inches from the fence line.

Brody and I both lifted our legs so they weren't crushed, and I shoved Brody off. He jumped to the fence at the end of the field, and she jerked aside.

She was too crazed.

I was running my hand down her neck, but she was beyond listening to me.

She reared up, and I let go.

I fell to the ground—hard—and heard Brody shout, but I rolled with it and went cleanly under the fence. I stood as Shiloh tore back through the woods.

I sighed. "She's pissed at me."

I saw people running down from the house, but I didn't want to waste more time.

I thrust a hand at Brody. "Give me your pack."

"What?"

I nodded at his sweatshirt tied around his waist. "That too. The girls will need warmth when I find them."

He didn't move, so I unclipped his pack from around his shoulders. It fell into my hands, and I started riffling through it.

He had all the essentials, even a lightweight tent and blanket.

I nodded my approval. "This is good. Really good."

"What are you doing?" His voice rose. He gestured in the direction Shiloh tore off in. "She just took off. You have no fast way to find the girls."

The people were closing in. They were through the first fence and would be down the field to us in no time. Finn, Abby, Gayle, and another woman I didn't recognize.

I climbed back over the fence before securing his pack on my back. "What are your niece's names?"

"Wha—" He cursed and then rubbed a hand over his face. "You aren't joking, are you?"

"I have to go now. I can't wait and answer their questions. I only have so long before dark falls. Their names, Brody. I need to know what to call them."

"Ambrea and Alisma."

I nodded and moved to step away, but he reached for me.

"Wait! They both have blonde hair. Ambrea's is almost white, if that helps."

It did. Any little bit did. "What do they like?"

"Brody!"

"Morgan!"

They were almost to us.

"What do they like, Brody?" I raised my voice.

"Uh—" He looked back at the impending arrival and then snapped back to me. "Unicorns and mermaids. They used to like princesses, but I don't know if they still do."

Unicorns. Mermaids.

I could work with that.

"I have to go."

"Morgan!"

I ignored Finn and started running away.

"Morgan!"

I kept going, and once I was through the first line of trees, I started calling, but I changed my whistle. I kept going. I kept calling, and after I walked a mile, I felt the steps before I saw her coming.

She was walking toward me, among the trees, with her dark eyes and her ethereal white coat. She wasn't fearful or frantic. She was calm. She was steady. She was coming because I needed her to help me save two little girls the same way she once saved me.

Shoal had come.

# CHAPTER FIFTY-FOUR

## Morgan

I made my decision.

As I rode Shoal and she picked her way over the land, I knew this was the first of my last rides with this mare. It was nearing her time when she would go. I knew Shiloh was extra touchy because she would have a foal next summer. It was time. I felt it in my bones, and when he came back and I saw him again, I knew it was my time too.

This had come full circle.

I was the little girl who ran into the woods so long ago.

I was the one they sent a search party to find.

Shoal was the one who took me away then, and it was right that she was the one to go with me to find the girls.

I didn't know if they would be alive when—or if—I found them, but I felt they would be. I glanced down at Shoal and corrected myself—when she found them. I was trusting her. If she picked up a new scent, she would alert me, but until that time happened, I was near tears.

I loved this mare.

She was my mother in ways, and most of the time, I felt as if my mom was a part of Shoal. Shoal always cared for me. She always watched over me, and after she had Shiloh, she guarded me from a distance. She was content to let Shiloh be my sister. And just like any other sister, Shiloh would forgive me for forcing Brody onto her. It wouldn't change what I felt coming, though.

Change.

As soon as he stood on that walking path, I knew I would be leaving with him.

She began resisting me then.

After all this was done, I would go and find Shiloh. I would make sure things were okay between us. I needed her, and even if my return trips back to her took longer, I would still need to come.

Shiloh was as much of me as Shoal was . . . as Brody had become.

There was a part of me that would remain wild. But there was a part of me that remembered I was also human, and that was what Brody unleashed before he left.

I didn't understand it.

I would never understand why it was Brody who brought me back to life any more than I would understand the connection between us. It didn't make it any less real, and I could no longer live without it.

I wanted to tell him about these changes and the decisions I had made. I knew there was a chance he had already moved on. He may have. Millions desired him, but I had plans.

I kept thinking about them as Shoal and I searched. Then, I didn't know how much later, her ears perked up and she paused.

I looked up. There was a small hill toward the farthest corner in the south. I knew what was beyond it. It was the end of a creek that had wound its way around the mountain, the mouth of the creek that opened into larger river flowing toward the south. The current was strong, and if a kid played in the water there was a good chance they would be swept up.

If they were indeed up there, the only saving grace would be the logs that sometimes clogged the creek ahead. If someone were to get swept up and wasn't able to break free, they had a good chance of grabbing on to some of the logs and pulling themselves to safety. It would leave them wet and chilled to the bone but alive. If this was the route the girls had taken—they were probably chilled to death.

I listened and heard nothing but the trickle of the water. Still, I urged Shoal ahead, and we crested the hill.

And there, like I thought, were his two nieces.

And they were alive.

Just like I had been too.

# *EPILOGUE*

I was waiting in Brody's bed for him. I knew he needed to be at the main house for a bit, to hug his nieces, to talk to his sister-in-law, or whatever else he needed, but I was waiting for him.

And that was when I told him my decision.

"Are you sure?" He could only stare at me.

I was kneeling on his bed, the sheets pulled back already, and I nodded. My heart was in my throat as I nodded. "Yes," I rasped out. "I've lived most of my life with Shiloh and Shoal. It's time I formed my own family, and if that's just you and me, I'm ready."

I didn't tell him about how I felt like dying when he left or how I sat and watched his car take him away, weeping the whole time.

I hadn't just cried for him, though.

I had cried for losing my mother.

I had cried for never having a father.

I had cried for the loss of my siblings when my mother died.

I had cried because I had kept Finn, Abby, and Matthew away.

I had cried for closing myself up.

I had cried for turning my humanity off.

When Brody had left that night, I had already been starting to change. I just hadn't changed enough or quick enough to go with him.

And I waited because I wanted to know if everything would go back to normal. If I would be content again with Shiloh and Shoal, but it never went back to the way it used to be. I think both mares knew I was changing. It was in how they looked at me. They would watch me, waiting for me to leave and not come back.

Bringing those girls back was like I was bringing myself back. I was returning to a life that was interrupted when I was ten years old. I was returning to make my mother proud of me. I was returning to someday have my own little girl.

And that time had come.

It was four weeks later.

Finn and Jen married. Peter was convicted. Matthew took over the Kellerman company.

The day before I was supposed to fly to Iceland with Brody, I spent from sunrise to sunset with the herd. Both Shiloh and Shoal were glued to me. I barely got off Shiloh the whole day. When it was time to go back to the house and to Brody's arms, I got off Shiloh and walked to Shoal.

She was watching me with those big dark eyes, and as I stepped toward her, she lowered her head. My forehead rested against hers, and I held her face. We stood there a long time, both knowing we wouldn't see each other again. I would be gone when she would pass, so it was a forever goodbye.

I wept that night like I had when Brody left.

I hadn't been able to stop crying, even after Shoal stepped back and Shiloh moved into her place. I reached blindly above and lifted myself up to her back, and I couldn't stop crying in order to see if Shiloh was even taking me the right way, but I knew she was. She always carried me the right way.

Brody was waiting for me when I slid off my sister.

He waited as I threw my arms around her and then pressed my forehead against hers, saying goodbye.

When Shiloh stepped away like Shoal had, Brody stepped forward and swept me up in his arms.

He carried me to bed that night, and my heart ached.

I was starting a brand new life.

"Look," he said the next morning when we were in the car that would take us to the airport. We were going down our driveway. Gayle was with us, and I heard her gasp before I looked.

The herd was in the woods, running beside us.

Brody opened the window for me, and leaned across his lap and half out the window so they could see me.

Shoal stayed among the herd, but Shiloh veered off so she was the closest to us, still running. We got to the gate and went through, and as we turned left onto the road, the herd went right toward the mountains. They fanned out over a clearing, and I watched until I could no longer see them.

Brody squeezed my hand and leaned over to brush a tear away. "Do you regret coming?"

I ached for them, but there was no regret in my body. I loved him. I chose him. I shook my head because he was my new chapter.

## THE END

For more stories by this author, head to:
www.tijansbooks.com

CPSIA information can be obtained
at www.ICGtesting.com
Printed in the USA
BVHW06s2008230418
513925BV00004B/6/P